Jackpot!

ROBERT BRUCE KENNEDY

Outskirts Press, Inc.
Denver, Colorado

This is a work of fiction. The events and characters described herein are imaginary and are not intended to refer to specific places or living persons. The opinions expressed in this manuscript are solely the opinions of the author and do not represent the opinions or thoughts of the publisher. The author has represented and warranted full ownership and/or legal right to publish all the materials in this book.

JACKPOT!
All Rights Reserved.
Copyright © 2010 Robert Bruce Kennedy
v2.0

Cover design by Robert Aulicino

This book may not be reproduced, transmitted, or stored in whole or in part by any means, including graphic, electronic, or mechanical without the express written consent of the publisher except in the case of brief quotations embodied in critical articles and reviews.

Outskirts Press, Inc.
http://www.outskirtspress.com

ISBN: 978-1-4327-6304-6

Outskirts Press and the "OP" logo are trademarks belonging to Outskirts Press, Inc.

PRINTED IN THE UNITED STATES OF AMERICA

ALSO BY ROBERT BRUCE KENNEDY

THE PATENT

Acknowledgements

ONCE AGAIN I wish to acknowledge the assistance provided by two fellow retirees, both of whom helped me with my first novel, *The Patent*. These are Bill Kuh, my good friend and neighbor, and Patty Conley, my legal assistant in my former professional life in Atlanta. To my surprise while I was writing this novel Patty had been working on her own and beat me to publication with her *She Came From Alabama*. To my chagrin, rather than having turned to me for enlightened assistance, she had enlisted that of her 95 year old mother! For the cover design thanks again go out to Robert Aulicino. The author's photograph was made courtsey of Bonni Shuttleworth and Joan Ussery.

Prologue

They met literally by accident in a bar review course lecture hall in midtown Atlanta. Distracted by the lanky young man with long, dirty-sandy colored hair jaunting his way up the stairs towards her, she picked up her folder upside down. Out spilled its contents of bar review materials, some falling on the landing and some slopping over onto the top stair. He knelt and helped her retrieve them to end her fluster. Jimmy escorted Sheila into the hall and took the seat next to her. She was a curly-haired brunette with her hair styled as a page boy, and a very pretty yet strong face.

After the three-hour lecture they had a drink at Lulu's Bait Shack, a watering hole on Peachtree Street in Buckhead that featured fishbowl size drinks and alligator tail munches. Their personals were quickly dispensed with.

"I was born at an early age," began Jimmy with a laugh. He continued on telling her that he was officially James Delano Davis, but known to all as Jimmy, a bachelor, and an electronics engineer working at Lockheed-Martin in Marietta, a northwest suburb of Atlanta. He had gone through law school at night at John Marshall. Although John Marshall was an approved law school in Georgia, it was striving to become nationally accredited. It was a primary source of legal education for those who held down day jobs in Atlanta and were seeking a new career path.

Sheila Frazier, on the other hand, had just graduated from prestigious Emory University which was located in Decatur, a close-in old suburb. She was now working as a summer intern at a large, silk stocking law firm in Buckhead. No spouse yet for her either.

The bar review course was essential for Jimmy as the pass rate for John Marshall graduates was not that good for only about half passed. After all, law studies for most there had to be worked around the demands of their day jobs. For Sheila the bar review was optional. Having already received a first rate legal education, Emory law grads took the course mainly to focus on the materials that would be covered by the big test, the Georgia bar exam. But she was taking no chances. No, she would not be the only Emory law graduate to fail.

The bar review course ran *its* course. There was no exam; no passing or failing it. It would be followed by the grueling, multi-day bar exam itself which in turn would be followed by an almost three-month wait for the results.

Jimmy could only guess at his outcome. What if he had failed? He would simply retake it. Lockheed didn't care. It would just be a big pain in *his* ass. But the next time he wouldn't waste all that time in driving to and from the review course. No, he'd restudy the course materials at home. That way he would have even more time available for study.

Sheila felt confident that she had passed. But what if she failed? That would be an absolute disaster. Her standing at the firm of Ramsey, Ivy and Prince would plummet, regardless of what they would actually say to her. An Emory law grad who failed the Georgia Bar? Failing the New York or California bar exam would be one thing, but Georgia? The waiting finally came to an end.

"Hello," answered Jimmy.

"Well?"

"Well what?"

"Sure, don't tell me it didn't come," said Sheila in her rapid-fire way of speaking.

"Oh that thing; let me take a look. Hum. Georgia Power, The Salvation Army; someone gave them my name. Then again, the army might be an alternative. I might even make Major one day."

"Will you shut up? Did it come or not?"

"Well, not yet, I guess. No, wait. Here's something: Office of Bar Admissions. Must be from that bouncer down the street at the corner bar."

"Funny; now you didn't steam it open, did you? I can tell, you know."

"No, I've kept my part of the bargain," said Jimmy. "The question is: Have you?"

"I have. I have, indeed. I couldn't wait to see if it had come so I came home for lunch. It's here – and unopened, as promised."

"Then it's Alfredo's at five for the opening ceremony."

"See you there."

Alfredo's was located on Cheshire Bridge Road amongst tattoo parlors, strip clubs and gay and lesbian ones. She found Jimmy in a booth by the window studying the Italian menu with his envelope standing upright between the salt and pepper shakers. She took a seat facing him and placed her envelope alongside his.

"Where is your drink? That's no show of confidence," said Sheila.

"What do you think? The *quesadilla* or the *quiche d' hemlock?*" asked Jimmy in his slow manner of speak.

"I asked about our drinks."

"Hemlock can be drunk."

"What will it be, folks?" asked the waitress.

"Well I do need some courage." They ordered two exotic mixed drinks from the menu.

As the waitress left Sheila took Jimmy's hand in hers. "Don't worry, you passed."

He looked at her. Her expression appeared to be one of actual acknowledgment rather than merely a show of confidence.

"How do you know that? Do I detect a little ESP going on here?"

"Feel your envelope."

His eyes shifted from her to his envelope aside her envelope. He picked it up and carefully read the address and return-address.

"I said feel it, not read it. It's the thickness, Jimmy. It's too thick to be a fail."

Seeing that hers was of the same thickness as his, he ripped his open. She had had it pegged! He beamed and leaned over to kiss her just as their drinks arrived.

"Congratulations, Jimmy," she said as she raised hers in salute.

"Marry me, Miss Sheila. Marry me."

She looked deeply into his eyes. Then a smile began to form and grow wider in acceptance as she lowered her drink.

An open-mouth smile lit his face. He stood and leaned over

and kissed her and kissed her. "This is the greatest day of my life."

Jimmy sat back down. They clicked their two fishbowls together in mutual salute and drank.

"Hey, aren't you worried about my results?" asked Sheila.

"Why bother?" he said as he took hers and dropped it on the floor beneath the table.

She quickly retrieved it. "I'd best take a look – just for the record."

Chapter 1

"Once upon a time there lived in a land far away, an evil sorceress named Gretchen," began Sheila as she opened the large, picture-filled book of children stories beside the twins' bed. She paused while thinking to herself that the evil sorceress *should* be Abigail, her boss at work. Abigail Carmichael was not only head of the taxation law section of Ramsey, Ivy and Prince, LLC where Sheila worked, but also her self-appointed, personal tormentor.

She turned from the story book in her lap to her two twin boys lying there in bed together, eyes closed with expectant smiles on their faces. Bedtime stories read by their mother were an all-too-rare treat for them. Her hesitation brought a slow opening of their eyes. She continued to read while wondering if the story wasn't too frightening for two-and-a-half year olds.

"The evil that Gretchen possessed could be seen in her fiery eyes that glowed red whenever she practiced her sorcery." On and on she read until she saw the heads of the twins tilt to the left and then nod again almost in unison as if executing a rehearsed eye choreography.

Sheila read until she was certain that both Andy and Alec were asleep. She knew which identical twin was which since Andy always slept on the right side of the bed. Other than that she wouldn't have known as they lay there without turning one of them over to see which bore that small, brown birthmark on the back of his neck at the base of his hairline. Only Alec bore the mark. Of course when awake and active, identification was simple. Andy had a devil-may-care attitude while Alec was reserved and methodical, at least for a boy in his terrible twos.

She closed the book, gave each a silent kiss and sat back. Her mind returned to the office and to Abigail, that real-life sorceress.

"These extensions that you approve, Sheila, they've become addictive. The accountants don't care. It's a quick-fix and a quick bill for them, you know. Put your foot down. Make them justify these infernal extensions – *in advance*. Everyone knows these deadlines far ahead of time. When they become a habit it needlessly runs up the bill for the client. The accountants have to figure the tax twice, once to pay a close estimate on time, and once again for the final tabulation at the end of the extension. It's just a habit; a bad habit."

Never mind that more often than not it's the clients themselves who push for extensions, thought Sheila, but she had held her tongue.

Sheila wasn't actually the sole target of Abigail's wrath. Had that been the case she would have long since been out of there. But she treated some of her colleagues the same way. In fact one had recently left and set up his own practice. No, Abigail was simply an unhappy woman. That was the root problem she thought as she turned off the light and stole out of the children's room. It would be a long, tedious, uphill path to make partner while working under her.

Downstairs she found Jimmy watching a pro football game with a beer in hand and his feet propped up. She plopped herself down in the other easy chair beside his.

"What's with the long face, girl?" he said as he looked at her tired face with her hair pinned up as usual when she was at home.

"Abigail; what else?"

Jimmy looked at her and then turned back to the game.

"Maybe I should talk with Ted. *He* broke the cord. Maybe I should team up with him."

Jimmy turned back to her. "That's a bad idea, at least for now. Your income would drop to zilch. We would have to make do with my salary which already is less than yours."

"It couldn't hurt to talk."

"Talking won't change the fact that you have a client-following of exactly zero. You'd start with no client base. Your income would be negative. Your overhead would be paid by what, a loan? Paid from my income? No girl, this isn't the time.

"So it's a client base problem."

"No shit." He turned back to the game. "Shit *he* fumbled."

"Jimmy, cut the TV."

"Might as well, now.

"Sheila, you've got three years in now with one of the bigger firms in town. You are doing what you want – and what you are good at. You are making good money, maybe not the kind to support you in the lifestyle that you were raised, but that will come. You know you're on track to make partner in another three or four years. That's the lot you've cast. Don't try to change it now in midstream. Chin up, girl."

Sheila thought; three or four more years of working under Abigail to pay car loans and credit cards; three more years of working into the night, raising twins. Hell, three or four years like this and I'll be burned out.

"Three or four more years of not being here for the boys, is that what you want?" She knew that would strike a chord. "On my own or with a small firm, I could care less. No two thousand plus billing hours a year. You know, maybe something part-time."

"On your own or part-time you would have to spend time marketing yourself. How much time do you spend now cultivating clients? No, any business of your own would only require *more* time; more time away from the boys. Besides, our credit card is maxed out again."

She grew silent. "What if I got a commitment from a good client, one like say J and M? Then I could make the break."

J and M was J and M Gaming, Inc. It was a local manufacturer of slot machines out in Peachtree Corners. Sheila named it as she knew full well that Jimmy did a lot of work for them at the firm where he now worked as a patent attorney. They provided a steady stream of patent and trademark work in the highly competitive field of gaming machines. Sheila's firm was their general counsel and handled most of their work, but so far they had farmed out all of J and M's intellectual property law work, that is all of their patent, trademark and copyright work, rather than handle it themselves. Thus Knight and Macguire, where Jimmy worked, also had J and M as a client. In fact, it was the only client that Jimmy had personally generated so far and that was thanks to Sheila's position with Ramsey, Ivy and Prince. The rest of his work there as an associate was working on cases handed down to him by the partners.

Sheila chuckled. "If I got J and M your bosses would then become beholden to me. How would that be for job security, Sonny?" She called him "Sonny" or "Sonny Boy" whenever she wanted to give him a jab. She couldn't recall its origin, but it had always proven to be effective. "Or maybe I could grab Excelsior, J and M's competitor."

"Sure; sure thing. From what you've told me about Excelsior I think they might just need more than a tax lawyer - a *consigliore*, no doubt."

Sheila chuckled again. "Slot machines to casinos to the Mafia; that's always the scenario. Don't think so; only in the movies. But just like in the movies slot machine production is a business – another business segment in that big wide world out there called entertainment. It's all show business, Sonny Boy."

The next morning Sheila dropped the twins off at KiddyKare, a day care center located just a couple of miles from their home in Dunwoody. Miss Clara, their black, live-in nanny, would be picking them up later in the afternoon in her vintage, two-tone, 1975 Chevy Impala. Back at the house they would nap before living out their afternoon terrible-twos' playtime until dinner. For Jimmy and Sheila, and Miss Clara also, the "terrible-twos" term had a dual meaning.

From the day care center Sheila took Georgia 400 into Buckhead in her BMW 328i sports wagon. After flying through the toll gate with her cruise card she took the Lenox Square exit in route to her assigned underground parking space in the Financial Center Building adjacent the mammoth Lenox Square Mall, the Southeast's premier shopping mall. As she exited the elevator at the thirty-eighth floor directly into the reception area of Ramsey, Ivy and Prince she was waved over by the receptionist.

"Ms. Davis, Ms. Carmichael asked that you come to her office as soon as you got in."

Sheila gave her a perfunctory "thank you" as she swore to herself under her breath.

She hung her coat in her office and grabbed a legal pad and pen. As she entered Abigail's spacious office she found her standing in her black and blue tweed business suit leaning back against her desk. She was twirling her granny style eyeglasses with one hand while her other arm was outstretched behind her with her palm planted atop the desk. Two men in sport jackets and ties were standing, looking out the floor-to-ceiling window at the Atlanta skyline some five miles away. The short, pale one was the first to turn towards her.

"Sheila, I'm sure that you remember Mr. Bianco here of Excelsior," said Abigail without shifting her position against her desk nor slowing the eyeglasses twirling.

"Mr. Bianco, it's good to see you again."

Bianco's eyes lit up and he smiled as he walked over to greet Sheila.

"Ah, it's our charming tax lady. Sheila, right?" he said as if he had remembered her name anyway. He held out his hand. As Sheila raised hers to shake, the rather frail and very pale Bianco instead embraced it with a kiss, European-style. As he raised his head he revealed the color of his eyes to be a pale pink.

"And this is Mister Recos. I don't think you have met Mr. Recos before."

The other man, who looked like an NFL linesman packaged in a dark suit, was over six feet, had also now turned around from the window to face Sheila. He wore a black shirt and white tie but that detail was eclipsed by the sight of his enormous, hairy hands.

"Charmed," was all that he said without any facial expression. He did have the courtesy though of taking his smoking cigar out of his mouth.

Sheila gathered up her courage and walked over to the physically intimidating Mr. Recos. Rather than a handshake it was more of an emersion of her hand into a human sleeve. He gave her hand a slight squeeze and quickly released it to her relief. For a moment she remained in front of him mesmerized now by his single eyebrow which apparently serviced both of his black eyes

"Thank you," she said as the odor of the cigar enveloped her. "It's nice to meet you."

What a pair of eyebrows, she thought, or more accurately, what an eyebrow. Recos, noticing the barely missing eye-to-eye contact, smiled more to himself than her and then turned back to resume his gaze out the window.

"Do you live down there?" he asked as he nodded at the downtown skyline.

"No, actually I live the other way. It's in a section called 'Dunwoody.'"

"Everyone here seems to live in the burbs."

"They used to call Atlanta, New York - South. Now it's become L.A. - East."

"How far is this 'Dunwoody' from here?"

"That depends on the traffic, which depends on the time of the day. It can be fifteen minutes – or fifty."

"I meant as the crow flies."

Sheila stared at him. Rather odd question, she thought.

"I don't know. Five or six miles, I suppose." The pause that followed was ended by Abigail.

"Mr. Bianco and Mr. Recos flew in last night from Las Vegas

on their way to Atlantic City. So some strong coffee is on the way to help reset their watches."

Just as that was said coffee did in fact arrive and was placed on a small conference room table. The men followed the coffee over and took seats on one side of the table while the lady lawyers took seats facing them. Sheila positioned her yellow-pad for note-taking as Recos poured himself a cup and slid over an ashtray.

"Sheila, Mr. Bianco here has come to us with a somewhat sensitive situation – actually a problem."

"With our good friends at the I.R.S., no doubt," she replied.

"No, no; not at all. For once it's not the I.R.S."

Sheila waited for Abigail to continue. After Abigail had eyed each man for a moment, she did so.

"Sheila, it's about J and M Gaming. It appears that Excelsior may have a little patent problem with them."

"J and M? A patent problem? I'm afraid that's a bit out of my field," she said as she put down her pen.

"Ordinarily that would be true, but not in this case."

"Let me explain this to the lady here," interjected Bianco. "This here J and M is going around telling people that it's getting this here patent on smart cards. You know about them smart cards?"

"I'm not sure what you mean. Do you mean bank cards? Cards like credit cards?"

"Yeah, those kinds."

"I find that kind of odd since J and M is a slot machine manufacturer. They are not into banking."

"You are right about that. They sure ain't. They'se a slots-house just like us. You know, like a competitor-like. Not our biggest; no way. But still they got a pretty good line. That J and M, they do come up with some pretty good slots. 'Bout time somebody did."

Sheila took a sip of her coffee while wishing that that infernal cigar smoke would drift the other way.

"Anyhows, our slots these days have done away with pay tickets. You know, those paper, pay-out tabs that you can carry from machine to machine, or cash out. These cards is a big hit now with the houses – the casinos. That's all they'se gots to have. Fact is we've been retroing like crazy."

"So J and M uses them too, now?" asked Sheila.

"They just started. You know, they saw what we was doing and hooked on."

"And?"

Bianco glanced at Abigail before continuing.

"And? And fuck." Bianco paused as he looked Sheila over. "Sorry, my mouth sometimes disconnects – disconnects from my brain." He chuckles as his business colleague looked at him and gave a knowing wink.

"I know this is all new to you, miss, you'se beings a tax lady and all. Here, let me explain.

"When we first puts the smart card modules on our 'chines we don't think it's a big deal. I means we didn't invent the damn thing; we only puts them on our slots that's already in the big houses. At least, that's what we thought. But then our attorney here, he goes into Caesars one night and sees our retrofits. So he jumps on my ass. Why hadn't I checked with him? That might be patentable, he says. So I tells him to search it out for us. Guess what? He comes back to me telling me that J and M already has a patent on it!"

"A patent?" asked Sheila.

"I think Mr. Bianco means a patent application," chimed in Abigail.

"Oh, yeah, a patent application. They hadn't come at us just yet."

Sheila pondered a moment and then spoke. "Well they might get turned down, you know. As you said, you didn't think it was a big deal – an invention. Maybe the Patent Office will agree with you and not grant them a patent."

"Maybe? Maybe? I can't live with no 'maybe.' You see, last week Mitt Casey, you know, the Pres of J and M, is over at the Bellagio spouting off about them patented our retros. Tells 'em that they will be having to get those from them."

"What did they say?" asked Sheila.

"Honey, they've been around the block. Well I guess there are blocks on The Strip," he says with a chuckle. "They've heard that crap before. Besides, their P.O.-s comes with a warranty. It's our ass if any of our 'chines causes 'em any legal problems."

There was a pause while Sheila mulled this over too.

"Since you put them in first, maybe you could go to the Patent Office and have their application killed. I'm no patent lawyer, but it might be worth a try."

"Already been there. Our attorney has already checked that out. No, they went after their patent way back - ways back before us. Seems that J and M has what's they calls a 'submarine patent.' You know, one that they just sits on while waiting for some ship to come sailing by. Pretty damn sneaky; wish we'd thought of that."

After an awkward silence Sheila spoke. "Well how can we, eh, how can *I* help you?" The two men looked at Abigail who then turned to her.

"Sheila, that raises the sensitive matter than I mentioned. It seems that the attorney on J and M's patent application is none other than your husband."

The room went silent as Sheila stared at Abigail, who returned the stare, and then looked at the two men. Bianco was quietly nodding at Abigail while Mr. "Recos's eyes and eyebrow were riveted on Sheila.

"Well, I guess he might be. I mean, I guess he is. But what, what . . . "

Finally Abigail took charge.

"Sheila, I think that this is something that we should continue in private; that is if Mr. Bianco doesn't mind."

Bianco turned to Recos. "Jal, what'ch think? Let the ladies have a go?"

Recos stood and leaned over Sheila with one hand supporting him on the table and the other supporting his cigar and his eyes appearing to be dead like shark eyes.

"Yea; yea. Let 'em have a little chat." Bianco reached up and gently tugged one of Jal Recos's arms who stood his ground for a moment before retreating.

"Then we stand adjourned, gentlemen," said Abigail with authority.

Chapter 2

Jimmy made his way into the parking garage of the Concourse and found a space on the third level. The Concourse is a Class A office building complex at the juncture of Georgia 400 and I-285 which is a 60 mile-long, eight-lane highway known as "the perimeter" that encircles Atlanta. The Concourse's two signature, high-rise buildings are known as the King and Queen buildings since their domes looked like the crowns of two giant chess pieces. Well illuminated at night, they can be seen from miles away and serve as a landmark.

Knight and Macguire was no Ramsey, Ivy and Prince where Sheila worked. It had no army of lawyers working in different states in multiple fields of law. Rather it was a small, boutique, IP firm that only handled intellectual property law work. In fact it marketed itself as such to the larger firms so that they would farm-out to them the occasional IP case that came their way without risk of losing their client. Of late however the big firms were handling IP litigation themselves since it was lucrative and the litigators didn't need to be professionally registered patent attorneys. Often though they would associate Knight and Macguire and have one of their lawyers serve as second chair and advise the first chair, referred to as the lead counsel, on the applicable patent law and technology at hand.

Jimmy enjoyed working at Knight and Macguire with its

small firm feel. Here technical proficiency counted more than personal flamboyance and one-upsmanship. He felt comfortable with an office practice and normal work hours and the lack of tension and irregular hours that came with litigation. Drafting patent applications was a positive and creative pursuit, where litigation had so much negativism associated with it.

Once settled in his office he pulled up J and M's patent application docket. Six pending applications popped up on his desktop computer screen:

8J01-1-011 Centralized Smart-Card Money Management Method and System for Gaming Machines
8J01-1-050 Cashless Gaming Apparatus and Method of Use
8J01-1-070 Method and System for Using Time-Sensitive tickets as player awards in Gaming Machines
8J01-1-080 Gaming Device with Joystick and Trigger
8J01-1-090 Gaming Device Having a Masked Award Game
8J01-1-100 Gaming Device Having Independent Reel Columns
8J01-1-110 Gaming Device Having Multiple Transverse Rotating Displays

In adjacent columns appeared what action was required, its due-date, and the number of extensions that remained available. Jimmy took satisfaction in seeing the digit 8 in the client identification number 8J01, the 8 identifying him as the attorney whose client this was within the firm. Most docket numbers, of course, bore 2, 3 or 4 leading digits which identified one of the firm partners as the lawyer that had originated the client and brought it into the firm. The digit 1 had been that of Cecil Knight, but it had been retired when he had died. As he was finishing scanning the docket Charles Macguire appeared in his office threshold.

"Got a minute, Jimmy?" he asked.

Jimmy stood, surprised to see the senior partner coming to see him. "Of course; come on in."

Charles Macguire was probably the only member of the firm that looked like a polished trial lawyer. He was a handsome man in his mid-fifties, a bit over six-feet tall; a man who radiated self-assurance and inspired confidence in both clients and jurors alike. He took a seat in one of the two armchairs that faced Jimmy's desk.

"Jimmy, I had a call this morning about a client of yours – a J and M Gaming out in Peachtree Corners."

"It's funny that you mention them as I was just looking over their docket," he said as he nodded to the screen. Macguire rotated the self-standing screen and looked over the docket.

"This application here - this one on smart cards; it's been pending quite awhile now, I see."

"Yes, we had to file a continuation-in-part on it. They wanted to add a little to it."

"I see. Yes, that's the one of interest. It seems that this one may have some real commercial value. We want to get it right. Don't want to leave anything on the table on this one."

"I'll make sure of that."

"Tell you what. If you don't mind I'd like to look over your next response on it before it's submitted. I see that it's coming due in two weeks."

"We can get an extension. That should be no problem."

"Yes, it's best to take our time and get it right. As I said, it's become quite important to J and M."

Macguire left and Jimmy turned the visit over in his mind. It was nice to have the senior partner come to him but why had his own, and so far only, client gone to Macguire? That's not good, he thought. Then again Macguire hadn't actually said that – only that he had received a call about J & M. Strange, but then it was good to see that he recognized that Jimmy had brought in a client that was giving them steady work. Patent prosecution work wasn't lucrative like patent litigation, but it was good, steady pay. Also, the more patents secured, the more likely that there would be crossed swords in the future with some competitor which in turn could led to more work - to more billing hours.

Jimmy pulled the J and M smart card application folder from a file cabinet and started his review of the Official Action that needed a response. The application now had 27 claims. Each claim defined the monopoly that the applicant sought in different terms. Generally, the fewer the words the broader the monopoly claim since each word provided a "limitation" which any product accused of infringing would have to have. Jimmy recalled an example that was given when he was first introduced to the world of patents. It went something like this.

Suppose that you were the first person to have invented the chair. What would you claim? How would you define your product – your invention? At first you might think to simply claim "a chair." But what is that? It had never existed before so the word itself would mean nothing. You would have simply coined a new but meaningless word. So you must think of the parts that make up this "chair" and how they are all interconnected in order to define this new fangled thing.

So you think, well it has a support upon which a person can sit. And it has these four legs that are mounted to one side of the support. So there you are. Thus you claim a product upon which a person may sit that has a support of a size and shape to be sat upon from one side of which four legs extend. Since such a product would have never existed before, the government grants you a patent. Now no one can make, use or sell such a product until the patent expires without your consent.

So you think that you are now really *sitting* atop the world with this chair. But then comes along this smart aleck with his new three legged thing that he calls a "stool." Having one less leg it is cheaper than your chair. So you take the jerk on and what happens? You lose. Why? It's because his stool does not have the construction that is defined in your patent claim. It does not have a support from one side of which *four* legs extend. The stool only has three legs! So your claim had one too many elements making it unnecessarily narrower than it should have been. You as the patent attorney had left something on the table, something that Mr. Macguire had just warned to be on the lookout for.

Not only that but this other inventor of the stool might even get a patent of his own since the triangular arrangement of his three legs would differ from your chair and be novel. To rub salt into the wound *your* chair would infringe the stool patent since it did have three (plus an extra) legs. Not only that but these three legs – any three of your four – formed the bounds of a triangle. Crazy stuff these patent claims! But that's why patent attorneys earn their keep by authoring these tangled and often esoterically worded patent claims. Jimmy turned back to his modern-world patent claims.

"Claim 1. A cashless gaming machine comprising electronic

memory means for storing credits available for play, the amount of credit being determined by the outcome of a game played or an amount of inputted credit; a reader for . . . . "

On and on the claim went in electronic systems language but the essence was that the gaming machine, which included slot machines, was designed to generate game credits from inputted coins and currency, game wins, as well as from smart cards and to pay out credits back to smart cards whenever the player cashed out. The player could then use the same credit bearing card at another such machine or cash in.

This and the other claims stood currently rejected by the patent examiner who had referenced patents that existed before Jimmy had originally filed. These prior patents showed the existence of slot machines and the existence, of course, of smart cards. Although the smart cards were shown for use in payment for goods and services, the examiner had taken the position that it would have been "obvious" to use them with slot machines.

Non-obviousness was a requirement for the patentability of any patent claim. Jimmy's counter-argument had been that the slot machine could pay out credits onto the cards as well as pay in credits from the card, and that all of this was done in conjunction with plays on the slots that added or deducted credits. Moreover slot machines were highly imprecise mathematically, quite the opposite from debits and credits. They were games of chance that actually used random number generators. His job remained to convince the examiner that such would not have been obvious at the time that the application had been originally filed just because slot machines and smart cards themselves had been independently known.

Just as he was beginning to think this through and frame his argument his phone rang. It was Joe Turner, the Vice President at J and M who was his regular contact there.

"Jimmy, Mitt is breathing down my neck about the smart card patent. How's it coming?"

"How about that for timing; I'm sitting here studying the file as we speak."

"What can I tell him?"

"Tell him that it is still pending. This latest action is another rejection but it's not final. The examiner has come up with a couple of new references. I don't think they add anything new. I'll point that out. I mean it is encouraging that she felt she needed more ammo to support her earlier rejection. But again these new prior art patents look to me as just more of the same-old, same-old."

"How can we speed this thing up?"

"Joe, I'll move this to the top of my list. I'll get right on it."

"What if you call him – the Examiner?"

"It's not a 'him'; it's a lady - a Chinese lady, I think."

"Look Jimmy, we really do need to hustle on this. What if you go up there and talk to her. You know, a little one-on-one. Can't hurt can it?"

"No, it can't hurt. But it might hurt your pocketbook a little. You know; the airfare and all."

"Jimmy, you aren't listening. This is important. We want this done and we want it done as quickly as possible. Look, you can make it a day trip if you want or not. We don't care. We just want this job done."

"Yes sir. I'll get right on it."

So much for Macguire's go-slow-but-sure spiel.

Chapter 3

That night it was Jimmy who put the boys to bed. At first he resisted their pleas for a story but finally relinquished. Another chapter from Dr. Seuss's *The Cat in the Hat Comes Back* was read. Both children were asleep within minutes.

Back downstairs he found Sheila plopped on the sofa in front of the TV that was turned off. As Jimmy entered she looked up at him. She looked exhausted.

"Rough day, huh?"

When she didn't respond he sat down and put his arm around her. Her head fell over onto his shoulder.

"A weird thing happened today." She paused and stared far off at the darkened TV screen. Jimmy waited.

"We had a meeting with a couple of men from Excelsior. God, what a pair they were." She continued to stare off into space. "You know Excelsior, right?"

"Vaguely; I've seen a few patents of theirs on slot machines. Guess they probably are a competitor of J and M."

With that Sheila turned to face him. "Yes; yes they are."

He didn't respond.

"Jimmy, both Excelsior and J and M are clients of Ramsey Ivy. I know that they probably shouldn't be - at least not now, but Ramsey, Ivy and Prince is big. Excelsior came in through our west coast office way back when. When J and M came in, the days of extensive conflicts of interest checks for new clients had barely begun. Actually, Abigail first took them in while working in L.A. since it was a tax problem that had generated the client. I doubt that she even ran a conflicts check. Tax lawyers don't think that way since their work involves one client and one government. Private clients rarely go around knocking heads over taxes."

"So? Is there a problem?"

"When you got J and M as a client it was my doing; my referral. Remember?"

"Of course."

"That was when they had gone to Abigail and said that they needed some patent work done - that they had been using a D.C. firm but now wanted someone local to be on-hand. Abigail checked and found out that Ramsey, Ivy and Prince was handling patent matters for Excelsior. The conflict was obvious. Knowing that you were a patent attorney she farmed it out to you, through me."

"Yea, I know all that. But I still don't see a problem."

"The problem is that you are working to get J and M a patent on a slot machine that takes smart cards; right?"

"Yes, that's right. Did I mention that one to you?"

"No, not you; it was those henchmen from Excelsior that just so happened to *mention* it today."

"Well I guess that's no longer any secret since we also filed internationally on it. It's been published."

"That's not how they found out. They found out a wee bit more directly. It seems that Excelsior's own slot machines now use smart cards. J and M now is going around to the casinos in Vegas with warnings over that."

"Well that explains a lot. I was about to tell you that I have to go up to Washington for J and M on their smart card application. Joe Turner called me today on it and said that it was important to get it through, and to get it through fast."

Sheila looked Jimmy in the eye and moved out from under his arm. "There's more, Jimmy. Excelsior doesn't want that to happen – for obvious reasons."

"Of course they don't but that's business. After all, the patent isn't directed just against them, you know; it's there to hold *all* competitors off. Let the chips fall as they may – especially in the casino business." He chuckled at his pun as he was often prone to do.

"Jimmy, there's more I'm afraid. Excelsior wants you, *Jimmy Davis Esq.*, member of the bar, to back off; to let this application run aground."

"You're kidding, right?"

"I wish I were."

Jimmy now moved further away from her and put his hands on his knees. Now they both found themselves staring at the darkened screen.

"Did the two goons say this, or did Abigail?"

"They told me about their problem. Later Abigail spoke to me in private."

"What exactly did she say?"

"For once she tried to be diplomatic. She said that she well knew that this was a sensitive matter - that legal ethics were involved. Nevertheless, she said it really would help her out if I could see it in me to see if you couldn't help us out. She emphasized that it would be just this once. She actually softened her armor and looked at me almost pleadingly, if you can believe that."

"Do you want me to accommodate her?"

"Oh, I don't know."

"Well you know my answer."

Sheila sighed, reached over and placed a hand on one of Jimmy's.

"Let's not worry about it right now. I've seen that getting patents takes time. By then things may have resolved themselves on their own," she said wearily.

Jimmy kept his eyes peeling out the window as the Boeing 767 continued its approach into Reagan National. What had been a smooth flight from Atlanta's Hartsfield airport was no more. There was nothing to see but the light-grey soup. It took another three minutes of turbulence before he began to make out the terrain below. About that time he heard the wheels being lowered, followed by a jolt indicating that they were securely down and locked. Moments later they were over the field and onto the runway. The low buildings of Crystal City flew pass as the plane decelerated under the reverse thrust of its engines.

Being right in the Washington metropolitan area, a mere three miles from Washington's central business district, Reagan National's three runways are short. One is actually less than five thousand feet and its longest doesn't even reach seven thousand feet. The airport had been called by many names in the past from "National," "Washington National", "Reagan" to "Reagan National."

For patent and trademark professionals the airport had been the most convenient airport in the country for them to ply their skills. Before its move recently to Alexandria, the Patent and Trademark Office had been located in Crystal City just across railroad tracks from a runway. One could literally walk there from the airport terminal.

Examiner Fang and Jimmy had scheduled the interview in her office for ten-thirty. That way this could be just a day trip. He had prepared by reviewing the application file and the prior art references. He had also gotten an affidavit from Joe Turner testifying as to the commercial success that the invention was enjoying in the casinos. He would use this to support his position that the invention had not been "obvious to one skilled in the art," and thus was entitled to patent protection. He had discussed with Joe Turner the option of bringing the inventor along but in the end they had decided against that as this was more of a legal issue than a technical one. Even though he had prepared well, at least in his mind, he still was rather new at all this. He hoped his apprehension wouldn't be too apparent.

Not surprisingly his nightmare overnight had involved the upcoming interview. In the nightmare Madam Fang had lived up to her name. There he had been standing in front of her desk looking down at the diminutive Chinese dragon lady in her mustard colored, patterned silk dress. As he made his pitch she would smile and nod in agreement while repeatedly saying "no, so solly, Mr. Havis. No, so solly."

"But Ms. Fang, surely you understand . . ."

She had continued merely to nod while smiling as she repeatedly hissed "no, so solly, Mr. Havis," all the while exposing the two fangs that straddled her upper incisors. This had continued until she had finally stood, pointed to the door and hissed through her fangs: "You speak with forked tongue, Mr. Havis; now out, please." And out of the nightmare he had come with such a jolt that it had woken Sheila.

The real-life Ms. Fang proved to be entirely fangless. Her dominant facial feature was her thick, rectangular eyeglasses with bold black rims that matched the black design of her pantsuit. There was no visual anomaly in her mouth.

Jimmy found her in her small office studying an open file. He knocked on her open door and she greeted him professionally. The open file proved to be his. After brief small talk he took a seat and started to give her his pitch.

"Ms. Fang, as you see from the file here . . ."

"Mr. Davis," she interrupted, "Your claims here are very broad. What you basically claim is merely the use of smart cards with gaming machines. That is too broad."

Wow, he thought, Ms. Fang was pointed, albeit without benefit of fangs.

"Well yes, that's basically it. We were the first. This concept originated with my client."

"That may be true, but that doesn't make it patentable."

Ms. Fang looked over the young Mr. Davis up and down before continuing.

"As you know, under 35 USC 103 your claims have to be non-obvious. It seems to have been quite obvious to me."

"Whether it is obvious to you is not the point. The question is whether it was obvious to one of ordinary skill in the art at the time."

Ms. Fang glared. Oops, thought Jimmy, what a stupid thing to have said to this seasoned professional.

"I'm sorry, of course you understand that. I grant you that electronic gaming machines such as slot machines are well known. I also agree that my client makes no claim to have invented the smart card. But there is no suggestion in any of the art of record here to a workable combination of the two."

Ms. Fang remained silent, inviting further argument.

"At the time of the filing of the parent application smart cards were used for payments. Back then a smart card would be inserted into a card reader and a personal identification number entered. The card reader would read these and deduct an amount keyed in from the card." Jimmy paused and studied Ms. Fang's face which seemed to express a "so what?" look.

"But here we have, shall we say, a two-way street. With our invention monetary units are deducted from the card and entered as credits for play. The same card also *receives* credits back from the machine whenever a player hits a cash-out key. The player then can go to another machine and continue to play. The player may also turn in the card whenever he or she wants to, and receive actual cash. The cards have proven to be very popular in this unusual application. Both the gamblers and the casinos love them." Jimmy paused.

"Mr. Davis. You seem to say that it is this two-way street that is new. Correct?"

"Yes, you could put it that way."

"Mr. Davis, this prior art reference here shows how credits are entered onto a smart card. Correct?"

"Yes, that's right."

"And this reference here shows how credits are subtracted from a smart card. Correct?"

"Well yes."

"That is a two-way street, is it not?"

"No, not really, you see these transactions are done at two different locations. The smart card is issued in this prior art reference at a bank and used elsewhere at a retail store terminal. We are claiming a cashless gaming machine where credits are both subtracted and added. This renders the machine a cashless one; one in which cash need neither be inputted nor extracted."

"So it is your position that your cashless gaming machine is non-obvious simply because credits may be extracted and added to a smart card as it is associated with the machine?"

"Basically yes, although the gambling environment should also be factored in; it is far afield from the mathematically precise environment of commercial accounting for debits and credits."

"I must disagree. Your client did not invent the cashless slot machine as the patent here to Hendrix shows."

"Hendrix shows a typical tito machine — a ticket-in, ticket-out, slot," said Jimmy. "True, it is cashless, but it generates a lot of paperwork. Those machines have to be supplied with paper and resupplied. They are electromechanical and thus subject to wear and malfunction. With the smart card there is no paper; no issuance, destruction and reissuance, over and over, of paper tickets. That's why both the casinos and gamblers love them."

"Isn't that inherent in any use of smart cards?"

"Yes, in a way, but again this is in conjunction with our two-way street feature."

"Ah yes, the two-way street analogy. Mr. Davis, some highways are divided. They have grass or even trees between lanes going each way. Some highways are undivided; they have no mediums of grass or flowers. Your position is simply that it would be non-obvious to do away with the medium. I don't think so. Highways with mediums came along *after* the medium-less highway. The Lamb reference here shows how credits are entered into a smart card by a bank. It also shows how they can be redeemed by the same bank, a la a two-way street."

Jimmy stared at her. She had turned his own analogy against his position. He tried to recoup.

"But again, this is all for bill paying. These references are not in the field of gaming machines at all."

"Mr. Davis. This tito - this ticket-in, ticket-out reference shows cashless gaming machines to have been old. The other references show both the adding and subtracting of credits from smart cards to be old. You have merely substituted smart cards for printed tickets. Your claims are too broad. Now if you have brought a proposed amendment with you that further limits your claims I will consider that. Have you?"

"No, not exactly, but I have however brought this affidavit that attests to the commercial success that this invention had met almost instantaneously. Both the casinos and the players love it. This shows that if it had been all that obvious it would have been thought of and used before in lieu of the titos."

He handed the affidavit to Ms. Fang. She read the single sheet.

"Mr. Davis. This affidavit of Mr. Turner merely says that slot machines with smart cards have been commercially successful. It does not state by whom. It does not state here that it has been his company, this J and M, I believe, that has accounted for this success."

"Well, no. But does that matter?" At once he realized his error. Trial lawyers are always taught never to ask a witness a question that they didn't already know the answer. That probably applied here too.

The dragon lady smiled.

"Do you have anything else to offer?" she asked.

"Ms. Fang, please remember that our invention was made some time ago. Smart cards were hardly even known back then. In hindsight they might now be considered obvious but I assure you that that was not the case back then."

"Mr. Davis, I will enter this document into the record along with a record of our meeting. And I thank you for coming," she said as she glanced at her wristwatch.

With that Ms. Fang stood. Jimmy followed suit and with a rather meek and tentative "thank you" and walked to the door.

"Oh, and Mr. Davis," she smiled. "If you look into it I think you will find that it was a company by the name of Excelsior that has actually accounted for this success. We do subscribe to the trades, you know."

After Jimmy had had a bite to eat in the cafeteria he made his way to the public search room. He filled out an access form at the security office and was issued a pass. He entered the room through a secured entry.

The huge, cavernous facility was a beehive of activity. Times Square may well be the crossroad of the world, but the U.S. Patent Office's public search room was the equivalent for its technology niche. It was filled with regulars who made searching their trade, most of whom knew each other.

Before the days of the cell phone there had been a bank of telephones along a wall of the room. When they would ring a regular standing nearby would pick up and yell out the name of the person being called. When these professional searchers weren't working the stacks, or doing on-line searching, you could find them chatting. Whether talking shop or gossiping, they would abide by their own unwritten code of conduct of not looking at paperwork laid out on the tables or patents displayed on screens by their fellow searchers, although sometimes they would be invited to do so in helping out a colleague. Beside the pros there were people from the four corners of the globe using the gigantic technology resources that the search room provided. Many babbled in foreign tongues.

Jimmy put down his briefcase and coat at a table that was vacant save for a couple of spots where a chair was pulled cocked open in front of a briefcase and a pile of patents.

He opened his briefcase and took out a sheet which described an invention of one of his clients. From that he formed a few key words in his mind and took off to find a classification manual. Identifying a couple of classes and a number of subclasses that the invention probably belonged in, he made his way into the stacks. It took him ten minutes before he located the most promising one. Unfortunately the very "shoe" of printed patents that he wanted was missing. Apparently someone else was now going through it.

Jimmy returned to his work station and relocated the subclass on a computer terminal. He booted it up but decided on a visit to the somewhat distant restroom before beginning his searching.

After that he took his time in exploring the search room facilities to get better acquainted with it before returning to his terminal. Boy I wish I had more time, he thought to himself. He had only been here once before and that had been for training with one of the searchers that the firm regularly used.

But this time he wanted to bill out at least one search himself before returning to Atlanta.

He sat back down at his terminal. The screen was dark. Guess the time had run out he thought as he clicked the screen back on. Rather than the index being re-displayed, there was a message:

MR. DAVIS. GUESS YOU DON'T GET IT. THE NEXT THING YOU HAND
FANG HAD BEST BE AN
ABANDONMENT NOTICE.

Jimmy stared at the screen in shock and bewilderment. As he did so he became super-conscious of the sounds all around him, especially including those directly behind him.

Slowly he looked over his screen. An oriental man straight ahead raised his head and eyed him for a moment before returning to his own screen. Jimmy looked to his right and then to his left; nothing. Slowly he pushed his chair back, stood and turned around. He could find nothing out of the ordinary. He looked at his watch. He probably still had time to do his search or to return to Ms. Fang, but not both. He decided on Ms. Fang.

Jimmy walked quickly back to her office. At its threshold he found a man in a white shirt and necktie standing in front of Ms. Fang's desk, talking softly with her.

"Mr. Rossi, this is Mr. Davis, the gentleman I was just mentioning."

Rossi glanced back at Ms. Fang and then turned to look Jimmy over.

"Mr. Davis, Mr. Rossi is the primary examiner on your application," she continued.

"Ah, Mr. Davis, we were just reviewing your file. I am glad to meet you," he finally said as he extended his hand.

"That was fast, Mr. Rossi."

"Examiners have to write up a summary of what was discussed and agreed to at interviews. We were discussing just what to include."

"I see," replied Jimmy. "Tell me, have you all discussed this with anyone else? I mean since the interview."

Rossi and Fang exchanged glances before Ms. Fang responded.

"Why do you ask?"

Jimmy studied them both for a moment as they studied him.

"Would you please answer me?"

"Mr. Davis, we do not discuss internal office business affairs with applicants, or with their attorneys," said Rossi.

Jimmy thought for a moment.

"Mr. Rossi, I have just been threatened."

"Threatened?"

"Yes, threatened."

"Physically threatened as by a robber? Are you alright?"

"No, not by a robber; I was ordered to abandon this patent application. A threatening demand was made that I drop it."

"Where? Here in the office?"

"In the public search room."

"Did you recognize the man?"

"The threat appeared on the screen of the terminal that I was using."

"Did you print it out?"

"Uh, well no, I didn't. I guess I should have. But what would that prove? I mean, I could have typed it myself."

"Did you tell security?"

"No. I came right back here. Hey look, you are grilling me. Someone knew I was here in your office. They even knew Ms. Fang's name. Tell me, are your computers tied in with those in the search room?"

As soon as Jimmy had said that, he wished he hadn't. Ms. Fang stood.

"What exactly are you implying?"

Jimmy retreated.

"I mean if they were, someone up here in your examination unit could have been the one."

To this no one responded. With all three now standing in Ms. Fang's small space Mr. Rossi brought this to an end.

"Mr. Davis, I will ask Ms. Fang to add what you have just told us as a subscript to her interview record. Now I suggest that you return immediately to the search room and report this matter to security as you should have done at the time. It *is* right there, you know."

"Yes; yes sir, I will. I am sorry if I sounded like I was accusing anyone up here. It's just that I am upset. I am sure you would be too had this just happened to you."

Chapter 4

"Bam!" came an attack from Jimmy's left; "Bam!" came a synchronized attack from his right.

It was Saturday morning and the twins were making the most of it. Andy had initiated the action by jumping on the bed next to his sleeping father. Alec had followed his lead by jumping on Jimmy's other side. As one boy reached the zenith of his bounce the other would land. Just like a seesaw, had they known what a seesaw was, but along with high-diving boards and now even low-diving boards, plus Jungle Gyms and carousels, the seesaw was now banned from playgrounds. It was just *too* dangerous. Lord, some schools were now even starting to ban dodge ball. It *is* a contact sport, you know. So much for fun; someone might scratch a knee.

Jimmy grabbed Andy and put his arm around him. "Now just who is the ring-leader here?"

"Me," screamed Andy as Alec continued to bounce up and down.

"Are you sure?"

"Me, me, me," he yelled. Then Alec changed his cadence from bounce-bounce-bounce to bounce-sit-bounce-sit-bounce.

"Wow," said Jimmy. Andy would not allow Alec to take center-stage so he wiggled free and joined his brother. Jimmy surrendered and got up.

A few minutes later he found Sheila downstairs at the breakfast table sipping coffee as she read *The Atlanta Constitution*. "G'morning. What's new?"

"Same old, same old – Iraq; Iran; Afghanistan; you know."

"America does not go abroad in search of monsters to destroy."

"Hey, that's not bad," said Sheila.

"Know who said that?" She looked up.

"John Quincy Adams, our sixth President; that's not bad, huh?"

Sheila looked back down as Jimmy grabbed some juice and cereal and took a seat. She slid the sports section over to him without so much as a glance.

"Hey, how about this for news: The Falcons lost!"

Sheila glanced up only to return again to her reading.

"It was so late last night that I didn't tell you about something that happened to me at the Patent Office."

Sheila looked up while holding her finger on the newsprint to mark her place.

"Hey, this will take a few minutes, if you don't mind."

She relinquished and sat back.

Jimmy filled her in on the threat that had been made in the search room and what had followed. As she was in the midst of asking for details Alec came in crying.

"Andy broke my pirate ship. He broke it."

Sheila pulled him to her and sat him on her lap. "There now, how did that happen?"

"He broke it. He hit it with his rocket."

Sheila took a napkin from the table and dried his eyes. "There there; it's going to be alright."

"It's not; it's broken."

"Let me take a look," said Jimmy as he stood and left. He found Andy still attacking Alec's pirate ship with his rocket in hand.

"Wham, wham, wham; the model ship's mast was bent. Jimmy took it and straightened it out.

"Take it easy, pal," he said as he returned to the kitchen with ship in hand. Alec was mollified and ran back. It would no doubt continue on like this, this being Saturday with Miss Clara off for the day.

"What should I do, Sheila?"

"I don't see that you can do anything. Besides, people say nasty things on the internet all the time."

"Sheila, this was done by someone that was watching me; stalking me. It's hardly the same."

She took a moment to respond.

"You gave me a quote, by Adams, as I recall; now I'll give you one. 'The art of life is to deal with problems as they arise rather than destroy one's spirit by worrying about them too far in advance.'"

Jimmy studied her. "I think you are quoting Mrs. Abigail Carmichael here."

"More like Cicero, I'll have you know."

Cicero, indeed; another lawyer thought Jimmy. "Look, this didn't happen to you. I don't think you would feel the same if it had."

"Jimmy, people don't go around knocking off lawyers over matters concerning their clients, and for good reason. That inherently involves risk and doesn't accomplish anything. Clients simply hire another.

"This is a problem for J and M. If I were you I would get my butt over there Monday morning. You don't need this worry. Get them on it."

"Who wants to go to the playground?" asked Jimmy.

"Me; me," responded Andy.

"Then let's do it!"

Sheila bundled up the twins good and warm. Jimmy broke out the two-seat stroller from the garage. The twins got in with their toy guns in hand and they were off.

Jimmy pushed the stroller along the sidewalk under a cold, cloudy sky. A cat that crossed their path was gleefully targeted by the boys.

"Chink; chink; got him," said Alec.

"No you didn't; I got him first," responded Andy.

"Did not . . . Did so . . . Did not . . . Did so."

The cat calmly ignored them as only cats can.

After some six blocks or so they arrived at the public playground which was under a canopy of barren oak tree limbs adjacent to a grammar school. Dead leaves from autumn still covered the surrounding grounds.

Jimmy unloaded the boys from the stroller and herded them through the small gate after pocketing their guns.

Inside the fenced-in area was an oversized wooden Jungle Gym. It had an elevated playhouse that was connected with a turret via a crawl-through, arched, tunnel-bridge. It had an abundance of swings and slides and handlebars all set atop a field of moistened bark.

Jimmy closed the gate behind them and made his way over to a vacant spot on a bench. A black nanny sat at the opposite end of the bench. In all there were about a dozen adults milling about trying to keep warm as they watched the children at play and occasionally went to their rescue.

"You must be Mr. Davis," said the nanny.

"Why yes. How did you know?"

"You don't see many twins here. Clara brings them here."

"Glad to meet you Ms. . . . ?" he said as he leaned over and extended his hand.

"Ida May; I have the Jenkins' boy - the one there making mischief, as usual. He's a pistol, that Tommy."

Jimmy saw that her Tommy was the one chasing the little girl wearing the pink parka.

"Yea, he's a real pistol; already a'chase'n."

Jimmy smiled as he reflected on his own early youth, at least as it had been told to him. He had been a notorious kisser in kindergarten. "Well I'm glad to meet you, Ida May. I'll tell Miss Clara."

With that he reached in his coat pocket and extracted a pocket novel as he stretched out his legs. He read a few pages but then his interest in the book lapsed. His mind was back again on that monitor in the Patent Office and on that message that he couldn't stop replaying in his mind. Surrender, indeed; by damn he would not be filing any white flag.

He laid the book down and looked about. He located Andy in the midst of the children, at least he thought it was Andy rather than Alec since he was engaged in a bark-throwing battle with another child. Jimmy marked his place, re-pocketed his book, and with an "excuse me" walked over to the fence.

"Andy, stop that; stop that right now."

Andy obeyed. The other boy looked at Jimmy for a moment and then let fly with another piece of bark at Andy before he turned and ran off. Andy gave chase.

Jimmy scanned the children to try and spot Alec. Not finding him he walked around one corner of the fence to gain another view of the large, rambling Jungle Gym. There still was no Alec to be found.

"Alec," he called out. No response. He returned to the front of the playground and entered the gate just as Andy came running by still chasing the other boy. He grabbed him.

"Hold on there, fellow," he said as he swung him back and forth between his spread legs. Andy squealed with delight.

"Andy, where is your brother?" Andy continued to squeal.

"Andy, come on now. Where is Alec?" Jimmy stopped his swinging and plopped Andy down who immediately took off again.

Jimmy walked towards the Jungle Gym. "Alec," he yelled. "Alec."

"Looking for the twin?" asked a woman wearing a knit cap.

"Yes; have you seen him?"

"I have; he was talking with a man over there at the hut."

"Man? What man?"

"I don't know; just a man. He was standing there talking with your boy who was up in the playhouse."

"Thank you," said Jimmy as he walked over to the hut. He walked around to its open side, but no Alec. He turned around as he felt a rush of adrenaline. "Alec. Alec."

"Boo." Alec's head appeared out of the tunnel-bridge in which he had been lying.

"Alec, you scared me. Now come on out."

Alec stood and came out as Jimmy walked over to the railing of the hut.

"What were you doing?"

"Hiding."

"Hiding from whom? Hiding from me?"

"No, just hiding."

"I heard that you were talking with a man. Is that right?"

Alec swayed back and forth but said nothing.

"Well? Were you?" Then Jimmy saw that he has holding something tightly in his little hand.

"What are you holding there?" What have you got?"

"Nothing," he said as he continued to sway.

"Come on now. Let daddy see."

Slowly Alec opened his small hand to reveal a pack of Juicy Fruit. Then he re-griped his small treasure.

"Where did you get that? Did the man give it to you?"

"It's mine; mine."

"Yes, it's yours. But tell me, did the man give it to you?" Alec nodded.

"He's a nice man."

"Did he talk with you?"

Alec nodded again.

"What did you talk about?"

"About me; about me and Andy."

"What about you and Andy?"

"If we were the same; you know."

"Oh, he asked if you and Andy were just alike?"

Alec nodded.

"And what did you say?"

"You know – the spot."

Jimmy knew that he was referring to Andy's birthmark. Standing on the ground with Alec standing on the elevated hut Jimmy drew him into a close embrace and gave him a long hug.

"Let me see the gum."

Alec slowly handed it over. Jimmy carefully examined it. It was sealed like new. Jimmy handed it back.

"Alec, if you ever see the man again you let me know. Okay?"

"Okay. He's nice. I like him."

Chapter 5

Jimmy did as Sheila had said to do and presented himself to the J and M receptionist early Monday morning, which for him was nine o'clock. The receptionist called Joe Turner who told her to send him on back. So she had him sign in, gave him a badge and he was on his way. He found Joe seated at his desk talking with Jack Partus, an engineer who was a named inventor on a few patent applications. "Good morning, Jack; Joe."

"Good morning, Jimmy," replied Jack as he stood to greet him. "Have a seat. Like some coffee?"

"That would be great," said Jimmy as he looked at the huge picture of the Las Vegas strip at night that adorned Joe's office wall behind his desk. Though it was only about three feet high, it was over ten feet long. It was straddled by two antique, nickel-fed, one-arm bandits that were lit up and raring to go. Another wall bore some industry awards and pictures of mega jackpot hits including a staged one with a local Elvis.

"So how's business?" asked Jimmy.

"How's business?" Joe answered. "How would you say business is, Jack?"

"There's no business like show business."

"Right."

There was a pause. So much for the small talk, thought Jimmy.

"How was your trip? Hope good news is what has brought you over this morning."

"I did get to speak with the examiner in person. In fact we spent almost an hour on the smart card application. I, uh, I also got to speak with her supervisor." Well *technically* that was true, thought Jimmy.

"And?"

"Well; well nothing was finally resolved but she's going to consider it further."

"You did give her my affidavit, right?"

"Of course."

"What was her reaction? That must have impressed her."

"She read it in front of me and said that she would accept it and enter it into the record."

"That's all? She's just going to stick it in the file?"

"Oh, no; I'm sure it's going to help."

"She didn't comment on it at all?"

God, here we go again, thought Jimmy.

"Well yes, she did comment on it." As Jimmy hesitated Joe and Jack maintained eye-to-eye contact with him. "She pointed out that the commercial success had not been made by J and M but by Excelsior."

"She told you that?" Jimmy nodded. "Let me see the damn thing. You've got it with you, right?"

Jimmy opened his briefcase just as the coffees arrived, which served to somewhat break the tension a little that Jimmy felt was developing. As Joe added some Sweet and Low to his coffee Jimmy pulled out the smart card application folder and extracted the affidavit. He handed it to Joe who read it slowly.

"Just as I thought; this doesn't say who had been putting these retros on. There's nothing about that. In fact I had caught the fact that you had not actually said who it was when you wrote the thing up."

Lord, thought Jimmy. That wasn't by design; it just came out that way. "Thanks."

"Does it matter that someone else has been the one putting these in?"

"No, I don't think so. Commercial success is commercial success." Jesus, I hope I'm right, Jimmy thought. I've got to look that up when I get back to make sure.

"Well?"

"Well?" responded Jimmy.

"Well, how did she know about Excelsior? Did *you* tell her?"

"No sir, but she did mention trade journals. Apparently it's been reported in one of those."

"You say that you also talked to her supervisor. How did that go?"

"That brings me to the reason that brought me over this morning, Joe."

Jimmy and Joe both took sips of their coffees as Jack walked over to take renewed interest in a couple of details in the Las Vegas strip photographic scene.

"Joe, while I was at the Patent Office I received a threat, a threatening demand that I abandon this application." Jimmy proceeded to tell them what all had happened. Joe listened intensely as Jack paced back and forth, still preferring to look at The Strip rather than at Jimmy.

"Jimmy, I wouldn't take this as a personal threat. No, I wouldn't worry myself over it. This is business - business between Excelsior and us. It's just that — it's just that I don't see how they found you up there. That doesn't compute." Joe paused to think.

"Who knew that you were there?"

"My wife knows, of course, and my secretary."

"That's it?"

"Yes, unless one of them told somebody else."

"Check on that, will you?"

"And you all, of course," replied Jimmy as he saw Joe take a look at Jack.

"So that's what you took up with the supervisor?"

"Yes, it just came out that way."

"Then you didn't push our case with him."

"Right, but I'm sure she will. In fact she was going over it with him when I intruded.

"Joe, I've never been threatened like this before. This is a first. Is there something here that I should know?"

"Not that I can think of. Look Jimmy, I don't know anything about what happened up there in Washington. Wish I did. But as I said, I wouldn't get too exercised over it. It could have been a prank. It could have been anything. I've never been to the Patent Office. I don't know a damn thing about it, but let's move on. Jack has something I want you to take a look at."

After the meeting in Joe Turner's office Jack took Jimmy back to the engineering spaces to see a new project. They made their way back through the assembly line area that occupied a cavernous, thirty-foot high manufacturing area where sounds echoed and reverberated. Some of the space now went unused, which attested to the transition of slot machine designs away from electromechanical to the modern world of electronic operation.

Where actual reels and reel drives had existed before, now there were projected images of reels spinning and locking on. On many machines coin registers and dispensers no longer existed either, having been replaced by currency and ticket readers and printers. And now, albeit belatedly by J and M, smart card readers and encoders were going in.

They finally reached their destination space which was set off from the assembly line area. No manufacturing echo or high ceiling lighting in this product development space.

Jimmy followed Jack over to a bench where Jack motioned him to a stool in front of a shrouded object. Jack took a seat on the other stool and faced the shroud. For a moment both men just sat there staring at it. Then Jimmy turned to Jack who gave him a chuckle.

"Any guess?"

"Our lunch?" quipped Jimmy.

"In a way, I suppose, since we may well be eating our competitors' lunch with this little sucker. But before all is revealed let me gave you a little background.

"Until now slot machines have been the bread-and-butter for the casinos. But you know that. More revenue is normally generated by them in casinos than by all of their other games, combined. They are the venerable mainstay and have been for a long time. But things are a'changing. The new generation of twenty and thirty- year olds is not content just to sit mindlessly by and watch reels spin. No, twenty minutes is about all they can take at a slot. They have grown up on eye-hand coordination games; video games of all sorts. Also they are used to communal play - play in competition with others. They want interaction, with the emphasis on action."

"Yes," replied Jimmy. "But gambling games of skill are illegal."

"Up to now they have been, but that is about to change. At least we are gambling on that," Jack joked.

"But a casino is not going to go up against a good player, one that outperforms the average over and over. No way," said Jimmy.

"True; of course that's true. They are in business to make money, not to continuously lose to a skilled player. But neither can they sit back and watch their aging slot-client base dry up. So here, take a look at this little sucker."

With that Jack lifted the shroud. There stood a five-reel slot machine all lit up and ready for play. It looked conventional enough, but at its base was centrally mounted an upright joystick.

"A joystick?" exclaimed Jimmy.

"You got it."

"But how? I mean how . . . What are you going to try to do, guide the reels in for a safe and winning landing? You know, like trying to line up the symbols on the reels?"

Jack chuckled. "No, but that's an idea. Guess again."

Jimmy gripped the joystick and moved it in every direction – omnidirectionally. Nothing happened. But then the machine had not yet been credited for play. The five reels remained still.

"I don't get it. This has to be based on skill. Let's see here. I guess more and more as a player wins the machine makes it harder and harder, perhaps even requiring higher waging. Yes, that might work."

"Matter of fact we thought of that too," said Jack. "The

problem with that is that the machine thinks the same player is playing all the spins in sequence. That might not be happening – even by design."

"So the machine would have to recognize the identity of the player on all plays."

"Right; and how would you do that? Have a fingerprint constantly monitored on the joy stick? No, people would find a way around that."

"Here, give the thing a try."

With that Jack inputted a number of credits. Jimmy punched in the number of credits that he wanted to play and then hit the play button. The reels spun – that is an electronic image of reels spinning came up on the screen. One by one they came to a stop. Only a couple of the five symbols that lined were matched. Jimmy looked at the field of images in play. They were the same as those of other J and M machines save for one that bore the word "bonus" in bright red.

Jimmy continued to play. On his fourth spin he made a hit and some credits were posted both visually and audibly. On and on he played. About a dozen spins later a red "bonus" symbol lined up. Immediately the screen image was transformed from that of a slot machine to that of the well known video game of Pong.

The Pogo game pictured a vertical paddle along each side of the screen, one of which could be moved vertically with the joystick. A bouncing ball was in the field of play between the paddles. "Select Paddle" appeared. Seeing no select button on the machine, Jimmy gripped the joystick and wiggled it to the right. The paddle on the right side changed from faint to bold. "Please wait" then appeared. After a few moments the other paddle went vivid too and the ball began to bounce off the four borders or walls of the field of play similar to a handball court. The game was on. Exactly one minute later the game was over. Jimmy had lost 4 to 1. The screen then returned to the five reels and Jimmy saw and heard his credits increase by the one point that he had scored.

"Well it has been a long time," he said sheepishly. "It's a pretty good idea, though, to combine a slot machine with a video game. And the other player - It's not a player for the house, is it?"

"No, it's another player at another slot – all in real time. Makes it communal – just what the younger generation is used to. Thus the skill is not in competition with the house but against another player. The house doesn't care which player wins or how often.

"But what if another player isn't available? The casino doesn't want any down time."

"It's all on a network, a large network that includes a large number of slots from many locals, at least we hope so."

"So the casino doesn't care about skill here. The skill is just between two players."

"Right; the casino's take remains the same."

"But what if better players went to one casino and the losers to another? Wouldn't that make one casino mad?"

"There is no incentive for players to do that."

"Then this might satisfy the gaming commission?"

"Right again; we are counting on that. They too don't want to see slot play steadily decline any more than us."

"You'll probably need a license for Pong."

"That's in Joe's area. But believe me, folks like Atari will be eager to sign and rejuvenate Pong."

"And there are a lot of other video games that you could use."

"Yes; and the timing is right for spinoffs to use, what with the Sony PlayStation, Microsoft's Xbox and Nintendo's Wii all fighting for market share. Body motion directed games is behind a lot of their current R and D. They are even trying to develop emotional surround sound where you actually feel things – things like being rained on. These are interesting times."

Chapter 6

A few days later Abigail was back again on Sheila's case. Sheila could do nothing right. Why so conservative here? Take an aggressive approach. Stand up for the client; we're their tax lawyer, you know. Now why did you do this? Surely you knew that would invoke penalties, right? Well guess what? They have, and big time. Didn't you read that new reg? On and on it went. Finally Sheila defended herself.

"Abigail, this is trivial. This isn't what's bothering you. Just what is it?"

Abigail took a long look into Sheila's eyes before she answered. "You know what it is, I'm sure. We all here are supposed to be team players, including the Davis family team."

"The Davis *family*, you say?"

"Are you deaf, girl? No, I don't think so. And speaking of families, Ramsey, Ivy and Prince, LLC is a family too, you know. And if you want to become a tenured member of it, you *will* find a way to satisfy our good clients. Understood?"

"By that you mean Excelsior."

"Precisely."

That evening Sheila found no relief at home from the day's tension. She and Jimmy bickered over Abigail and her preaching. Why was she on his case? What was her problem?

"Maybe she is right. Ever considered that?" asked Jimmy.

"Right? Right? Are you out of your fucking mind?"

"Well she does have a hell of a lot more experience than you, you know."

"Yes, she does have a lot of experience at intimidation."

"What's that supposed to mean?"

"You know what that means. I suppose that you've forgotten about Excelsior. I suppose that nobody has been watching you or watching our children or threatening you."

"She's back on that again?"

"Yes, she's back on that again."

"Well you tell her to go kiss my white ass." With that Jimmy stood and walked out.

The next day Jimmy could think of nothing but the J and M – Excelsior matter. Damn it all, he thought, I can't believe this shit.

He pulled the Smart Card application folder and tried to review it with freshened eyes. He recalled his conversation with the dragon lady and her position that the claims were too broad. He studied all of the claims as objectively as he could in his current state of mind. Yes, he could see that the broadest claims were indeed probably too broad. They probably did just mirror the ticket-in, ticket-out machines with the mere substitution of a smart card for paper.

He looked over the more specific and detailed claims that depended from the broad ones. A few of these spelled out the electronic protocol that linked the single smart card that was physically held by a slot machine during play only to release it back to the user once play was ended with remaining credits encoded back onto the card. This was clearly different from the tito protocol.

Next Jimmy researched the issue of whether or not commercial success had to be orchestrated by the inventor or his successor or partner in interest. He found that the issue had indeed been litigated before. No, it did not matter whether or not commercial success had been achieved personally by the inventor, or by a successor in interest, or by a licensee or by anyone else for that matter. As long as the success was directly tied to the claimed invention, such could be used as an indicator that it had not been obvious at the time the invention was made. Why else would it have taken off so fast? Jimmy reached for the phone.

"Ms. Fang; it's Jimmy Davis here."

"Yes, Mr. Davis."

"Do you remember me?"

"How could I forget so quickly? It's not very often that we hear of one of our registered patent attorneys being threatened, much less of being threatened right here in the Patent Office. I hope that you are well and that no harm has actually come to you."

"Oh yes, that. Well so far nothing further has happened to me along that line."

"I see."

"Ms. Fang, I have revisited the claims in the application with what you said in mind – about they're being drafted too broadly. While I still feel that all of them really merit approval I do want to advance this case as quickly as possible." He paused but Ms. Fang remained silent.

"Ms. Fang, what I propose is to cancel all of the broad, independent claims and to proceed with just those that relate to the physical capture of the smart card during play. As you know this is not done with tito, with ticket-in, ticket-out machines." He paused. He waited. Finally the dragon lady spoke.

"I see."

Jimmy waited. Was that it? Was that all? She sounded like a business man waiting out an offer.

"Ms. Fang I might add that I did research the point that you raised about the nexus of commercial success with the inventor or the assignee of the inventor's rights. There's no requirement for such a nexus."

"You have citations to support this?"

"I do, by the Federal Circuit."

"Then I suggest that you prepare and file an amendment by which your claims are amended as you say. You should also brief the commercial success matter. I suggest that you fax it to my group. I will give you the fax number."

Jimmy's heart skipped a beat. By damn maybe she was buying this!

"Yes ma'am. You can expect it by the end of the day."

He hung up the phone and tilted back his swivel seat. Hot damn; hot damn! Then the realization crept in – as well as the implications. If these threats were more than idle ones, what was he facing now? I just don't know, he thought. But this was the only right thing to do. And yet it wasn't a *fait accompli* just yet; not until he received something in writing back from the Patent Office. In any event he felt some solace in the fact that the deed was done. Now there would be no indecision or the slightest thought of becoming corrupted by Sheila or her boss. Yes, the die was now cast.

That evening Jimmy came home in high spirits. He even gave Miss Clara a hug as she turned the twins over to him in leaving. He romped with them for a while and then popped a beer and turned the TV on for the evening news. The time passed without

Sheila. Where was she, he wondered. He picked up the house phone and dialed her cell.

"Oh, I was just about to call you. I'm afraid that you are going to have to fend for yourself tonight. I have to go to dinner with a client from out of town."

"Well that's alright, I guess. It's just that I have some good news to share. At least I hope that you will take it as good. There was a delay before Sheila responded.

"And what might that be?"

"The patent for J and B; you know, the one on the smart card."

There was a prolonged silence before Sheila spoke: "And?"

"Well the Dragon Lady and I spoke again. I gave a little ground and it looks like we may have a deal. At least she held her fiery breath." Jimmy chuckled.

Again there was no response from Sheila.

"Oh. Oh yes, I'm still here."

The line went very quiet much like Sheila or someone else had put their hand over the receiver.

"Well, asked Jimmy?"

"Oh. Yes, that's great. Congratulations. I'm sure J and M will be pleased."

"Yes. But I think I'll wait for the written confirmation before I break the news to them."

Chapter 7

Miss Clara spied Ida May sitting on the park bench just outside the fenced area of the playground and made her way over with Andy and Alec in tow.

"G'morning to you, Miss Ida."

"Why good morning to you too, Miss Clara. How you be?"

"Can't complain, I guess. Here, let me put these two inside."

With that she lifted each off the stroller and walked the twins over to the gate which she swung open. Andy ran in and Alec followed but only after Miss Clara had given him a gentle shove. She then returned to the bench where she found Ida May lighting up.

"You know that that weed is going to kill you, don't you?"

"Hush, woman. Don't want to hear about it."

"Lord-a-mercy, soon it'll be five bucks a pack. Why don't you just take a gun? Bullets are cheaper."

"I now tolds you, I don'ts want to hear it. I gets my preaching in the good Lord's house."

Miss Clara sat down and stretched her legs. She shook her head as she watched Ida May exhale alternately smoke and vapor, it being that cold in the morning air. "Un-huh; un-huh," she hummed in sync with Ida May's exhales. Ida May ignored her for a spell but then suddenly turned her head towards Miss Clara and blew a huge puff of smoke into Miss Clara's face.

"Un-huh, yourself."

Miss Clara just waved the smoke away and laughed. But that did succeed in getting her to back off.

The two nannies settled into their usual gossiping while keeping their coats drawn tightly about them. Both also wore knit hats for warmth. Ida May's was a rather stylish tweed while Miss Clara's was a more functional woolen head scarf that was draped over her head and shoulders. The two watched their small charges playing, with only Ida May occasionally shouting out to hers, "Tommy, leave that girl alone now."

The two women relaxed. Dropping small children off into the enclosed play area was much like taking pets off their leash at an enclosed dog park. Let'um romp! The place was designed with safety foremost in mind.

As time passed the two nannies became more engrossed in their gossiping and less focused on their charges as they mixed with other children and went from one play gym to another. Occasionally one would move out of sight only to pop up again as he reemerged out from a crawl pipe of a jungle gym set. The weather began to deteriorate as a very light rain materialized accompanied by a stiffening breeze.

"It's getting cold. I think I'd best be heading back," said Ida May.

Together they walked to the playground gate when Miss Clara had left the stroller. They went inside and separated. Since many of the other children were being rounded up to head home, it didn't take Miss Clara long to locate one of the twins. From his robust behavior it appeared to be Andy, although that mattered little. She took his hand and looked about for the other.

"Where is your brother, Andy?" she said as she pulled his coat hood over his head. But Andy didn't reply.

"Where is he? Where is Alec?" she said gently.

Andy shrugged his shoulders.

Miss Clara looked back at the gate. She didn't want him to be leaving. Except for a couple of older ones, the exiting smaller ones were all being escorted by other nannies or parents. She turned around and called.

"Alec? Alec? It's time to go."

Miss Clara began to become concerned. The dreary weather had darkened the sky. There was just a couple more children left inside the gate while the ones outside were being hurried away.

"Alec; Alec; come on, it's time to go."

Nothing.

"Where did you last see your brother, Andy?"

"I don't know."

With Andy in hand Miss Clara walked the perimeter while looking both inside and out and all the while calling for Alec. The only sound however was that of the light rain and breeze.

Completion of her check of the perimeter fence brought her back to the gate which she went through to put Andy in the wet stroller. "Now you stay put while I finds your brother, you hear? And if you see him you call me."

Miss Clara found that she now was the only person inside the playground. She went to each of the crawl tubes while calling for Alec. Each was empty. She went to the jungle gym. No Alec. She called up at the little hut or tree house on top. From the ground she could not see inside it. She looked at the small child steps leading up and decided to give it a try. She reached the elevated platform and walked to the hut and looked about. No Alec. But then something caught her eye at her own eyelevel just outside its entry. A white envelope was taped to the wall. As she approached it she saw that there were three words written on it as with a black marker: FOR ALEC'S DADDY

Miss Clara stared at the envelope in amazement. Good God Almighty, she thought. She took it off the wall and turned it over. It was sealed. She stuffed it in her pocket and hurried back to the gate and stroller where she found Andy splashing rainwater that had accumulated on its floor with his shoes.

She hurried back to the house with tears mingling with the rain drops. She felt herself now shaking in the wet cold. She was scared. The child was gone! Little Alec had been snatched right out from under her nose. She couldn't stop looking at the empty seat beside Andy and its dangling seat belt as she pushed the stroller towards home.

Sheila was the first to arrive back home in response to Miss Clara's frantic call. Miss Clara's report of what had happened at the park was delivered fitfully and mournfully. There wasn't much for Sheila to ask. The child had obviously been abducted as evidenced by the envelope which the nanny had handed to her unopened.

Sheila studied the envelope. Should she open it or wait for Jimmy whom she had already phoned? Should either one of them open it? Her thought process was broken by the sound of Jimmy's car screeching to a halt in the driveway. She met him at the door. No words were spoken as they looked each other in the eye before embracing, awkwardly.

Inside Jimmy found Miss Clara standing beside the breakfast room table with her hands folded. Her face was distorted in anguished despair. She appeared to be on the verge of breaking down.

"Miss Clara, don't blame yourself. I know that we hadn't mentioned anything to you before but we have been threatened recently. I just can't believe that they've actually gone and done this."

"You knew that the boys were in danger, Mr. Davis?"

"Oh no; not the boys; it was me I thought they were after. Oh no, if I had had any notion that one of them might be in danger we would have never had you take them out."

"I'm just so sorry Mr. Davis. Is there is anything I can do."

"Well, just tell the police everything you can."

"The police?" asked Sheila.

"Of course, the police."

"But; but."

"But what?" asked Jimmy.

"Nothing; it's just that . . "

Jimmy looked at Sheila. Then the envelope caught his eye. He picked it up.

"Where did this come from?" he asked no one in particular.

"It was at the playground," said Sheila.

"Yes, sir; I found it at the little hut up on the jungle gym," said Miss Clara.

"You didn't open it?" he asked Sheila.

"I was just about to when you drove up."

Jimmy stared at the envelope and its "FOR ALEC'S DADDY" address. He started to tear it open but then decided to use a kitchen knife. Inside was a printed message.

> YOU KNOW WHAT WE WANT
> AND WE KNOW WHAT YOU WANT.
> MAKE IT HAPPEN.
> POST COPY ON COUNTYCOURT
> HOUSE LEGAL BOARD
> NO POLICE

He handed the note somberly to Sheila and sat down.

"Where is Andy?"

"He's asleep, Mr. Davis," replied Miss Clara.

Jimmy nodded and sat there in thought. Then Sheila spoke.

"Miss Clara, why don't you run on home, now. I know how tired you must be."

"She had better wait here for the police."

"Jimmy, you read the note; no police!"

"To hell you say."

"Jimmy, please!"

Jimmy felt his pulse rate rising.

"Miss Clara, I guess you should go home. Please just stay there until the police show up. Okay?"

She looked at Sheila and then went to get her coat.

"I'll be home if you need me."

Chapter 8

To go the police or to the FBI, or not? That was the question that Jimmy and Sheila argued about that evening. You can't deal with kidnappers was Jimmy's position. You can't trust them. Paying a ransom or not paying a ransom has little to do with the outcome. That may not be true when kidnapping is a common extortion practice as in Mexico, but not here. They're going to do what they're going to do.

Sheila's counterargument was that there was nothing to pay in their case. The kidnappers simply demanded that Jimmy file a legal paper which would take the form of a notice of abandonment or withdrawal of the smart card patent application. "Was that too much to do in return for a child? Good God, man, get your priorities straight," she had shouted.

Jimmy had been raised as an army brat with all the accompanying moves that that entailed. While his father had been stationed at Fort Benning, near Columbus, Georgia, his parents had separated. Not long afterwards that they divorced and she returned to her native Germany. He decided to turn for advice to his father, a now retired army major who lived in South Carolina.

Jimmy explained the situation by phone. His father listened intently, only interrupting a few times with questions. Once finished, Jimmy asked him if he should he meet the kidnappers' demand? Not unless his client agreed, came the reply. Should he go to the authorities? Of course he should go. End of conversation; simple questions called for simple and decisive answers.

Sheila drove to her parents' home in Virginia Highlands, an old, upscale residential section located just minutes north of downtown Atlanta. There the old guard had once reigned on high. Today it was quite cosmopolitan with youth-orientated coffee houses and places like Blind Willie's Blues Club and the Dark Horse Tavern and Grill. She had told Jimmy that the drive would give her time to think.

Her parents heard her out. Both complimented her on how well she was handling the situation by showing deep concern without tearful carrying on. In the end they echoed Sheila's position, as she felt they would. Certainly Jimmy should file the legal paper. Under these conditions of coercion surely the paper would not be valid. But definitely they should keep all of this quiet. The last thing they needed was for their daughter to make the front page of the *Atlanta Constitution* or headline news on CNN whose world headquarters was virtually right down the street. No network would pass up a kidnapping of one of two twins. There would be endless on-air speculations and interviews with psychologists and other specialists about the reason and the choice of which twin. This thing would be broadcast all over the world. Reporters would be camped out at Sheila's house as well perhaps at their own. Their privacy in Virginia Highlands would be at an end. Foremost of her action, or rather, inaction, must be to keep this quiet.

Once back home Sheila found Jimmy sitting on the floor with his back propped up against the twins' bed. Andy was sound asleep. She motioned for him to leave and come with her. He shook his head. Quietly he told her that he would stay there for a while. "We'll talk in the morning then," she said. He nodded.

Later that night she felt him climb into bed but they kept their distance. Just before dawn Andy climbed in between them.

The next morning Sheila gave Jimmy an ultimatum-like demand. File the abandonment and bring her a copy home that evening, she demanded. No child was worth this.

Jimmy was shocked; so much for their talking this out. Had she delivered this demand emotionally through a veil of tears, that would have been one thing, but her delivery had been cold, uncompromising and out of character. Just when they needed mutual support and comfort she had done the opposite. What was going on with her? Her parents had to be behind this, he concluded.

Upon arrival at the office Jimmy checked his phone and email messages but found none concerning the kidnapping. He then made his way to Charles Macguire's office where Macguire heard him out.

"Jimmy, this is terrible; I've never heard of anything remotely like it."

"What should I do? What would you do?"

"I can't tell you that. It is your child that has been taken; not mine."

"If I file an express abandonment do you think it would be valid and irreversible?"

"As I said, I've never heard of such a situation before and frankly I don't know but I would guess that it could later be reversed since it was made under duress - under extreme duress. Why don't you look it up?"

"I will, but what good will that do? Once they found out that it had been cancelled or withdrawn we would be right back where we started."

"Except that in the meantime you would have your child back and be on guard against any repeat of this.

"Jimmy, my advice is that you go talk with your client about this before you make any decision. But find out first for sure if an abandonment would be reversible."

"What about bringing in the FBI?"

"Ordinarily I'd say yes. But if you do you may well be putting your child at risk. No, I wouldn't just yet. See if the mere filing that they want brings your boy home." Hearing himself say that, Charles was pleased and thought that his own advise was actually sound. "Yes, that is what I would do in your place."

Jimmy took Macguire's advice and phoned Joe Turner at J and M and told him that he needed to see him right away.

"Jimmy, I can't today. I'm booked solid."

"Joe, this is urgent. They've taken my boy, my boy Alec."

"Good God, are you serious?"

"He's been kidnapped. There is a ransom demand."

"For money?"

"No, it's the same demand that they made at the Patent Office."

"Good Lord, just over a patent application?"

"That's it."

"That's just unbelievable. Jimmy, come on over at noon. I'll cancel my appointment. We can talk over sandwiches."

Once at J and M, Joe heard Jimmy out, saying nothing while he listened and ate his sandwich.

"This is unbelievable. To think that anyone would steal a child for a legal document is crazy. It doesn't make sense. There must be more to this – or there will be more. And you say that this "Express Abandonment" that they want wouldn't even be valid?"

"That's right. Any document that is signed under a gun is invalid, provided that you can prove it. And that applies here. I looked it up before I drove over."

"I don't get it. Surely they must know this."

"I don't get it either, Joe."

"Perhaps this is just a test."

"I hadn't thought of that. Yes, perhaps that's it."

"Well the paramount thing now is to get your child back home safely. I suggest that you go ahead and do what they want. Let's take this one step at a time to see just where it is going. As I said, I doubt this will be the end of it."

"And the authorities: What about bringing them in?"

"If Excelsior is behind this, as it appears, then I would leave the cops out of it, at least for now. I don't want to come to work one day to find this place burnt to the ground. Let's try to keep this on a business level."

"On a business level," repeated Jimmy quietly as he turned his head and looked out the window. "On a business level," he said as he shook his head.

Joe put his hand on Jimmy's shoulder. "I didn't mean it to come out like that, Jimmy. I just don't want to see this ramped up any further than it already is. Now if you have any better suggestion I am all ears."

"I guess not. Okay, I'll do it quietly."

"Jimmy, we won't be forgetting this. Once we weather this I'm telling you that we are going far together. Just wait till you see what we are coming up with now. It's one innovation after another here. For so very long there wasn't anything new in the field of slot machines. Now we are in the process of revolutionizing it and we will be wanting you to protect and preserve our little revolution."

That swept through Jimmy's mind like a fresh breeze. He beamed. What a great client to land so early in one's career.

Back at the office he had his secretary Patty prepare a Notice of Express Abandonment. Patty's services were split between him and Tom Bouldin, a fellow associate attorney in the office. When Patty questioned it, he swore her to secrecy and retold the kidnapping story yet again.

Patty was dumbfounded. She started to question his decision to file but he quickly cut her off. So she went ahead and brought up the abandonment form on her computer screen, filled in the particulars as they related to this specific application, and printed out several copies. After reviewing it Jimmy signed the document as attorney of record and signed a Certificate of Mailing to the Patent Office affixed to it. He placed it in an envelope, sealed and stamped it himself and placed it in the outgoing mail tray along with a copy to Joe with a cover letter that confirmed their conversation. A little covering of his rear end wouldn't hurt.

After telling Patty that he would see her in the morning he was off for downtown. The traffic outbound from downtown was already building.

He made his way to the staid old Fulton County Courthouse which was located not far from the State Capitol building geographically, but quite far esthetically. Around the courthouse concrete had been substituted for shaded grounds. He located a prior notice that had been posted the longest and tacked his on top.

An hour later he was pulling into his home driveway thinking how happy Sheila would be to see the copy of the abandonment notice that he had brought for her. She read it word for word. Once finished he reached for it but she waved his hand away and put it in her briefcase that lay close by. He looked at her questionably and she returned the look. Then her face softened into a smile.

"This should do the trick," she said as she gave him a maternal kiss on the cheek.

Chapter 9

The next day passed without any word from the kidnappers. Maybe they haven't yet gone to the courthouse. Maybe the document had been taken down. Maybe the owner of the document beneath had gotten pissed and thrown his away; maybe anything.

That the kidnappers had always used notes gave Jimmy little to expect from the telephone. That nothing came by email was also to be expected since that could be traced. Not knowing how they would contact him, nor how they would be returning his child, was driving him crazy. All that Sheila would say was to give it time.

The following morning he got up early and drove into the city and back to the courthouse. He found that his notice was still right where he had pinned it. In frustration he drove back out to the office and called Sheila.

"I told you that you couldn't trust these people."

"Relax, Jimmy. Just cool it."

"How can you, as his own mother, tell me to cool it?"

"Just what good would it be for me to lose my cool? Just be patient; things should break anytime now."

"They'd better, and fast; or I'm off to the FBI. I already have their phone number and local address."

"So you have the telephone number of the Federal Bureau of

Investigation. Why that's just great. That's really just great, Sonny Boy. Here we are about to get our Alec back and you want to go and stop it."

"Sheila, I am getting sick and tired of this." With that he hung up.

Jimmy sat at his desk fuming. God damn it; God damn it all to hell.

He swiveled his chair and stared out the window. Down below he saw the two white geese that made the lake at the Concourse their home pond. How serene *their* lives were.

"Excuse me sir," came a voice from behind him at his door. He turned to see a maintenance man in a workman's jumper bearing an embossed company emblem standing at his threshold with a bag and a box of fluorescent lamps in hand. "May I?" he asked as he motioned for permission to enter.

"Sure," replied Jimmy as he glanced up at his ceiling where there were several fluorescent lamp fixtures. All of them appeared to be working.

The man entered and closed the door behind him. Jimmy looked at him questionably and the man returned his look with a broad smile that revealed a missing tooth. Without hesitation the man leaned the box up against Jimmy's desk, plopped his bag on the desk and sat down in a side chair facing him. He took off his work cap while continuing to smile. Seconds ticked away as the two men just sat there eyeing each other, Jimmy in his dress shirt and tie and the older, stocky and hairy maintenance man across from him with that incessant smile and tooth that remained absent.

"What do you want?" finally asked Jimmy as he studied the man's single eyebrow that overlaid both of his eyes.

"I think you've been expecting me, Mr. Jimmy Davis."

Jimmy studied the man further. He was a big man with large, hairy hands. When the man saw Jimmy looking at his teeth he stopped his smiling.

"Are you here about my son?"

The man took a cigar out of his pocket. The uninvited visitor then took a box of wooden matches out and lit up.

"Nice office you have here, Mr. Jimmy Davis." The man looked around and then blew smoke up at one of the ceiling fixtures. "Very nice indeed and I bet you would like to keep it so."

"Where is my son? Where is Alec? Have you brought him? Is he here in the building?"

The man slowly stood and walked over to the large windows that extended almost floor to ceiling thus providing a panoramic view of the Concourse complex and the surrounding area.

"Very nice indeed; you've come up in the world since your days at Lockheed." The man retook his seat.

"No, your boy is not here but he is just fine. He's been no problem."

"Look. I did just as you asked. Don't you know that? Didn't you see the notice I posted at the courthouse?"

The man sat there eyeballing Jimmy. Slowly he took in a big drag and blew a giant smoke ring directly at Jimmy who watched it as it encircled his head. Then the man gave a repeat and again flawless performance before tapping some ashes onto the wood desk.

"Yes, we saw it. And I am happy to tell you that you passed our little test."

"That I passed? Passed what test?"

"Lawyer Davis, we don't want just one thing done here. What

we want here is a relationship. You understand? A relationship. But we have to establish trust and respect. I don't see no respect in your eyes.

"Anyway, as I says, you passed and since you passed I am here to tell you that you will have your precious Alec safely back by this time tomorrow. You see, we want you to trust us too. Then you'll know that we keeps our promises."

With that the man stood up and snipped off the burnt end of his cigar into a cup of coffee that Jimmy had let go cold on the desk before him. He grabbed his box of lamps and headed for the door with his cap back on. As Jimmy started to rise the man motioned for him to stay seated.

"Not to worry; I'll see myself out. I know my way. Now you take care of yourself and behave."

The man left the law offices via a back door that was off the combined office kitchen and lunch room. He made his way to a utility closet down the hallway. A couple of minutes later he emerged wearing a coat and tie, sporting a mustache and carrying a briefcase. The missing tooth had miraculously reappeared. He made his way down a stairwell three floors, which was one floor below where one bank of elevators ended nonstop service from the ground level and another bank began floor-to-floor service to the next higher tier. By doing that he avoided any chance encounter with anyone from Jimmy's law office.

Jimmy called Sheila on her back phone line. She answered and heard him out without comment or interruption.

"Well there we are," she finally said. "It looks like I've been vindicated."

"Time will tell."

"Yes, time will indeed tell, Jimmy."

"This isn't what I expected. I don't know what I expected but it wasn't being visited right here in the office by that goon."

"Jimmy, you are not in control. They are. Whoever they are, and we don't know for sure just who they are, they are in their own element and you aren't. They are calling the shots, so behave."

Behave? Didn't I just hear that word, thought Jimmy? Have I been misbehaving here?

"Yes, I'll try to *behave*."

It was 2:30 a.m. when the telephone rang at the Davis's house. Jimmy sat up, startled.

"Hello?"

"Good morning, Mr. Davis," came a familiar voice. It was *the* man, again.

"Yes, what is it?"

"I have some good news for you."

Jimmy now thought that he recognized the voice of the "maintenance man".

"You will find that we fucking-a kept our promise. Your Alec is now back safely in his own room there with you." With that the man hung up.

"What was it?" asked Sheila.

"They say that Alec has been returned. But I sure didn't hear anything."

Jimmy got out of bed and made his way to the hall where he switched on a light. Sheila was not far behind. He walked to the children's room and opened the door. The night light was enough for him to see that there still was but one boy asleep in the bed. The only change was the child's position. He was sleeping on Andy's side of the bed.

Jimmy turned around to find Sheila staring at the bed.

Sheila walked over to the bed and bent down. The child was lying on his side facing her. She studied the boy's face carefully while gently stroking his hair. Her eyes slowly made their way down the back of his head to the hair baseline. And then she saw it; the birthmark! This was Alec asleep on his side of the bed as he always had. She rose up and gave Jimmy a look of both anguish and anger.

"This is Alec. They've returned him; returned him, *as promised*."

"What?" exclaimed Jimmy.

"Yes, they have returned him in exchange for Andy."

Jimmy quickly looked for the birthmark. She was right. Alec was now back home, back home alone with his brother now gone. The kidnappers had made a switch.

Sheila's eyes narrowed as she looked at Jimmy. Her narrowed eyes were devoid of tears. Jimmy had never before seen the look on his wife's face that he now saw. It took on a look of disgust; it was a look of contempt.

Sheila picked up Alec and a blanket that lay thrown on the bottom of the twins' bed.

"You can have the bed," she said as she left the room leaving Jimmy alone and perplexed.

What had he done? What's really going on here? He scanned the room.

"Andy," he said quietly. "Andy?" There was no response. He looked under the bed and then in the closet and bathroom. No

Andy. Slowly he returned to their bedroom where he found himself alone and cold and wide awake.

Meanwhile Sheila had gone downstairs, flicked on their gas log fireplace and laid down on the sofa that faced it with Alec wrapped snuggly in the blanket with her. She fell asleep with an odd look of contentment.

Chapter 10

Jimmy thought the morning would never come. What sleep he managed to get was fitful. When the wintry dawn finally came it came cloaked in a cold, grey mist.

During the night, when his mind wasn't dwelling on the new loss of Andy, it was dwelling on the estrangement that had developed with Sheila. Just when they needed the support of each other the most, she was acting as though all this was his fault. What had happened to their love and affection for each other?

And then there was that smug "we keep our promises" bit of the goon. How clever; how cute; that was someone else's doing. Yes they did return Alec but only in exchange for Andy. And why? For a long term relationship, the man had said. There would be no end to this. Thank God they hadn't had triplets.

Oddly, Sheila was gnawing on him more than *the* man. There was no pleasing her.

In one sense the switch had shown that the kidnappers were rational. At least they weren't in some sort of cult. The kidnapper could have been a deranged individual or a sexual pervert. Since they had apparently taken good care of Alec, they could be expected to do the same with Andy. On the other hand Sheila was becoming a new person to him. A wall had now replaced love. Jimmy wondered if that would return even if this kidnapping business, and it did appear now to be a business, were to be resolved. He had heard that after the first two or three years of marriage the fire waned but this was more like the aftermath of a fire extinguisher's spray.

Their first conversation that morning had been about Alec. When Jimmy started gingerly to quiz Alec on what had happened to him, Sheila interrupted. She had already put him through that, she said, and he didn't need to be interrogated again. Alec, she said, had told her that he been visiting his aunt, his aunt Bessie, who lived on a farm out in the country. He had had fun. Aunt Bessie had dogs, lots of chickens, a red cat and some big cows. He had even helped milk one of the cows. He liked his aunt Bessie and his Uncle Sam, too. They were nice. But he was scared of one of the big dogs. As Sheila told the story in front of Alec, without his interrupting or commenting, Jimmy decided just to accept it as is. He picked him up.

"I'm glad that you had a good time. Farms are fun and we don't have them here where we live. But I sure did miss you. Did you miss me?"

"Yes Daddy, I missed. And I missed Andy. Where is Andy?"

Jimmy looked at Sheila.

"As I told you," said Sheila, "it's Andy's turn now on the farm. He'll be back in a few days. Now I've got to get Alec ready for KiddyKare."

"Sheila," we have to talk.

"I don't see that there is anything to discuss. There's nothing you can do. And don't start up on going to the police again. You would look like a complete fool. Do you make it a practice of only reporting every other kidnapping? They would think you were crazy. You, as the man of the house, allowed someone to steal your child? Not once but twice?"

"Hey, if you remember I had wanted to go to the police in the first place."

"Come on Alec. Let's get ready." With that they walked out.

Jimmy was finishing a second cup of coffee when Sheila came back down with Alec in tow. Rather than sporting a business suit she was dressed in jeans and a leather jacket. When he looked her over in surprise she told him that she had some errands to run before she went to work. With that they were gone.

When Sheila arrived at KiddyKare she took Alec to the door where a teen helper stood greeting the children and helping them off with their coats and caps and scarves. After the girl had taken Alec's wraps and he was off to join the other children Sheila spoke.

"Carolyn, that is Alec."

"Alec? But where is Andy now?"

"Unfortunately he has now come down with the same ailment that Alec had had. I guess Alec passed it on to his brother. Anyway, it will just have to run its course as it did with Alec. But don't worry, he's well beyond the contagious stage now. In fact you will find him to be fully recovered."

"Okay," she replied as she turned to the next two children that were now being ushered inside. As Sheila passed by the new arrivals Carolyn called back over her shoulder: "I'll tell Mrs. Stallings."

―――――※※※―――――

Again, time drug for Jimmy at the office that day. He just couldn't concentrate. With each incoming phone call he held his breath expecting a new demand, or worse. When he detected movement in the hall outside his open door he would tense up. He wanted to leave early but felt that he couldn't for fear of missing a call. To make matters worse he felt he couldn't share his burden with anyone else.

Mercifully the work day finally came to an end. He hoped that he would only find Miss Clara and Alec at home so that he could talk with both of them without Sheila. When he arrived he found that Sheila indeed was not home, but neither was anyone else. There was a note on the fridge:

> Jimmy. Alec is with me. I have taken him to my parents so don't worry about us. Right now I don't feel safe at the house. I need some separate time and space, alone.

Jimmy took down the note and placed it on the kitchen counter where he read it over several times. He took off his coat and went upstairs. He looked in Sheila's closet but couldn't really tell for how long a sojourn she had packed. Then he went to the children's room but that was even harder to decipher since the clothing was for two boys of the same size.

Jimmy looked up the phone number of Sheila's parents and called. Her father answered.

"We've been expecting your call, Jimmy."

"Can I speak with Sheila, Mr. Frazier?" He still called him "Mr. Frazier" because neither "Buz" nor "Dad," nor anything else, had felt right.

"Jimmy, Sheila asked me to take this call. She's too upset to speak to you tonight. I'm sure you can appreciate how she feels at the moment."

"Mr. Frazier, I need to talk with her. I don't know if Miss

Clara will be coming tomorrow. I don't know about the day care for Alec tomorrow. I don't know . . . "

"Listen up Son, Sheila has already told me to tell you that she will take care of all that. All you have to do is to fend for yourself and to let us know as soon as you have heard anything about Andy. Okay?"

"Yes sir. I mean I guess so."

"And Son, for God's sake get that house of yours rigged up with the best home security system that money can buy. That should have been done long before now."

The morning came silently. There was no sound of Sheila bustling about, nor sounds of the boys. It was so quiet that Jimmy even heard the refrigerator cycle on and off. He didn't recall having ever heard that before.

Before breakfast he walked throughout the house, taking in each room with fresh eyes. With a family no single person arranged things or decorated to just one person's taste. For better or worse it was a group effort. But alone now he could see how he would change many things to suit himself.

The morning at the office brought no word from Sheila or the kidnappers. Jimmy ate the brownbag lunch he had brought from the house in the office break room while reading the *Wall Street Journal* and making chitchat with a couple of the legal assistants.

Back in his office he found that Patty had placed some files on the corner of his desk with incoming correspondence attached to the outside cover. The one on top grabbed his attention. It was a formal Notice of Allowance and Issue Fee Due Notice from the Patent Office on the smart card application! Apparently it had crossed his Notice of Abandonment in the mail. Jimmy stared at it in silence. All of his modified claims had obviously been accepted. The Dragon Lady had come through. For that matter he too had come through with his advocacy. He reached for his phone.

"Joe? This is Jimmy Davis."

"Good afternoon, Jimmy."

"Joe, we just received a formal Notice of Allowance on the smart card application. That little trip to Washington paid off."

"Hey, that's great news. Good job."

"Thanks."

"Is there any news on your child yet?"

Jimmy had anticipated that question and had thought out his response. He figured that it would look bad were he to tell J and M that he had regained one of the twins only to lose the other – from right there in his home – again. That, plus the new "relationship" that had been foretold, had led him to decide to underplay what had just happened, at least for the time being.

"No, not yet."

"So you can't yet withdraw that Notice of Abandonment?"

"That's right, I suppose. But we have plenty of time; we have three months in which to pay the issue fee."

"Three months? We'll don't even think in those terms. We here sure can't and I'm sure you can't either in terms of your child."

"No, of course not, but the ball is in their court. I've done all that they have asked." So far, he thought to himself.

"Tell you what. It's time anyway for you to take a trip to Vegas and meet some of our customers. So print some copies of that Notice of Allowance. I'll let our sales rep there know that you are coming. In fact you can carry the new flyers we've just printed to him which announce our new smart card retrofit package. It's got 'patent pending' on it as we had discussed. How about it?"

"Oh yes, sure, I mean."

"You don't sound very enthusiastic about Vegas. Would you prefer Buffalo?"

"Oh, no; Vegas sounds great. I just hadn't thought about a trip, any trip right now, you know."

"I understand but life goes on."

Chapter 11

Jimmy felt the main gear wheels of the airliner contact the runway. That was followed by a slow rotation of the nose until the front wheels also touched down. As the reverse thrusters began their noisy work Jimmy watched the outside landscape as it flew by at diminishing speeds. Lord it was flat, but then this was a desert in which man had made his unnatural intrusion. And there it was, the Las Vegas Strip seen just a few miles distant by its line of mega casino-hotels rising above the desert floor against the mountainous backdrop and the brilliantly blue sky.

A taxi whisked him away from the airport, not to the Strip but to an address in the downtown industrial area a few blocks south of Interstate 95. The address proved to be a warehouse with a few small offices in the front. The front door bore the name Moreno Distributors.

As Jimmy opened the building door with his bag in hand, a bell announced his entry. The small reception room was Spartan. No one seemed to be home.

"Hello? Is anyone there?"

"Just a minute," came a female response.

A moment later an attractive young lady came through a door located behind the counter. She had long, solid black hair that was matched by strikingly beautiful, black eyes. Her smile appeared to be warm and sincere and made Jimmy feel comfortable right off.

"You must be Mr. Davis," she said as her smile broadened in completing her demeanor change from back room worker to front office worker.

"Yes; I'm Jimmy Davis from Atlanta; I'm here to see Mr. Moreno."

"Of course, we were expecting you. I'm Juliana, Mario's wife," she said as she extended her hand. "How was your flight?"

"Flight? Oh, yes; good and uneventful."

"Better that than an eventful one," she said with the slightest Hispanic accent. "Here, let me have your coat and bag. I'll put them here behind the counter."

"Thanks. Is Mr. Moreno here?"

"Yes, Mario is in the back." With that she picked up a phone and dialed a single number. "Mario, Mr. Davis is here," she spoke into the phone which relayed the message to loud speakers back in the rear somewhere. As she replaced the handset she asked if he would like a coffee, which Jimmy accepted.

A couple of minutes later Mario Moreno came through the door wiping his hands on his faded blue coveralls. He was short, about the height of Juliana, but quite heavier. He had his black hair tied into a ponytail with a red leather band that matched the color of the portions of his shirt that were not covered by the coveralls. At any time, removal of the coveralls readied him dressed for his job as a sales rep. Apparently both of the Morenos had some chameleon genes with their multitasked jobs.

"Ah, Mr. Davis; I'm Mario," he said with a slight smile that twitched his thin mustache.

"It's Jimmy, Mr. Moreno."

"Good; then it's Mario to you. Have a nice flight?"

"Good and uneventful," he repeated.

"That's what you want and expect when you leave your earthly cares at 35,000 feet. Now come on back; I need a break and bring your coffee. Would you get me one too, Julie?"

Mario led the way to the back and to an office with a dirty glass wall through which the warehouse floor could be viewed. A forklift truck could be seen some distance away scurrying about in between rows of cardboard boxes and larger containers beneath fluorescent lamp fixtures suspended from a high, trussed ceiling. The noise from its engine could barely be heard.

Mario motioned for Jimmy to take a seat in one of the two well worn leather armchairs that faced his no-nonsense aluminum desk.

Jimmy sat and immediately was struck by the half dozen, large calendars that were mounted to the wall opposite the glass one. They were mounted chronologically by years. Jimmy's gaze and appreciation of their Latin, poster-girl beauties was broken by Juliana's entry with Mario's coffee mug.

"I love, I love, I love my calendar girl," she sang to the Neil Sedaka song as she smiled at Jimmy's abrupt turn-away.

"Calendar *girls*," corrected Mario.

"Most sales reps have Vegas show girl calendars, but not Mario."

"It's a cultural thing. Besides, which are you? I don't see any feathers, girl," he teased.

"Is this your first time here, Jimmy?"

"Yes, first time."

"Then you've never been to a G2E."

"No. I mean I've read about the gambling industry's annual trade show here, but I've never been to one."

"How about to an E3; ever been to one of them?" You've got to make one if for no other reason than to check out them booth-babes."

With that comment Juliana glanced back over her shoulder at Mario as she was making her exit. He winked back in return. After no response from Jimmy, Mario explained.

"It's the Electronic Entertainment Expo; the video game industry's annual trade show.

"Actually I already knew that this was your first trip out here. You see our good client here will be wanting you to attend the upcoming G2E and maybe the next E3, too. J and M didn't want you to look like a greenhorn to these folks."

"They told you that, but not me?"

"Hey, amigo, they are grooming you. Be happy; they are investing in you, Jimmy Davis."

"Well, tell me about the E3."

"It's big; real big. This is a $30 billion global industry, Jimmy. Today it rivals the music and motion picture industries in size. Last year Nevada's casinos took in $13 billion and two-thirds of that was from the machines. While the overall industry has been on the move away from the young, 18 to 30 year old pathological players' base, we are a bit of the contrarian."

"By that you mean making the slot machines more attractive to boys as they mature?"

Mario gave a serious look to Jimmy. "Yes, that's right. That's exactly right - and the ladies.

"Now the main action at the next E3 will not be of much interest to J and M. No, that action for the most part will be in the price slashing area. Will Sony cut its price on PlayStation 3? Well of course they will, but by how much? How will Microsoft respond with regard to its three models of the Xbox 360? Will Nintendo touch the price of its Wii? I think not. Anyway, that's where the main action and interest will be for the honchos."

"What about for us?"

"Us? Well I hope we'll be there to play catch-up. Look, little old J and M isn't in the league of a Bally or an IGT, or even a Mikohn, but if it doesn't nail some good video games for its slots, it's going to be run over. Frankly I don't think that J and M has enough experience with video games to be able to keep up with the changes that are coming. After all, IGT has been making both slots and video games all along."

"But J and M is working on the games now."

"Yes, so they say. But I'm worried that they are way behind. In my humble opinion they need to make some deals at the next G2. You know, get some rights to some games the kids already like. WMS already has a slot based on the movie Top Gun. Cyberview is already showing a prototype game that they call, well I think it's called Glaxium. You pay for play time and do your best taking on fighter planes, dodging asteroids; you know; that sort of stuff. It uses random number generators to keep it legal, but you know what? My bet is on skill-based game slots becoming legal next year anyway. After all, video poker already involves skill. It's just that the skilled player loses less to the house."

"You sound worried, Mario."

"Damned right I'm worried."

"But what about our cash card invention?"

With that Mario came off his lectern.

"Oh yes; the cash card. Well, as you say, that now is a horse of a different color."

Jimmy looked Mario: how much did he know?

"What do you mean?"

"Excelsior has it now installed in their slots. They march to a different tune, a tune in a minor key; in a *very* minor key. They've also been hitting on the video game people for some licenses but have struck out so far. The video gamers just don't really know about Excelsior, I guess.

"Now I could go on but you need to be seeing and not just listening while you're out here. I realize that you are three hours ahead of us so why don't I get Juliana to drive you to your hotel. Check in, check out the town a little on your own, and I'll pick you up in the morning. By the way, where are you staying?"

"The Las Vegas Hilton."

"Good choice. It's a stop on the monorail and close to the Strip and to the Convention Center. Tell you what, I'll park there in the morning and we can ride the rail in together. Let's say nine o'clock in the Lobby."

With a push of a button on her car key the Morino Distributor Honda gave a short beep as it unlocked itself. Jimmy put his bag on the back seat and climbed in. As soon as Juliana got in behind the wheel Jimmy was smitten by her perfume. I don't usually notice perfume, he thought, but this really *is* nice. She cranked the engine and they were off.

"Tell me about Jimmy Davis," she said straight off.

"Is the Mr. Davis married?"

"Separated." Jimmy caught his breath as that word came out spontaneously and surprisingly effortless. He had never said that before to anyone, not even to himself.

"Children?"

"Yes, twin boys, of the smaller size."

"Are they with their mother?"

Jimmy began to feel uncomfortable, which Juliana noticed.

"Sorry, I don't mean to pry."

"For the moment he, that is they, are with her. Our breakup just happened."

"Sorry; again. It must be hard."

"And you? Any bambinos?

Juliana laughed. "Sin hijos. No, no bambinos. Why? Do you think I'm Italian?"

"Oh, that's Italian?"

Juliana laughed again.

"Are you planning on kids, Juliana?"

She glanced over at Jimmy with a studious look but said nothing for a moment.

"Mario was married before. He had that little operation, you know."

"A vasectomy?"

"Yes."

"They can reverse that, you know."

"Sometimes."

They drove on in momentary silence.

"Look, I shouldn't have told you that. Please keep it to yourself. It's just that I'm a real upfront type and I felt comfortable talking with you right off. I don't know why."

"Me too; consider it done. I *am* a lawyer, you know."

"Mario also had a severe heart attack several months ago. Poor guy had to have a defibrillator surgically implanted in his chest. That has slowed him down, physically and spiritually."

"Was it work-stress related?"

"I think so. This business can be ruthless."

As she drove into the Hilton she gave Jimmy a parting admonishment.

"Now behave yourself here in Sin City."

"I *SINcerely* will."

As she drove off Jimmy saw here shaking her head with a smile.

Chapter 12

After checking in Jimmy freshened up and decided to head for The Strip for he was having an adrenalin rush from the excitement of being here in Las Vegas for the first time. Not only that but he was on his own, not due to his own fault but due to that of Sheila. They were now *separated*. And it was all her own doing. He did not feel guilt. In fact he felt rather good. The gloom of his missing boy, over which he had no control, had lifted for the moment. It would be a stag night out like before he had met Sheila.

He caught the monorail which headed south. It was noticeably clean and modern. There weren't many riders at this time of day.

The train went past the Convention Center and then on to The Strip. He marveled at the structures of the Venetian, Harrah's, The Imperial Palace and The Flamingo.

At Bally's he exited and walked to The Strip. It seemed that he had arrived right at its heart. Here was The Bellagio, Caesars Palace, and The Paris all within an easy walk of each other in the clear, crisp, desert air of winter. He checked all three out without spending a dime until he stumbled across a sports bar and the smell of fried food, where his stomach took control for after all, even though it was only afternoon here, his stomach said it was dinnertime.

Dinner alone was no problem. There were several other loners eating at a bar in front of a giant screen mindlessly watching a game of hockey.

After a couple of beers and some spicy chicken wings he made his way through the casino at Bally's. A few minutes of video poker proved to be enough. He wasn't a gambler and viewed gambling as just another form of entertainment much like seeing a DVD. Instead of buying a ticket to see a movie or show, the same amount of money could be spent at a gaming machine or by playing blackjack. If you happened to win, fine, but after the "ticket" money was spent, that was it for that night for the conservative Jimmy.

The monorail delivered him safely back to the Las Vegas Hilton early. He made his way through the crowded lobby and to the elevators. Soon one that serviced his floor opened to disgorge a full complement of riders on their way out for the evening. He and a little old lady were the only ones to go up.

"Good night," she said with a smile as she reached her floor.

"Good night, ma'am," he replied as he continued alone on higher to his floor.

As he opened the door to his room he sensed the smell of smoke. Funny that he hadn't smelt it before. He reached for the light switch.

"Leave it, kid," came a voice from within the darkened room. "And close the door."

Jimmy stopped at the threshold and looked where the voice had come from. Faint light from the hall revealed the figure of a man seated in a chair near the drawn window curtains. A draw on the man's cigar caused it to flare and momentarily reveal a dark skinned face beneath a cap.

"I said close the door, kid."

Still standing in the threshold Jimmy looked back over his shoulder both ways down the hall. It was empty. I can close the door and run, he thought.

"No point in that, counselor," said the telepathist.

Jimmy stood there undecided, his hand still on the doorknob.

"It's now or tomorrow. I don't care."

Jimmy looked at the figure of the seated man but couldn't make out the face well, his eyes still accustomed to the lighting in the hallway. Then he resigned himself to the inevitable, walked inside and closed the door behind him. Obviously the man wasn't just a chance opportunist.

"Lie down on the bed."

Jimmy sat on the side of the bed.

"The other way," commanded the voice as Jimmy started to swing over and put his head on the pillows. So instead his put his feet there and his head on the foot of the bed just a couple of feet from the armchair.

Jimmy lay there in silence. Then a ring of cigar smoke came floating over his head which he could see from the drawn window curtains that were softly backlit by the outdoor lighting. Then another ring floated over his head in silence which oddly brought to mind the Fox Theatre back home in Atlanta where the theatre ceiling was a star-filled sky beneath which fair weather clouds drifted in silence.

"Well?" Jimmy finally asked.

This was responded to with yet another ring of smoke being blown over his head and then over his body until it dissipated at the headboard. Still the man said nothing.

"Well come on," said Jimmy as he started to get peeved and lifted and turned his head back towards the chair.

A hand grabbed his ear and yanked his head back down onto the bed. Then another muscular hand grabbed his other ear to pin his head down firmly on the bed.

Jimmy looked up to see the bottom of the man's chin beneath the cigar. The chin then tilted down towards his face to bring the burning end of the cigar right between Jimmy's eyes, which instinctively closed. Then the man nodded which flung a few hot ashes onto his eye lids and forehead. Again instinctively Jimmy raised his arms towards his head. They were met forcefully by two hands that had been made into fists upon being released from Jimmy's ears. Jimmy's arms were driven back onto the bed. Jimmy curled his lower lip and blew the ashes off as he shook his head from side to side.

Jimmy lay there in silence. He wanted to wipe off some residual ashes on his eyelids but was afraid to lift his arms which were both smarting. Finally the man sat back down and spoke.

"Welcome to Vegas, Mr. Davis."

"Who are you?"

"Shut the fuck up."

Jimmy blew over his eyelids and then brushed them with one hand.

"Mr. Jimmy, relax. You've been a good boy so far. No police. Keep it that way."

"So when do I get my boy back?"

"Your boy back? What-cha talking about, your boy back?"

"As if you don't know."

"Don't ya talk with your wife no more?"

"What do you mean?"

"Didn't she tell you that she picked up the twins, all of u'm, this afternoon from KiddyKare? Didn't she tells ya?"

"No, she didn't. Is that true?"

"You bets'ya. Cute little suckers. You'sa lucky man."

"So all of this is over now?"

"Now would I be here if it was? Do's I look like some fucking messenger boy?"

"Let me see," said Jimmy with a slow head turn towards the man's face. That was met by a stinging slap on his head.

"Here we thought that you were a smart attorney but you are nothing but a smartass. I have spelled it out for you, kid, about no cops or FBI. And you'sa took care of the patent. So far so good, and for that you'sa now been rewarded. Now you've got your precious little boys back safe and sound. They probably had more fun at the farm than at KiddyKare. Just ask 'um.

"You know we could have kept the kids on the farm until that cash card patent stuff was six feet under but that takes too long. So we've given you an early present, but try to go back on that and your little boys will be back at the farm only the next time they'll be not *on* it but *under* it. Got it? They'll buy the fucking farm."

"I got it."

"Good; now I's told ya before that we keeps our word, and we have – twice."

"I wouldn't call the first time keeping..."

"Oh yes we did. It was just our little joke. We *can* joke around, you know."

"So if I leave the cash card application abandoned this is all over?"

"Well, not exactly. Leave it alone and we leave the kids alone.

They can grow up to be big city lawyers just like their papa. Mess with that and they become country as dirt."

"Okay; okay. Other than that is all this now over?" As Jimmy waited for a response another smoke ring drifted overhead.

"We do have some more work for you, attorney Davis. Hey, young lawyers wants all the new jobs they can get; right?"

"What kind of new work? You want to open an account with me?"

"Don't get smart with me, asshole. J and M new work; just J and M. That's all we wants of you. We just wants you to do some work on those two other boys - the J and the M boys."

"Just what do you have in mind?"

"Not tonight but we'll be getting back to you on that. Now you just might be have'n to bend those nitpicking lawyers' rules a bit, but I'm sure you can handle that. You see the consa . . qencees for not helping out with this will lay just on your shoulders. Now I best be going." With that the man stood.

"Keep those eyes closed and spread your legs for tie-down. Then again . . ."

As Jimmy was spreading his legs a large fist punched into his groin with a thud. Unbelievable pain followed as he recoiled into the fetal position. His try at crying out was muffled by the inrush of air as he gasped.

"Don't bother Mr. Davis, I'll let myself out."

———•((◊))•———

It took several minutes for Jimmy to recover even though the punch had only been that – a punch. With the pain gone and his head now cleared he reached for the room phone that was on a bedside table. The handset was not on the cradle but in the table drawer atop a Gideon bible. He replaced it and waited for a dial tone and called Sheila on her cell.

"I've been trying to get you, Jimmy, but no luck on your cell or there at your hotel. Having too good of a time, I suppose."

"I just heard that Andy has been returned. Is that true?"

"You would know that if you weren't whooping it up in Vegas. Having fun out there, Sonny? Seeing all the sights?"

"Look, I forgot to bring my cell and my room phone has been disconnected."

"Cut off from the world, huh? Cut off all your worries. Head to Vegas. How are the chicks?"

"Will you shut up? Goddamn it; just shut it."

Silence followed.

"Is Andy back? Yes or no."

"Yes, he's back."

"Is he alright?"

"Yes, they're both alright - now."

Jimmy slammed the phone down in disgust.

Chapter 13

Jimmy awoke at 5:00 am, that being 8:00 am back in Atlanta. He had slept fitfully even though the room had been quiet and dark and the bed sheets freshly cleaned and comfortable. The rancid smell of cigar smoke would not go away.

After *the man* had let himself out and Jimmy had made the call to Sheila he had double locked the room door and pushed a table over in front of it. This wouldn't really matter if *the man* really wanted to return he knew, yet it still made him feel more secure.

During his fitful night he had had a dream generated by his unexpected visitor. He was on a wharf late at night in a cold fog with three men wearing hats like those in an old black and white John Dillinger movie. Two of them were holding one of his legs while the concrete in the bucket in which his foot was submerged was slowly setting up. He had tried to keep wiggling his foot and toes but his wiggle-room had kept shrinking. They were both kneeling while the third man stood behind smoking a cigar and supervising their work.

"Just a few more minutes, kid," the man had said, "and we'll be all set. Ha! All set; get it?"

Jimmy became frantic as he tried to kick his foot in the setting goo. At first the bucket did wobble a bit until one of the men grabbed it. More attempts at kicking became futile. Finally he mustered all his strength and gave one last kick that sent his bed sheet and blanket flying. The weight of the bed covers had been pressing all the while on the foot-of-interest.

Now awake he recalled what Sheila had said. Both of the boys were now safe. God, what a relief. When he thought of Andy and Alec only their joyful faces came to mind. There was no story nor decision nor doing associated with their visions. There were just happy thoughts of the boys themselves. Then his brain conjured up a recall of *the man*.

The man was a thug. There wasn't anything personal associated with his acts. He was just doing what he did like sharks and snakes do their things. On the other hand, with Sheila it was so personal and emotional with him; so confusing and unresolved. What had happened with her, or to her? Her better-than-thou parents merely came with the territory of the Virginia Highlands crowd and their membership in the prestigious, old moneyed, Piedmont Driving Club. But Sheila was no longer the same young lady he had married. Maybe it was the kidnappings. Maybe she had reverted to the society of her parents. No, that wasn't it. Perhaps it was her job that was getting to her. Whatever it was the change went to her very core. What a shame; what a pity for her falling out of love with him was involuntarily bringing about a reciprocal falling out.

Sheila's parents had never accepted him. They had but tolerated her Jimmy. From the beginning they had tried to talk her out of their marriage. An engineer from Lockheed? How many thousands of engineers did they have out there? And how long before he would be transferred, and transferred no doubt to that land of fruit and nuts called California. Good God. But he's a lawyer now, she had argued. Yes, her father had retorted; and how many of those are inside just the perimeter? But I love him! And how long will that last? Sheila, he simply is not one of us. He's not our kind. In the end, of course, they had relented and seen their daughter drive off into the sunset, quite literally at the Driving Club. Following the reception the drive-off had been made in a carriage pulled by a solid-white horse out from the Piedmont Driving Club clubhouse porte-cochere and through the adjacent Piedmont Park.

The Driving Club was, and still remains today, one of the most prestigious private clubs in the South. Founded in 1887 its original members would drive their horses and carriages out on the club grounds. Its bylaws from the 1920s capped membership at 500. Any new member had to be sponsored by three current members. A blackball from any member was fatal.

When Sheila's father had proudly mentioned to Jimmy at the reception that he might be able to get him in one day, Jimmy had said that the club was probably not for him. "Daddy" had tried. He would not be trying again. There was no genuine smile for the rest of the reception; just a forced one when required. This new husband of his daughter would definitely not be becoming one of them. No, he would be just another outsider living outside of the perimeter along with all those other transplanted Yankees and corporate gypsies. True, he was from the Midwest rather than the East, but he might as well be just another I've-been-moved-er, a.k.a. an IBM-er, spending a few years here before moving on and taking their children, which would be his own grandchildren, with them. In the process the grandkids would be moved from one school to another with no lasting friendships.

The thought of school shifted his mind back again to Andy and Alec. Apparently they had not been harmed. Indeed, at least Alec had had a good time on that farm. What a deal. Here he had been worried sick and here Alec had been seeing and enjoying new sights. When he saw him next he wouldn't be surprised if he asked when he would be going back.

So Sheila would be back at her home, the boys would be wanting to revisit the farm, and he, Jimmy Davis, would be - - - well he would be wondering when he would be getting another fist to his balls.

With that he got up out of bed. He needed to get some clothes on; something more protective of his privates than Jockey shorts. Anything but laying longer in the bed, thinking.

Jimmy finished his second cup of coffee and the newspaper in the hotel lobby. He looked at his watch and saw that it was eight forty-five. This Pacific Time seemed to be in slow motion, but then with relief he saw Mario making his way in. Today he was sporting a blue leather hair band that matched the color of his shirt. Jimmy waved him over.

"How did it go last night, Mr. Jimmy? Hit any jackpots?"

"No jackpots," replied Jimmy as he rose to meet him. "But tonight, for sure."

"Did Vegas live up to your expectations?"

"I suppose so, except for the fist to my balls." With that Jimmy elaborated by telling Mario about *The Man's* little visit to his room. Mario hinged on his every word.

"That's Jal; Jal Recos, I think, but I'm not sure. Anyway, he's known here as "The Hammer." Word has it that he once was a boxer, back East."

"Then he should know better than to hit below the belt."

Mario lowered his voice. "I wouldn't joke about him, Jimmy. He's bad news; real bad news. Believe me you don't want to have anything to do with him. Now come on; I've arranged a little show for you today."

Mario filled Jimmy in about the show he had arranged as they rode the monorail to The Strip. Today they would be initiating a field trial on J and M's new pro-active slot machine with a joystick. It was called Pong since the proactive play to which it progressed was the old well known game of Pong. The game was played on a screen with a ball and two paddles that two opposing players moved up and down with joysticks. Through Mario's efforts Caesars Palace was permitting J and M to set up two Pong machines and today was inauguration day. For Mario this was quite a coup. He had been able to leapfrog the competition in getting the first-of-its-kind Vegas field trial. Bally's and Excelsior field trials for rival pro-active machines was still two or three weeks off.

As they made their way to the entrance of Caesars Palace Mario pulled out his cell phone. "Sid; Mario; we'll be in the lobby in just a minute. What's say we meet at the exhibit in fifteen minutes? Great."

Mario led the way inside and then through the opulent rotunda beneath its beautifully lit dome, past the Roman statuary and onto the casino entrance. Once inside the casino and on its carpet he led Jimmy to one side where two shrouded slot machines stood positioned back-to-back all by themselves. Neither was turned on. Thus darkened they were hardly noticeable against the backdrop of the host of all the brightly lit others that were in loud play. A gold braided cord encircled the two. They had no sooner arrived there when a tall man in a business suit approached them.

"Good morning, Mario," he said as he held out his hand.

"Ah Sid, I'd like you to meet Jimmy Davis who is here from J and M. Jimmy, this is Sid Caesar."

"Don't worry about him, Mr. Davis; I gave up long ago. I'm Sid Riley, one of the floor managers. Glad to have you with us."

"Thanks, Mr. Riley." Jimmy noticed that Sid was wearing a thin headband with a mike and earpiece.

"Ready to rock and roll, Mario?"

"Just give me a moment."

With that Mario untied the gold cord and handed it to Jimmy. Then he flipped a switch on the back of one of the slot machines which immediately sprang to life. Pong was brightly lit and the sound of two ping pong balls being paddled back and forth could be heard even though traditional symbol-bearing reels were seen in the play window. Then he switched on the other slot which too sprang to life. Mario beamed.

"Pretty impressive huh, Sid?" said Mario.

"Not bad."

Next Mario pulled a stand-alone sign out from up against the machines and turned it around. It announced the introduction of Pong, an interactive slot machine where you can win a bonus bout against another live player in a game of Pong. The colored artwork showed three slot wheels with one wheel stopped at a Pong symbol from which an arrow was pointed to a display of the Pong game field. At the bottom in small print was the J and M diamond logo.

"All set?" asked Sid.

"As much as we'll ever be."

"Then it's show time."

With that Sid flipped down the small mike and positioned it over of his mouth. He touched a button on top of the headband beside a small antenna and spoke.

"We're ready; fanfare," he said distinctly.

A few seconds passed and then a chorus of trumpets could be heard throughout the casino demanding attention. At the end of the short fanfare Sid spoke enthusiastically into the mike with a voice much like that of a hawker at a circus sideshow.

"Ladies and gentlemen, Caesars Palace is proud to announce the introduction, not only to Caesars Palace, but to all of Las Vegas itself, a new breed of the venerable slot machine. With this revolutionary new slot machine you will be able not only to win the old fashion way that you all know and love so well, but also win the chance to compete with other players proactively in a game of skill – in a game of Pong for even more winnings! You here today are fortunate to have been in the right place at the right time to witness this first-time-ever event. So please make your way now over to the casino entrance by following one of the roving centurions to witness a truly unique and memorable demonstration."

"Sid, you really are a pro. That was great," said Mario as he gave a big two-thumbs-up hand gesture.

Over the next several minutes centurions in full regalia marched slowly towards the demonstration each with several of the curious in tow. Jimmy saw them as imperial Roman pied-pipers.

As they rendezvoused at the demonstration they lined up abreast and stood at attention facing their human deposits. At show time minus five Sid gave another short announcement. At time zero Sid surveyed the gathering of the some twenty-odd spectators. Seeing no more approaching he started the demonstration by picking up a portable hand mike from beside a small speaker that was set atop one of the slots.

"Ladies and gentlemen, I am Sid Riley. On behalf of Caesars Palace I want to welcome you to the first ever demonstration in a Las Vegas casino of a new generation of slot machines that we refer to as a proactive slot machine. I know you will find it fascinating. Mario?"

Mario stepped forward and took the mike.

"Thank you Sid, and on behalf of J and M Manufacturing I want to thank you for this opportunity.

"Ladies and gentlemen, you see before you two slot machines called Pong. These machines work just like the slot machines that you have been used to; you know - pull a handle or push a button and reels spin. Whatever combination of symbols comes up determines if you are a winner or not. That's all you do: Spin and watch. With these machines however you get the chance to do more than just watch. One of the symbols that can come up is PONG.

Now it will not appear until you have played at least three times, but when it does come up the Pong logo here will begin to flash. That means that you may enter a bonus round and go up against another player in an active, on-line game of Pong.

Now if you don't want to play Pong just hit the cancel button here or the play button here. The play button will cost ten coins – two dollars fifty. If you play just wait a few moments until another player, either here in Caesars or some other casino, also enters a bonus round. When that happens the screen will shift to Pong and the game is immediately activated and in-play. The winner will win five dollars – which includes your own two-fifty. You may elect rematches at two dollars fifty each before you are returned back to where you started. The payout for rematches is two dollars and a quarter.

"Rather than take any questions I think the game will become clear by your just watching a few rounds. I am taking this machine here. Oh and yes, I see my worthy is adversary arriving now."

Everyone turned to look in the direction that Mario was looking with his broad smile. Approaching was the Captain of the Guard with his flowing, red cape and red-plumed, crescent-shaped helmet. He was escorting a young vestal virgin in a flowing white gown. Her solid black hair and eyes were in sharp contrast to the gown. Spontaneously the gathering started to applause to the surprised delight of Sid and Mario. The Captain led her to the other machine and then took up a position behind her. Both machines were ready with prepaid credits.

"Let the games begin!" said the Captain with a flourishing wave of his arm.

On that signal Mario and the vestal virgin grasped their joysticks and pushed the button atop the ends of the sticks. Both machines went into play. Mario was beaming but the virgin remained demure. The reels spun only to come to rest with no winning combination of symbols. Again they played. On the third spin her machine came up with a small win with an accompanying sound of coins being delivered. The virgin's demureness changed to a sly smile.

Play continued for several more spins. Mario continued to lose. But again the virgin won and now her smile had broadened with excitement. A few more spins and Mario came up with a PONG symbol. As he was grasping the joystick in his right hand and working its button with his thumb he used his left hand to select PLAY PONG. The Pong symbol began to blink.

Three more spins by the virgin brought a PONG symbol up for her also. "Ah," she exclaimed. She quickly scanned the machine console and located the PLAY PONG button. She gave it a tap with one long, pointed finger. The spectators, who now were in two quarter circles inside the circle of centurions, interests now peaked with widened eyes.

The game of Pong came to life simultaneously on both machines. Mario's joystick suddenly felt like a hot poker in his hand. It had become electrified! He tried to let go, but couldn't. Alternating electric current flowed through his body as the screen showed the pong ball going to the right towards his opponent's sidewall.

Mario's hand began to shake the joystick violently. The shaking grew in intensity as the vestal virgin's paddle moved down to intercept the ball. Contact caused the ball to bounce back to her left towards Mario's sidewall and paddle. She squealed with girlish glee.

Mario's body began to thrash about atop the stool. He exerted maximum effort to release the joystick, but without success. A rush of sweat materialized. The lights on his machine began to flicker.

"I'm winning! I'm winning," squealed the vestal virgin with unbridled delight as she drove home the pong ball without noticing that Mario's paddle was remaining stationary and dormant. "See, I'm winning."

Another gyration of Mario's torso brought his hand that was still painfully grasping the joystick up against his chest and defibrillator. He and both machines lost consciousness, simultaneously.

The flickering of the machine's lights ended in darkness as it died with a smell of burnt wires. Mercifully it then released its death grip on Mario who fell to the floor. The burnt smell from his defibrillator was overpowered by that from his slot machine.

Chapter 14

Seeing that the lawyer was on the speaker phone, Sheila tapped lightly on the open door of her office. The lawyer, Patricia Devore, swiveled in her chair and motioned for Sheila to take a seat on the couch that faced her massive desk behind a coffee table. Sheila did so as Mrs. Devore picked up the phone handset to continue her conversation with a bit more privacy.

Sheila surveyed the senior partner and her office. Neatness was the operative word for both. Mrs. Devore was wearing a black, turtleneck sweater and black pants with a gold belt and oversized buckle. Her black, horn rim glasses were the color of her hair which was a bit long for her age. Her shoes were probably gold, Sheila guessed.

As for the office itself there were two facing arm chairs by the coffee table and some Egyptian art work on the wall behind the couch. The desk was almost devoid of paperwork. Two decorative feather pens straddled two ink wells that were set in an ebony stand boarded with etched gold. The gold matched the gilded frame of a wide Egyptian rendering of Ramses the Great, no doubt, accepting offerings amidst a field of hieroglyphics. As she ended her phone call Patricia stood and walked over to Sheila with her hand extended for a shake. And yes, her shoes were indeed gold.

"Sheila, Abigail tells me that you are a real comer in the tax department," she said while taking off her glasses and shaking hands in a womanly fashion with the now standing Sheila.

"That's good to hear, Mrs. Devore."

"Ms. Devore; you see I am divorced," she said with a faint smile. "Actually it's Pat," she said as she took her seat in one of the arm chairs while Sheila was sitting back down on the couch.

"Sorry that we have to meet again but in a professional capacity this time. Divorce is such an unpleasant and trying thing even under the best of circumstances."

"I wouldn't know. It's my first," smiled Sheila. As soon as she had said that she wished that she hadn't. But Pat returned the smile with a genuine one of sympathy. As head of the family law section of Ramsey, Ivy and Prince she understood full well this initial, frightening stage of a marital breakup.

"Ms. Devore, I really appreciate you taking my case. I'm flattered."

"For one of our budding star tax counselors I'm only happy to represent you. Trust me; it's in the firm's best interest."

"Before we begin could we discuss cost?"

"Now don't you worry about all of that. You have enough burdens on your mind already. The firm will be waiving all fees. I wish that we could also waive costs, but that we can't do as I'm sure you know."

"Oh, yes, certainly. Well I appreciate all this; I really do."

"Let's take it from the top then," said Patricia as she picked up a pad and pen from atop the coffee table and put her glasses back on all while sinking deeper into the armchair.

Patricia proceeded to take Sheila's case history as she had done so for countless other clients in the past, including practicing attorneys on occasion. Actually she usually found it easier to work with attorney clients. Sheila however had to relate her story without the ease of unbridled candor. Abigail had insisted that Sheila have Patricia handle her divorce case here inside the firm. At the same time however she had also insisted that Sheila not discuss any specifics of her tax work. There were certain secrets in the firm that simply were not to be revealed to other departments, and certainly not to the family law department. Divorces, custody battles and the like had nothing to do with corporate tax matters. So Sheila did her best to abide by Abigail's admonition, though at times she sensed that Patricia felt she was holding back. Patricia was used to that since intimate details of spousal behavior were so private, but Sheila's hesitations were not made in that regard, which Pat found odd.

Sheila explained that she had made a mistake in marrying Jimmy. Her parents had warned her that she was marrying beneath her station. But the cosmic timing had triumphed. Venus had been ascendant. Jimmy was so clean and innocent; so tall and good looking. He had been a breath of fresh air at that time when she had been under such pressure for so long to succeed with top grades from a top law school, to be followed by entry into a top law firm. Though she certainly felt the pressure to please her father, she also shared his drive to succeed. Now she wished that she had not brushed off her father's objections to Jimmy and had not bull nosed ahead. But she had felt that she and her Jimmy would rise together in their shared profession, and that along the way she would enjoy this young, fresh and good looking and rather witty young man. Also, she had expected to get her way on things of importance to her. He would only literally wear the pants.

But then life has that nasty habit of not following a script.

Jimmy's work was not of the slightest interest to her. It was too technical and she did not understand technical. He never brought home tales of exciting new enterprises on the breaking edge of technology. Hey, he would say, we live in Atlanta, not Silicon Valley. Litigation? Trial work? No, that's not for me, he would say. Marketing? Getting clients? No, I'm not the salesman type either. As for clients his only, personal client, J and M, had been delivered to him on a silver platter by Sheila herself. She now saw him as simply a patent scribe. Never mind that she spent all her days working on other people's taxes, which Jimmy found to be stiflingly boring.

But then there were the twins. Obviously they had not been foreseen either. In fact she had wanted to wait for a couple of years before trying to get pregnant. But Jimmy had starting pushing their having a child after they had only been married for a couple of months. Shortly after their birth she had found herself counting the months before they would be eligible for day care, and then eligible for preschool, and then . . . on and on. Her work took priority.

"What terms are you seeking?" asked Patricia after Sheila had finished her story.

"Not much, really; the house is in both of our names and the bank actually owns most of it. We can put it on the market and split whatever equity we get out, and the sooner, the better. He can stay if he wants until it sells provided he helps in its selling. If he does stay he simply carries its cost. If he doesn't, and splits, well then we split the house costs I suppose until it is sold. There's not much to hassle about in the furnishings. We can easily split what was bought.

"I see no problem with that; it's all reasonable."

"Our bank accounts are separate. We each just go our own way on money."

"What about child support?"

"Well, there is one thing that might be a problem with Jimmy. You see, the boys are at my parents now with me. My dad thinks that Andy and Alec should stay together, their being twins and all. He and my mom have a big house in Virginia Highlands. It's a nice old neighborhood with huge shade trees and sidewalks and yet today it is filled with young people. My parents think the boys and I should both continue to stay on with them. Right now I think that's a good idea, too, but I don't know about Jimmy; I don't know how he will react to that."

"So you have already moved out with both of your boys?"

"Right."

"Did your husband, Jimmy, agree to that?"

"Well, not exactly; I just left with them and left him a note."

"I see." Patricia tried to look into Sheila's eyes but she turned away.

"When was that?"

"Oh that was just now."

"Sheila, is there something that you are not telling me here; something else I should know?"

After a pause she responded "No; not really; I just didn't want a fight, particularly in front of the boys. It was the easiest way."

"Have you actually told him that you want a divorce?"

"Not yet; I just told him that we needed to separate."

"Surely you have discussed the twins."

"Look, this has just happened. I left him a note. Right after that he had to go on a business trip, a, quote, "business" trip to Las Vegas."

"A business trip, you say?"

"Actually it probably was a business trip. You see his best client manufactures slot machines."

"His client, you say?"

"Oh, he too is a lawyer, a patent lawyer. I should have told you that. That's how we first met – at a bar review course."

"I trust he's not in the firm here."

"Oh, no; he's with one of those small, boutique firms that specialize in IP law."

"Sheila, I suggest that you talk about all of this with your husband before you file. If the tables were reversed I think you would want it that way."

"No, I don't want to talk. I'll just get mad and so will he. No, in this case I think it best to go ahead and serve him with the papers. If you knew him you would understand."

Chapter 15

As soon as Mario fell to the floor Sid took charge in his role as floor manager. First he called a code over his mike and gave the location. Then he moved over to the collapsed Mario and bent down. Mario was in a modified fetal position with both hands clasped to his chest and his eyes wide open. His mouth was frozen in an open and rigid contortion. For an instant he thought of administering mouth-to-mouth resuscitation, but then found himself straightening upright in front of the now dark and smelly slot machine that had attacked Mario.

"Folks, please stand back. Let's give the man some air." Then he realized that he was preaching to the choir, the people nearest to Mario having already shrunk back away in horror from the unexpected fireworks.

Sid eyed two of the pseudo-centurions and gave then a hand gesture to disperse the assembly. As they began to do so the other centurions and the captain of the guard joined in. The bimbo vestal virgin remained seated as she looked around perplexed with her mouth open, still not comprehending what was happening.

Jimmy found himself amongst those being herded away while looking back over their shoulders at the scene. Quickly he recovered his senses and broke away to return to Mario. Sid stood aside as Jimmy bent down.

"Mario? Mario?" Good Lord, he thought, he looks dead! He

was feeling for a pulse just as two uniformed paramedics arrived and urged him aside. He stood back as they went to work.

Jimmy watched for a few moments and then turned to see Sid speaking again into his mike. He was quietly issuing instruction to have the area cordoned off and to move out those still playing in the area. When Sid paused Jimmy spoke.

"Sid, I think . . . . ."

Sid made a hand gesture to hush and started issuing more instructions in this mike. No more than seconds later another fanfare was sounded throughout the casino. Jimmy assumed it would relate to the horrible tragedy he had just witnessed. But no, the announcement that followed the musical fanfare merely announced that another exciting event would start in just fifteen minutes in another part of the casino. Sid watched Jimmy as he listened in surprise to the announcement and then put his hand on his shoulder.

"Jimmy, take heart. The last thing we want is to have people coming over here right now."

"Of course."

By now several casino security men in business attire had arrived to aid the centurions in cordoning off the area. Once Sid was satisfied with their actions and the results, he walked over to one of the paramedics who had just stood. The two quietly talked for a minute. Then he nodded solemnly and returned to Jimmy.

"It doesn't look good, Jimmy. I'm afraid that Mario is gone."

"My God, that's terrible. Hard to believe; it was so sudden. I mean; I mean that I just met him yesterday. He seemed to be a good man. I wonder what happened. Did you know that he had a defibrillator implanted in his chest?"

"Really?" That could be very useful information, thought Sid.

"That's what his wife told me."

"So he does have a wife."

"Yes; her name is Juliana. I just met her yesterday too."

"Jimmy, would you break the news to her? I don't mean to tell her that he has died. I mean that you can just say that he has had a serious accident, an accident probably related to his defibrillator."

"Sure; of course. I'll call her."

"It would be better to go to her. Do you have a car?"

"No; we rode the tram in. You know, this is my first time out here and I don't know the city."

"I'll have a driver take you. Accompany her to emergency at Sunrise - Sunrise Hospital. The driver will be at your disposal for the rest of the day. Here is my card. Please keep me abreast. I'll let the operator know to patch you right through to me at any time."

Jimmy once again found the reception room at Moreno Distributors empty.

"Hello? Juliana?"

"Mr. Davis, Jimmy. You are back already?" Then she saw how somber he appeared.

"Is something wrong?"

Jimmy nodded.

"Mario?"

Jimmy nodded again.

"I'm afraid that there has been an accident. Mario has been taken to the hospital."

"The hospital?"

"Yes."

"What kind of accident?"

"At the demonstration at Caesars - with the slot machines."

"The slot machines; what happened? Did one fall on him?"

"Juliana, I don't know. He was playing it when all of a sudden he fell to the floor. Paramedics were called and he's been taken to the hospital. I'm here to take you there."

"You could have called. Say, how did you get back here?"

"The casino has provided us with a car and driver. He's here now waiting. I think we should get going."

"The casino has provided a car and driver?"

"That's right."

"This is serious, isn't it?"

Jimmy nodded.

Juliana yelled out to someone in the back and then grabbed her handbag.

Jimmy sat with her in the back seat as they were driven to the hospital. Juliana was insistent with her questions.

"You saw the accident, right?"

"Yes, I was watching the competition between Mario and the other player."

"Just what did you see, Jimmy?"

"Mario was playing when all of a sudden he went into some kind of a spasm. He started shaking. He was holding the joystick and seemed unable to let go. Then he leaned forward over the joystick. The machine started sparking and smoking and then went dead – I mean that its lights went out. I guess some circuit breaker or other went off."

"Did anyone push him?"

"Quite the contrary; people were backing away from him."

"You're sure that no one pushed him?"

"Juliana, are you thinking that this was deliberate — that this wasn't an accident?"

This brought no response from her as she looked out the window at the passing traffic in contemplation.

"Who was his opponent? Was he close? Could he touch Mario?"

"No. And it wasn't a he. It was a girl, a showgirl in costume. They were well separated, for you see the two machines were set up back to back."

"So the people were actually watching her?"

"The men certainly were . . . . well . . . I mean . . . ."

Juliana continued on with her interrogation until the hospital came into view. Upon seeing it she fell silent and began to cry quietly as she looked out the window at the approaching building. Jimmy pulled out his handkerchief but hesitated in seeing that it was slightly soiled. Sensing that gesture Juliana reached to get her own hankie by intending to pull the more distant strap of her handbag to open it towards her. By mistake she took hold of the strap nearer her which caused several articles to fall out of the bag and onto the seat. Seeing her handkerchief now exposed Jimmy handed it to her which she took while still looking at the approaching hospital.

Jimmy started to retrieve the spilt articles which included a pack of gum, a lipstick and a blank card. In the process of returning them to the handbag he turned the card over. The other side bore a drawing. He turned it right-side-up for a better look. Of all things it was a Tarot card. It depicted a standing skeleton wearing a black shroud and holding a sickle over the skeletal remains of an animal. The death card – the grim reaper! Hurriedly he slid it back in her bag. He looked up at Juliana to find that she still was gazing out of the window. She hadn't paid attention to what had happened to her bag. Without turning she spoke.

"He's dead isn't he?"

"I don't know; perhaps."

Slowing she turned her head towards him. Her eyes were now filled to overflow with tears as she made no attempt to wipe them away. Jimmy returned her look and gently moved his hands from the handbag to hold her hands. With her hands now held softly by his he lifted them to his cheek compassionately.

Jimmy and Juliana waited together in the emergency room reception area. Finally a doctor came into the room and spoke with a receptionist who pointed Juliana out to him. He came over and introduced himself to her. Upon learning that Jimmy had simply accompanied her to emergency he led Juliana away leaving Jimmy alone with his thoughts. When she looked back over her shoulder at him he indicated that he would wait.

A half hour later the same doctor returned and fetched Jimmy. Once they were alone in a corridor he spoke.

"I'm afraid that Mr. Moreno has died. I'm very sorry."

"Yes; I thought as much. You see, I was there when it happened."

"You saw it happen?"

"Yes, that's right."

"Please tell me what you saw."

Jimmy repeated what he had told Juliana but in a more forthright manner.

"Now think back, Mr. Davis, and take your time. When this first happened was Mr. Moreno grasping the, uh, the joystick or was it the other way around? I mean, did the machine have him in *its* grasp?"

"Oh the machine was definitely in control. I mean Mario was gyrating all about trying to let it go."

"But he might just have been trying to hold on – you know, for support."

"Oh no; he used his left hand to try to pull his right hand free. I remember that when he collapsed his left hand was still grasping his right wrist."

"So he never grasped his chest? You see he was wearing a medical alert bracelet; he had a pacemaker."

"Not before he hit the floor. After that I don't know. I couldn't see then."

"Thank you Mr. Davis. Do you have a business card? The coroner's office may need to get in touch with you."

Chapter 16

Jimmy opened the front glass door of his firm's office and entered. "Good morning Alice," he said to the petite receptionist.

"Oh, Mr. Davis, Mr. Jones has been waiting for you," she said as she nodded to a young black man seated there in the reception room. Though Jimmy didn't recognize him he nevertheless gave the man his salesman's smile as he turned to meet him. Ah, a new client, he thought.

"Mr. Davis; Mr. Jimmy Davis?" returned the man with a smile of greetings too as he stood with his hand outstretched for a shake.

"The one and only, no less."

"That's great. Consider your one-and-only self duly served."

Jimmy's smile vanished as he saw the man extend an envelope to him in his other hand. He looked at Alice only to see that she was as surprised as he was. As the man continued to smile Jimmy could only stare at the envelope as if it contained a specimen of plague.

The man continued to stand there smiling with the envelope now just inches from Jimmy's free hand, his briefcase being held by his other. Jimmy was trapped. He took the envelope and walked away. Welcome home, he thought.

"Have a nice day," he heard from his rear as the man made for the door.

"Same to you," is all he could muster under his breath. Whereas a more seasoned member of the firm might welcome being served with legal papers, since that represented more work, more business, this was new for Jimmy.

Once in his office Jimmy looked at the envelope. Its return address read the Superior Court of Fulton County. That was odd, he thought, since the firm's intellectual property law litigation practice was done almost entirely in the federal courts. He opened the envelope to find that he had been served with personal divorce papers. His heart sank. Sheila had gone and done this without so much as a how-de-do. What a bitch, he thought.

He read the unfamiliar pleadings over slowly. Their marriage was said to be irretrievably broken. He stopped right there and considered the statement. Well if it hadn't been he guessed it was now. No point in arguing that point for what would be the alternative? Insist that it wasn't broken and keep on and on trucking? That would only make it even more irretrievably broken. No, he had too much pride to go down that road. He moved onto the proposed property distribution.

Sheila wanted the house sold and the equity in it split. Jimmy could live in it while it was up for sale provided that he paid all house expenses outside of the mortgage payments – which they would split. That sounded reasonable, he thought. Alternatively he could buy her half of its appraised value less the mortgage balance. That too sounded reasonable, as did the sharing of child support expenses. In fact all of the rest of the proposed financial settlement sounded reasonable to have come from such a bitch. Then too, they had not yet accumulated any significant wealth.

There was no demand for alimony.

It was the last demand that riled him. She wanted sole custody of the twins, but shared child support. He was to have reasonable visitation rights.

His mind switched to the boys. Andy's smiling face flashed before his eyes. After scanning the remainder of the petition he swiveled back in his chair deep in thought about the boys.

Jimmy reflected on the fact that it was Andy's face and only his that had immediately come to mind. He then thought of Alec only to find that his face was not as vivid. He seesawed back and forth between the two. Loving details of Andy's face, smiling and laughing, gushed forth. He was so vivacious in comparison with Alec and indeed even with himself. Opposites attract, he thought.

But he did love them both, just differently. Then they appeared to him playing together. They were on a seesaw. There was Andy on the top end with his head held back in an burst of laughter and Alex on the down end with his mouth wide open as he looked up in wonder at his brother. How symbolic, he thought as he turned back to the Petition for a reread of the child custody part. Then he picked up the phone.

"Sheila Frazier's office."

Damn, that was fast, he thought.

"Is Sheila there? This is her husband."

"Mr. Frazier, she hasn't come in yet. Shall I have her call you?"

"Yes, and it's Davis; not Frazier."

"Yes sir; yes Mr., Mr. Davis."

It was almost noon before she returned his call.

"I assume you got the papers."

"I could have waived service, you know. After all, I too am a . . ."

"Jimmy, I'm not handling this; my lawyer is. I suggest that you get one too."

"I didn't call you to argue. You want a divorce; you can have a divorce."

"Good. Have any problems with the petition?"

"By and large, no."

"By and large?"

"There is one thing that I won't go along with. In fact, there is only this one."

Jimmy waited for a response but none was forthcoming.

"This matter of custody; I don't think that it's fair that you have custody of the boys. That's simply not right. They are boys, after all, and I *am* their father. They need a father. They particularly need their own father."

"They'll get a father soon enough; it just won't be you."

Blood rushed to Jimmy's head in rage. There was a prolonged silence on the phone as Jimmy held his tongue.

"I'm sorry, Jimmy. I didn't mean that. It's just that all of this is hard on me too, you know."

"So there *is* someone else?"

"No, there's no one else. Look, the boys need a loving and stable home. They have that now with me and their papa and their nana. That's far better than their being the ward of a bachelor."

"The ward of a bachelor?"

"Sorry again," Sheila said in resignation. "Look, Andy and Alec are still in their terrible twos. Frankly I don't think you could handle two children in their terrible twos or even in their threes. Have you really thought this through?"

Jimmy hesitated. "Okay then, let's compromise."

"That's what the petition does – it gives you visitation rights. *That's* a compromise."

"That's not what I propose."

"Just what do you propose?"

"I'll take Andy and you can take Alec. We can get them together often, of course."

"I don't believe this. You want to split up a pair of twins - a pair of identical twins?"

"That's only fair; that's only just."

"Maybe that's justice for Solomon, but not for us."

"Bad example; this split would kill no one."

"And you think that that would be in *their* best interest? Is that what you think – that they should be separated?"

"I want one, and I'll have one. I'll be over tonight. Have Andy ready at six."

"Jimmy, the twins need each other. I'm sure the court would agree."

"I'll see you at six."

Chapter 17

Sid Riley was taking it on the chin. It was the casino manager that was delivering the punches.

"How could this happen, Sid?"

Pete Bianchi was not on Sid's back because of the Mario Moreno incident in and of itself. To the contrary Pete thought that Sid had handled it quite well at the time. The casino operations had not paused nor even slowed down for that matter. The actual observers to the incident had believed that the slot machine had simple malfunctioned and had frightened the man who had been demonstrating it, a man with a heart condition. No, Sid had handled that part quite admirably. It was what followed that Pete was all riled up about. Someone had gone to the authorities and the Coroner's Office had come calling. The slot machine was to be impounded. The problem was that the machine could not be found!

Caesar's Palace's procedures called for any machine that was damaged, accused of or found to be defective, or involved in any personal injury, to be specially tagged and promptly warehoused. In this case two men in maintenance clothes had arrived on the scene exceptionally fast, had applied a colored tag to the slot and hauled it off. When two other men arrived shortly thereafter with two substitute machines they were surprised to see that they only needed to haul off one rather than two. Someone else from their group had apparently already hauled off the defective one. They had thought nothing more about it at the time.

A check of the shipping department revealed nothing out of the ordinary. The guard at the loading dock remembered the burnt out mess of the defective machine. Its tag number matched the one on the requisition sheet presented by the driver of the van that had picked it up. So he had cleared it without hesitation. The van however never made it to the warehouse. It, along with the two maintenance men, had disappeared. All of this was recorded by the woman from the Coroner's Office who placed a hold order on the surveillance tapes made during that time frame and impounded the machine that the vestal virgin had been playing. She seemed satisfied with that for the time being.

After conferring with the general manager, the casino manager let Sid off the hook. This was clearly a matter for the police more so than for the Palace. Juliana Moreno wanted that, too.

Juliana's grief had quickly metamorphosed into anger. They would not get away with this; not this time. Her anger was not directed at J and M, nor at Caesars Palace. No, she knew that Excelsior had to be behind this "accident." And no doubt it had been Excelsior that had been behind that Tarot card with the grim reaper that she had found in Mario's desk just a mere two days ago. They had been crazy to think that they could scare Mario into submission. They really had not known him.

What a relief this was to Mitt Johnson for whom the J in J

and M was named. Their product liability policy just might not take a hit in this. Mario's widow was not blaming them, according to Jimmy. He gave her a call.

"If there is anything we can do Juliana, anything at all, just let me know."

"I appreciate that Mr. Johnson; I really do. You see, at this point I don't think this was an accident. In fact I have gone to the police."

"What did they say?"

"Well they didn't brush me off as some hysterical and bereaved Latino widow, if that's what you mean. No, the desk sergeant heard me out and then had me speak with the station captain. He took notes and all and said that he would look into it."

"You really think that Mario was murdered?"

"I do; I most certainly do."

"But why?"

"Mr. Johnson, I think you must know why."

Mitt started to respond but then thought better.

"I don't think this is the time to get into that, Juliana. When is the funeral?"

"I don't know. The Coroner's office has gotten involved. They have ordered an autopsy."

"An autopsy? I see. Has the press gotten wind of this?"

"Not as far as I know."

"I guess the casinos are pretty good at preventing this sort of thing from becoming newsworthy. Anyway, please keep me informed."

"I will. And Mr. Johnson, I'll be taking over the business. Mario would have wanted it that way."

"Good; that's the spirit."

"And I hope together we can push ahead with these interactive slots."

"Yes; yes of course." My God, he thought, she's already thinking business.

"As well as the smart cards; we have to move on that for Mario. We just can't let them get away with this."

"You know the risks, Juliana."

"Mr. Johnson, they will not get away with this. I just won't let that happen."

As soon as Mitt finished speaking with Juliana he phoned Charles Macguire at Knight and Macguire.

"Charles, has Jimmy told you what happened out in Vegas yesterday?"

"He sure did; quite bizarre; quite tragic."

"What was his take on what happened? I mean, did he see it as an accident or as something more sinister?"

"Of course he didn't see it as an accident, not with what all has been done to him. I mean it may have been an accident that Mr. Moreno died but with what all has been going on lately he feels that the slot was rigged purposely to malfunction. You should be able to tell that, I guess."

"I'm afraid not, for the machine has disappeared. Not only that but the Coroner's Office has taken the body and ordered an autopsy."

"You know, Jimmy is just a patent attorney; he was never hired to be a crime fighter. The poor guy has been really taking it on the chin – well actually, make that in the balls."

"I know; we plan to make it up to him."

"By the way, Mitt, I hope your product liability policy is in good shape. Somebody will be seeking compensation, I presume."

"I haven't said anything to them about this yet. The premiums are already high enough as it is."

"Well you better notify them or have your general counsel do so. Who is that by the way?"

"Dan Halsey. You probably don't know him. He's our corporate lawyer."

"The name is not familiar. Who's he with?"

"Big firm - Ramsey, Ivy and Prince."

Chapter 18

Dan Halsey, a mid-level member of the corporate section of Ramsey, Ivy and Prince, had the personality of the consummate corporate lawyer. He was trust inspiring, steady, competent and content with his status in the firm. He would readily acknowledge that the world of litigation was not for him. While he had his full allotment of the five human senses of sight, sound, smell, taste and feel, he failed to have that sixth sense that many trial lawyers had to their professional advantage – the sense of humor. Lacking that, however, was no more of a problem than lacking rhythm in making him a trusted confidant. One could feel sure that he would not ridicule nor chastise you regardless of how much you might have screwed up. His premature white hair and blue eyes offset his pudginess, not that that mattered very much, for little of his contact with clients was made in person. Incorporations, commercial contracts, mergers and acquisitions, those sorts of things were done at his desk working with an associate and an assistant.

"Dan; this is Mitt. How are you doing?"

"Can't complain; and you?"

"Did you hear about our debut in Vegas?"

"No; how did it go?"

"Disastrously; one of the damn things blew up right there on the casino floor in front of an assembled audience. Not only that, but the guy playing it died."

"Good Lord; what happened?"

Mitt proceeded to fill Dan in. He ended his recount by saying that the Coroner's Office had gotten involved.

"What's your advice?"

"I'll contact the insurance company. Leave it to me."

"Good; now what about Excelsior? "

"You think they were involved?"

"Of course I do."

"Mitt, you know they are our client too. That's why we had to farm out your IP work. We can't take any chance on a conflict arising between you two."

"Just what is it that you all handle for them?"

"I'm really not sure, but I think we mostly handle their tax work."

"Do you do any work for them?"

"No, in fact no one in our group does. As I said, the tax section seems to do most of their work."

"Dan, can you recommend a private eye?"

"No I can't; I've never had the occasion."

"Well just who there can? Don't you all do any criminal work?"

"No; not really; well there is a lady in our D.C. office that handles white collar crime. I could check with her. Come to think of it I guess our domestic relations group might employ private investigators. I'll check with them too."

"Good. Please get on it."

Needing to stretch his legs Dan walked down the hall to Pat

Devore's office, who he knew practiced domestic relations law. As he walked through her open door he saw that she was with a client.

"Sorry, I'll come back later."

"Come on in, Dan. This is Sheila Frazier. She's in our tax group."

"Oh, I thought she was a client. Hi, Sheila; I'm Dan Halsey – corporate."

Sheila stood and shook Dan's hand.

"I can come back," said Sheila.

"No," said Pat. "We need to get this done."

"Actually I only have a quick question. Can you recommend a good private detective?"

"Here in town?"

"Actually, it's for Las Vegas.

"Is it for a domestic problem?"

"No, it's more of a criminal nature."

"How are you involved?"

"It's not for me; it's for a local client of ours, J and M Gaming. They manufacture slot machines."

Sheila looked at him in surprise.

"J and M wants to hire a private detective for a criminal matter," asked Sheila?

"That's right. Why, do you know them?"

"Yes, I've worked on some of their tax matters. My husband is their IP lawyer."

Now it was Pat who looked surprised at Sheila, but she didn't speak.

"We use an agency that has offices all over the place," said Pat. Here, let me give you a name of a lady that I use occasionally.

I'll give you her name and number; just mention my name. I'm sure she'll give you someone to call in their Vegas office."

"Thanks, Pat. I appreciate it." Dan took the note and left.

"Small world, it appears," said Pat in mock amusement as she looked at Sheila's husband's name on the temporary restraining order draft lying there before her.

"As I said, Jimmy doesn't work for Ramsey Ivy. He's in another firm. There's no conflict here. This is just between Jimmy and me, estranged husband and wife."

"Yes; yes of course."

"Ms. Devore, I mean Pat, I don't mean to rush you but I would like to have this order before Jimmy comes over this evening."

"Shouldn't be a problem; can you take it by the courthouse?"

"No problem; that's not much out of my way."

"Come back in a half hour. My secretary will have it all ready."

"Thanks so much, Pat; I really appreciate it."

Pat watched Sheila leave. Something is not quite right here, she thought. But what else is new when it comes to the firm's tax department. There's got to be something to those rumors.

Sheila's brisk walk back to her office was interrupted by a man coming down the hall.

"Did you get it?"

"In half an hour."

"Good," he said as he caressed her cheek.

Once again the infamous Atlanta traffic had taken its toll. She was late. It was quarter past six as she drove into the driveway of her parents' home in Virginia Highlands. Good that she had taken the precaution of calling her mom from her car to tell her not to let Jimmy in the house, for there he was, swinging in the swing on the front porch having to make do with a Diet Coke in lieu of Andy. She pulled up by his car and parked.

Jimmy watched Sheila as she made her way up the few steps onto the end of the porch that ran the full extent of the house front. He recognized the black pants suit and matching briefcase. She looked tired and haggard; her hair was a mess. Jimmy made no effort to rise but kept on swinging until she was standing directly in front of him. He lifted his Coke for his greeting.

"Have a seat; take a load off."

He brought the swing to a halt and pated the vacant seat aside his.

This was not starting off as she had expected. Where was this new self-assurance in Jimmy coming from? She sat down with her briefcase in her lap looking straight ahead in silence until Jimmy started to rock the swing. She lifted her feet. The two swung while looking straight ahead with only the squeaking of the swing breaking the silence. Finally she spoke.

"Jimmy, I'm sorry about . . ."

"It's okay," he said with a gentle pat on her leg.

"Jimmy, I . . . I just. . . I just . . . oh to hell with it." With that she opened her briefcase and handed him the Court Order. He turned, looked her in the eyes, took and folded the document and put it in his inside coat pocket, all while maintaining eye contact until she broke that off.

"Aren't you going to read it?"

"I know what it is. Your mom was kind enough to . . ." A

commotion from the driveway interrupted as the twins threw down their scooters and ran up the stairs.

"Daddy! Daddy! Daddy!"

Jimmy stopped the swing and fell to his knees with his back to Sheila. Andy and Alec went into his embrace. Sheila watched as each child kissed him on the neck and then looked up to her with great big smiles of happiness. She couldn't help from suddenly feeling like a heel.

Chapter 19

Like Garrison Keeler's Guy Noir, private eye, the office of Nick Spenser was also in the Acme Building, but in his case it was the Acme Building in downtown Las Vegas, quite far from Lake Woebegone.

Nick was a loner. The larger firms of private detectives didn't take to his humor. When he had kept insisted on answering his phone with the slogan "We tries, private eyes; Nick Spenser speaking," he had been told to seek employment elsewhere.

Yet on occasion his old firm would still refer a case or two to him. So when the Las Vegas Office of his old, straight-laced firm heard that it was Excelsior that was to be investigated, there was no hesitation in their referring the job out. The folks there were addicted to breathing. In fact they were addicted to breathing regardless of the lack of hydration in the desert air. This was just the job for Nick Spenser. Once he learned that it was a paying client he would jump on it.

Nick found the job interesting but perplexing. A man had died while playing a slot machine at Caesars Palace. The machine had apparently malfunctioned and the man had suffered cardiac arrest, notwithstanding the fact that he had an implanted defibrillator. Well that didn't sound very sinister, he thought, but then it seemed that the County Coroner had gotten involved and ordered an autopsy and a search for the slot machine that had somehow become misplaced. This would have been a simple matter of Nick only having to report what the Coroner found and ruled upon were it not for the fact that the client wanted to know specifically if a Las Vegas company by the name of Excelsior had been involved. It seemed that Excelsior was a local slot machine manufacturer that was in competition with the client along with several others. Nick reached for his phone.

"Miss Jill, how the hell is my favorite medical examiner? It's Nick, Nick Spenser."

"Spenser? Nick Spenser? Doesn't ring a bell."

"Oh come on, Miss Jill, give a working man a chance."

"Well it has been awhile. Whatcha you up to these days, Nick? Isn't everyone in Vegas already divorced by now or are we already into re-divorce season?"

"I know you will find it hard to believe but I do occasionally handle something else."

"Well, what can I do for you?"

"I believe you have the remains of one Mario Moreno on ice."

"You too?"

"Huh?"

"Never mind.

"Well, do you?"

"Yes, we do."

"Another homicide, I trust."

"We haven't gotten that far yet, Nick."

"How about a cause of death?"

"His heart stopped beating."

"Cute; great insight! Have any idea as to just why that might have happened?"

"Nick, the man had a defibrillator which malfunctioned. It fibrillated when it should have defibrillated."

"Sounds like a juicy product liability case. Those people gotta have a ton of insurance."

"Maybe, but it's not that simple. The defibrillator was scorched; scorched on the outside of its case. Seem's that he was playing a slot machine when it went berserk. Sparks started flying. There was an arc from the Caesars machine to Mr. Moreno's own very personal machine. I'd hate to take that product liability case, at least on a contingency."

"Maybe throw both machines into the case and let the chips fall as they may. Chips, you know; chips."

"Nick, you'll never change. This *is* a serious business we're in, you know."

"What was the matter with the slot? Hadn't made a payout in so long that it finally exploded?"

"Don't know."

"When will you?"

"Don't know."

"Come on, at least give me an estimate."

"I can't until we find it."

"So that's why you all haven't yet ruled it a homicide?"

"You're a bright one, Nick; yeah, a real bright one."

"Who is the manufacturer?"

"J and M; it was a J and M slot."

Nick then heard a background voice speaking. He waited it out.

"Nick, I suggest that you turn your TV on right now as we

JACKPOT!

speak. Check out CNN. Seem's they have an exclusive of quite some interest to both of us."

―――⋙《◎》⋘―――

At that moment others also with a direct interest in the matter were also watching the CNN breaking news item. Those were Abigail Carmichael, Sheila Frazier and Ben Castleman who were all seated in front of a television screen in Sheila's office. The faces of all three were in broad, expectant smiles akin to those of children. What they were watching looked more like a pre-taped show than a news item. It was billed as "tragedy strikes slot machine player at Caesars Palace." The clip however certainly didn't start off as anything remotely connected to a tragedy. It was a professionally made recording of the entire episode that commenced with the flourish of trumpets which heralded the demonstration. Cecil B. Demille would have heartedly approved of what followed with the arrival of the centurions, the Captain of the Guard and the ravenous vestal virgin.

With some CNN editing, but not enough to remove the J and M name and logo, the clip quickly came to the contest between the smiling Mario and the giddy, vestal virgin. Then as if being directed by a film director the camera closed in on Mario's face and his slot just in time to capture the fireworks and Mario's calamity. After filming the collapse of Mario and dispersion of the spectators by the centurions the feature concluded with a CNN narration of events made against the backdrop of a statue of Caesar and a fadeout through the palace's fountains' mists.

"Fantastic! Absolute fantastic, Ben," said Abigail.

"Well I certainly can't take all of the credit," he replied as he kissed Sheila tenderly on the mouth. Abigail smiled her approval as Sheila returned the kiss.

"Our little Department of Dirty Tricks has struck again. But I'd say that this really went over the top."

Nick swung into action. First he called his new client and asked Mitt Casey if J and M had by any chance filmed the promotion. Hearing that they had not, but probably should have thought to do so, he filled Mitt in with what he saw as being bad news for him but probably good news for himself. No doubt this bizarre event would be aired again and again by CNN throughout the afternoon and evening, and they would be able to catch one of the next airings.

Then Nick called Juliana and again introduced himself. She seemed pleased to hear that he was on the case. Had they filmed the promotion, he asked. Again receiving a negative response he told her about the CNN broadcast.

Then he was off to the strip and the casino where he hit a wall as stone-hard as that of Caesars own statue. Security was in no mood to discuss the matter with him. Management was unhappy and when management was unhappy so was its security department. Surely their cameras had recorded the event, he asked. We record everything responded the stone wall. Then you recorded the guy who filmed the event from the floor. Silence. Look, I'm on your side, he had said. Silence. Hey look, I can help out here. Let me help you out here fellows, he had said as one of them grabbed his arm. Nick shook his arm free and in resignation turned and walked away. Another security man escorted him back to the public area. As the two walked from there to a side exit the man spoke.

"Sorry, friend, it's just a bad time."

"I understand, but I'm only trying to help. This thing was set up, you know."

"I can't help you but you might try the Coroner's Office. They just might have a copy of the film," he said with a comradely wink.

Chapter 20

A few months later

Robert Bianco, the President of Excelsior, was livid. Excelsior had been sued. It had been sued by J and M for patent infringement, for infringement of its just-issued patent on the smart card use in Excelsior's slot machines.

All of Bianco's efforts at intimidation to prevent this had come to naught. In the process a man had even been killed, though that had not been intended. The only saving grace so far was that J and M's patent attorney had not reported his kids as having been kidnapped, at least not yet. In actuality they had not really been kidnapped as their mother, Sheila, had been in on it all along. They had just spent a few days each on a farm of one of her relatives in North Georgia. Indeed, for them it had been a fun experience. Bianco had worried that this Jimmy Davis would go running to the FBI, but Sheila had been right that he wouldn't the way she would handle it. She still ran the roost. If he had though, Bianco wouldn't have given a second thought of turning on Sheila by turning it all into a just a domestic spat.

Robert Bianco had been born Bobby White. As a skinny, fair-skinned, little, red-haired boy he had had to endure continuous taunts from his classmates. First off was his name. Children would taunt him by calling him Bob White, Bob-Bob White, followed by the whistle call of a quail. Then there was his paper-white skin that wouldn't tan even in the summer. One day a kid started calling him an albino even though he wasn't. The others quickly took it up thinking that an albino must be some form of a deformed quail. Bob-Bob White the Albino – the foulest of the fowl. Run, here comes . . . whistle – whistle –whistle.

Just as he was entering the fourth grade his mother died. At the graveside service he had sat next to his father under a tent in a persistent rain as the preacher expounded on her life, a life that had been abruptly snuffed out while still in its prime. There had just been the two of them seated there alone before the casket in two, side-by-side folding chairs. The others in attendance had stood behind them. When the service ended his father had taken him by the hand and slowly walked over to a limousine holding a shared umbrella where a matronly looking woman stood holding a door open for him. His father gave him an unusually, and memorable, long hug before motioning for him to get in. He had assumed that his father would follow suit by getting into the seat beside him. Instead it had been the matron who had taken that seat. His father had just stood there with a couple of other men and watched as the limo drove off.

The limo had slowly made its way along a one-way lane that made a snaking loop before exiting that section of the cemetery. As they were completing the loop Bobby watched the two men escort his father to another vehicle. As he looked back over his shoulder he saw one man open a door while the other discreetly pulled out a pair of handcuffs and put them on his dad. Thus it was that day there in the cemetery that he had became an orphan.

At the orphanage he was told that his dad was being treated

for depression in a hospital, but he knew better. There had been no medical need at the cemetery to have restrained him for he had been thoroughly somber and withdrawn throughout the ceremony. No, he knew it wasn't a hospital to which his father had been taken.

At the orphanage the torments by other boys worsened. By the time Bobby reached the seventh grade he had convinced the orphanage to have his name changed from White to Bianco. He explained that that had been his Italian father's name before he had had it changed after immigrating. The orphanage was receptive to the idea. The name Bianco had thus now come full circle.

To his surprise the name change seemed to temper the tormenting and bullying. Spunky little cuss to have done that. "Bobby Bianco" had a ring about it quite different from "Bobby White." Even the "Bobby" part seemed to take on a new air. After all there had been a Bobby Kennedy who as Attorney General decided whether a condemned man lived or died - that is before he was rubbed out.

Bobby bought himself a spring blade knife with a pearl handle. This too seemed to impress the boys, in particular those few who themselves secreted switch blades of their own. This spring blade knife however was in a different league. It was one thing to watch an adversary menacingly rotate a single-edged switch blade out from its secure nest within the handle; it was quite another to see a double-edged blade suddenly spring forth seemingly out of nowhere from within an adversary's fist.

Of course it would be only a matter of time before someone had to put Bobby Bianco and his fancy spring blade knife to the test. That someone turned out to be a wiry, scrawny little punk called The Weasel.

At the orphanage there had been a rather pathetic cast-off called Albert. He was a real-life albino, frail and complete with glassy, flickering eyes and pale white skin. Albert, the Albino. His parents certainly had not thought it through in selecting the name Albert. Then again as a newborn it may not have been apparent. Anyway, one day The Weasel is on Albert's case. On and on he taunts and mocks the albino. Albert shrinks back. There is no fight in him. Other boys start to gather about but they aren't impressed with the Weasel picking on Albert and the Weasel soon realizes that. Big deal this picking on the albino again.

"Hey, I hear that albinos don't bleed red. Is that right Albert?" asks The Weasel in trying to up the ante.

No response.

"I'm talking to you, albino; is that right?"

No response.

"Well let's just find out," he says as he brings his switchblade out.

Albert shrinks up next to the nearest other boy on the scene, who just happens to be Bobby Bianco.

"Put that away," says Bobby.

The Weasel advances slowly towards the two of them with his now-extended blade slowly swaggering from side to side. In doing so he senses that his audience has at least become more interested, if not yet dutifully impressed with his prowess. Bobby pulls out his own knife and pops out its blade.

"Well, well; what do we have here?" sneers The Weasel, albeit with some apprehension.

"Leave him be," says Bobby as Albert shrinks further back.

The Weasel goes into a knife-fighting stance all bent over with his legs spread, his hands extended like a crab, and his head held high with his eyes focused on Bobby. Bobby just stands there as Albert makes his retreat.

The Weasel starts making jabbing feints as he sways from side to side. Still Bobby remains still with his knife aimed at the aggressor. With a sneer The Weasel starts to toss his knife from hand to hand as his sneer changes into an evil smile. With his eyes widely focused on those of Bobby he suddenly misses a toss and his knife falls embarrassingly to the floor. Bobby is quick to step on it just before The Weasel could retrieve it. Now Bobby finds himself towering over the empty-handed Weasel. The Weasel considers an attack to Bobby's crotch but Bobby's knife belays that. The kids begin to laugh. It now becomes The Weasel's time to retreat, but his retreat is made in humiliation as the boys laugh. Bobby realizes that humiliating The Weasel not what he had intended.

"Take your blade back," says Bobby as he put his own knife back in his pocket. He sheaths the switch blade and holds its out towards The Weasel who has now paused in his retreat.

"No hard feeling, Weasel; just leave Albert alone."

With the laughter now stopped the Weasel considers the offer. Finding it too tempting to pass up, he walks over to collect it.

"Don't give it back," says one of the other boys, a dark skin overweight boy with black, wiry hair that went by the name Jal.

Bobby looks at Jal and then back at The Weasel not knowing quite what to do. Then The Weasel holds out his hand while still looking at Bobby. Let's end this thinks Bobby to himself as he hands over the knife.

The Weasel takes it in hand and turns it over and over as if studying it. For apparent further examination he extends the blade. Bobby extends open his hands palms up in a "Well?" gesture.

"Yep, it's mine," replies The Weasel as he makes a slash at Bobby who instinctively rotates and raises his hands in defense. The blade strikes one of his palms. Bobby looks down to see bright red blood flowing from an inch-long cut. He can't believe his eyes. He looks back up to see The Weasel broadsided by Jal with a hit that any NFL player would be proud of. The Weasel goes down hard. Jal then cold cocks him as he lies on his back on the floor and retrieves the knife.

"I tolds you not to give it to him," says Jal as he hands Bobby a rag for his wound.

From that day on Jal took on the role of being Bobby's physical protector. In return Bobby took on the role of being Jal's social protector. For you see Jal was Jal Recos, an immigrant gypsy from Eastern Europe who had gotten separated from his mother in their early wanderings in America and who had a pronounced accent that most took to be Italian. He still was in need of social integration if his gypsy blood would permit. Thus the team of Bianco and Recos came into being, which was well before Jal had come to be reunited with his still gypsy mother.

Recos became Bobby's bodyguard which brought to an end his being called Bob-Bob White, The albino.

Thus it came to pass that education of the boys there at the orphanage was advanced a degree by their learning that albinos weren't really birds at all; those creatures were called albatrosses. Nor were albinos the people of Albania; those people were Albanians.

Bobby's mind returns to the present and to the damn law suit.

The strong-arm strategy had failed. He needed a new tact. He called Jal to his office.

"What's up boss?" said Jal as he stood before Bobby who was seated behind his massive desk.

"On this J and M thing I think we need to change gears."

"How's that, Bobby?"

"Well you see . . . you see we've gotten nowhere trying to mess with their attorney and sales rep. They have still gone ahead and sued us."

"Maybe we should stop beating around the bush and go for J and M, heads-on like."

"What do you mean?"

"It a be a shame if a fire somehow was to happen now, wouldn't it? I mean theys can somehow get out of control and burn a whole building down."

Bobby looked at the big ape of a man that stood before him with a big smile.

"Jal, take a seat. Here, have a cigar."

Jal took a seat and lit up. "Nice; real nice; thanks, Bobby."

Jal spread his big legs apart and then leaned over towards Bobby and his desk.

"Remember that time with the Smokehouse Grill? Remember? Man we were working together like real partners back then."

"Sure Jal, I remember. Not quite the same situation now though, is it?"

"Whats you mean," he said as his smile faded.

"Whats I mean is that the Grill was a rundown old wooden firetrap that was ready to go up any time. Whats I mean is that the J and M plant is a steel frame building with a fucking concrete floor."

Jal suddenly finds interest in his shoe lacings. He hated it when Bobby came at him with that fake accent that he could turn on and off at will. They had been together too long for that.

"So tell me, just how in hell are you going to burn J and M?"

Jal twitched his cigar until a burn cinder fall on his pants.

"Sorry boss," he said quietly as he brushed off the cinder and took a new drag.

Bobby turned his head and stared off to one side for the longest time while thinking. Jal kept quiet.

"Any other bright ideas, pal?"

"Yea; we stop beatings around the bush here. Let me take out those bastards."

"Stop; stop right there, Hammer. How many times have I got to tell you that's not how I works. Excelsior is no fucking mafia. Excelsior doesn't hire hit men. Excelsior may be tough and sometime overstep the law, but it doesn't make a habit of 'taking out' people, at least not on purpose."

Jal sat there taking it. The cigar was too good to get upset. Besides, this wasn't the first time he had had to hear this little lecture by Bobby; by the Boss.

"Look, if we start doing hits then I have to start looking over my own back all the time. You know, he who lives by the sword dies by the sword. Besides, the players here are two fucking companies. Kill off the bosses doesn't change a fucking thing. New ones just take over. You have to make an attitude adjustment – a change in their thinking.

"Jal, I've got to try something new. I want you to lay off the rough stuff for a while. You've got plenty to keep you busy working on the machines. And you are damn good at that when you are not busy trying to fry people. Okay, Jal-pal?"

Chapter 21

Charles Macguire sat in his office considering the Answer and Counterclaim that he had just received in the case of J and M Gaming, Inc. versus Excelsior Corporation. He found himself in a bit of a quandary on this one. His trouble lay not with the pleading itself. No, it was routine stuff. Naturally Excelsior denied all. It denied that it infringed the newly minted smart card patent owned by J and M. Excelsior claimed that the patent was invalid. It denied that it had deliberately infringed. It counterclaimed for a declaration of invalidity. It also claimed that J and M had engaged in inequitable conduct in having threatened Excelsior's customers on this very matter before the patent had been issued.

What concerned Macguire was that J and M, the plaintiff here, was a client of Jimmy, who wasn't a partner but rather a salaried associate. Jimmy had no experience in civil litigation of any kind, much less in the esoteric arena of patent litigation. He would have to tread carefully in handling this one so as not to cast Jimmy in a bad light in the eyes of his client. He could not have the client feel that this was a bait and switch tactic to put Charles himself to work here at an hourly rate double that of Jimmy. He knew that clients tended to focus on that hourly rate and not appreciate the fact that it would take an associate twice as long to do things. Clients rarely appreciated the fact that one hour at $350/hour was the same as two hours at $175/hour.

There also was Jimmy to consider. This case had already subjected him to intimidation, the likes of which he had never seen. The case may also have had a hand in the separation of Jimmy and his wife and the loss of custody of his two children. Macguire wasn't used to having such concerns about an associate. Was the young man worth all of this to the firm? Yes, he thought, I think so, what with his engineering knowledge and work experience. Heck even he couldn't understand all that computer stuff that Jimmy seemed to breeze right through. Yes he did have special value even if such were in nerd-land and an experienced replacement would cost more than they had been paying him. He reached for his phone to summons Jimmy.

"Thought this might interest you," Charles said as Jimmy came into his office. Jimmy took the pleading from Charles's extended hand and sat down. He allowed Jimmy time to read it through.

"What do you think?" Jimmy asked.

"About what you would expect; they could have thrown more back at us."

"Like what, for example?"

"For one thing they could have filed to have the patent re-examined and asked for a stay while that dragged on. That would have bought them well more than year during which time their slot machines keep plugging away."

"What about this inequitable conduct defense?"

"Depends on the facts; you need to get with J and M on that."

"Maybe we ought to get a preliminary injunction if this thing is going to drag on. J and M is looking for speed here."

"The federal court in Vegas is not known for speed. Theirs is no rocket docket like in Virginia or even Savannah."

"Savannah is?" Jimmy asked in surprise. "Well I'd better not let the client hear about that."

"It is if you can get the case there. Hell this Excelsior could have taken months just in fighting our having filed in Savannah rather than Las Vegas. And frankly, they would probably have won on that. There's no good reason for the case being tried in Savannah. That would just be blatant forum shopping. Don't think J and M would have appreciated six months or so passing in our just arguing where the case should be tried, plus having to have paid for that futile exercise."

Jimmy looked at Charles with renewed respect.

"Since we asked in the complaint for a preliminary and permanent injunction, why don't we move on that now. You know; file a motion."

"First off the court won't grant one on a patent that hasn't already successfully gone through all of the testing of litigation."

"But it's presumed to be valid."

"Yep; sure is. Second, J and M would have to put up a bond to cover all of Excelsior's expenses and lost profits were it to win the case."

"Okay, so where do we go from here? What can I do?"

"J and M ought to get a copy of this right away. And you need to find out about their alleged pre-issue behavior. You can also work up a set of interrogatories and requests for production of documents. Jinnie can give you some from other cases to massage. Have her get some from the Genuine case."

Jimmy spent the afternoon preparing a set of interrogatories and a set of requests for production. The ones from the Genuine case did provide a good model and made it easier than he had expected. The interrogatories would be useful in obtaining the names and addresses of potential witnesses that J and M might need to depose, like those who had been instrumental in producing the smart cards for Excelsior and those who would be knowledgeable in the financials. They would also want to see documents related to their smart card design and integration into the slots, plus the documents, mostly prior patents, that would be relied upon in attacking the validity of the patent.

That evening he felt good as he drove home. This legal fighting might be fun after all. In a way it was a nice break from patent prosecution. It had gotten his blood pressure up.

Once home however that feeling vanished. Home had become just an oversized, empty and lonely house. What was the sense in working all day only to face this in the evening? He missed his boys. He missed female companionship.

Jimmy checked out his mail: three ads, two utility bills, and a notice from the IRS about under-reporting of estimated income tax. There was also a business card from a real estate agent who had shown the house. To hell with all this, he thought. Mercifully the phone rang.

"Jimmy? It's me, Juliana Moreno from Las Vegas."

"Juliana! What a breath of fresh air. How are you doing?"

"Busy; I'm running the business now, you see. It's keeping me occupied. And you?"

"I've been busy too. I'm now working on the law suit against Excelsior. It's my first involvement in litigation so I've got lots to learn."

"Well I'm sure you'll do just fine. Matter of fact I was calling you about litigation. You see I've had several lawyers out here calling me about Mario's death."

"They are called land sharks. They are pretty far from the sea to be in Vegas."

"You got it."

"Just what are they saying?"

"They think I should sue for - - - for - - - what do they call it?"

"Wrongful death?"

"Yes, yes; that's it."

"Who do they want you to sue?"

"Caesars, and J and M, naturally. They say they'll take it on a contingent fee basis and it won't cost me a thing. But I know better."

"What do you mean?"

"Sue the company that we rep for? Just great. And sue the biggest customer of that company at the same time. Super great."

"So what are you going to do?"

"Well, I was sort of hoping that you might help me on this one. I'm all alone out here and could use some help; some advice."

"I don't know what to say, Juliana. Let me think on it."

"Will you be coming back out here soon?"

"We will be coming to Vegas to take some depositions, but not right away."

"Maybe you could speak with Mr. Johnson at J and M. I mean that insurance money is just sitting there. Maybe there is a way to collect it without having to sue."

"Don't you all have a lawyer out there?"

"Not really; Mario just had a friend incorporate us. We have an accountant that might be of some help, but I rather doubt it."

"How about life insurance? Didn't he have any?"

"Afraid not; you know we were busy with the business and didn't have any kids."

"And you don't want to talk with Caesars. I bet they would be happy to settle; to work something out."

"I don't know anybody there. Caesars, that's a big, big business. Jimmy, I'm all alone on this." Her voice trailed off into what he thought might be quiet sobbing. "You are the only one I could think of to turn to."

"Juliana I am going to try to help. I will; believe me. You have a good claim here, I feel sure. This will work out. There's no rush; just be patient. Take one day at a time."

"Call me back, will you?"

"You bet. I'll get back to you."

Chapter 22

Sheila's fears were coming true as she sat in her office hearing out one irate Randall Cunningham.

"You all told me that this was legitimate. I had my doubts but hell I'm no lawyer."

"Mr. Cunningham the lawyer you dealt with here is no longer with our firm."

"Where the hell is he?"

"I'm afraid I can't help you with that. I really don't know."

"Well this ain't right. Look, I was sent to Ramsey, Ivy. I paid Ramsey, Ivy. Now I want Ramsey, Ivy and Mr. Prince to take care of this."

"And we will, Mr. Cunningham. I have been informed that our insurance company will see that you are reimbursed in full for any taxes that the IRS requires from you. All you would have to do would be to bring in the delinquency notice and we would cut you a check. We would be the one to wait for reimbursement. Now isn't that satisfactory?"

"Your insurance company would pay, is it?"

"Right; now don't you worry, anymore. Just bring me the tax bill, if you actually get one, and we would take care of it in full," said Sheila as she gave the man an engaging smile. "But I doubt that that will be necessary. The agent wasn't even investigating you, right? He was investigating those medical companies."

"That's what he said but he did ask me what I was taking all those pills for. He also asked me the name of my doctor. You know, I didn't like that; I mean, well, would you? I mean what if he now goes to my doctor? What then?"

"He can't and he knows it. That's privileged information. That's protected by the doctor-patient privacy laws."

"Well I hope you are right."

"Mr. Cunningham you did the right thing in coming in and telling us about this little visit you had. Now I don't want you to go on worrying about this. So listen, don't use this program any more. If you do, you will be on your own from now on. The firm will be reviewing this medical rebate program. You know it is used by a number of people, not just you. So don't feel that you are alone."

"Will you be calling him – this agent?"

"We may just do that, but only after we have completed our review."

After showing the now mollified Randall Cunningham out Sheila sat at her desk turning over and over in her hand the card Cunningham had given her. The business card was that of a Hubert Smith, Special Agent, Internal Revenue Service. This was not good; not good at all. This was not an auditor; no this Hubert Smith was no doubt a criminal investigator.

Sheila knew the scheme. It was a self sustaining computer program that virtually ran itself, thus eliminating the human error factor. Each month its participants would be billed for medical services and pharmaceuticals. She well knew their names, names such as Oxford General Insurance Group, Premier Pharmaceuticals and Organics, Secure Oxygen Reliance, and Albright Brothers Chiropractic Services. The participants didn't actually receive bills. No, these "bills" would merely be automatic debits to their credit cards. The full names of these companies being too long to spell out on a Visa or Master Card statement, they would be abbreviated often to the point of non-recognition, leaving an encoded transaction number as the only identifier. But well before the participants had to pay their monthly credit card bill they would have already received a rebate for 96% of what they had charged in the form of a money order from a company called The Physicians Adjustment Group. That little monthly self sustaining routine provided quite a nice deduction each year come tax time, and a tidy sum to the firm's client when their small fee was multiplied by the substantial number of participants in the scheme. And it had worked; at least it had worked up until now.

When Sheila had originally questioned it, Abigail had said that it was just too simple for the IRS to uncover. No, they were focused on complex schemes, schemes like those that involved offshore bank accounts, partnerships and trusts. Just the mention of an account in the Bahamas or The Caymans and their interest would be piqued. But medical expenses? Too mundane; and very unlikely because sickly taxpayers tended to be chronically sick, year in and year out. No, if a regular IRS auditor ever did ask to see proof of these payments, a copy of the monthly credit card statements had always marked the end of it. The auditor's job would be done and his or her work record completed. Theoretically they could of course investigate deeper but that was not their job. No, their job was to meet their monthly goal of processed returns. The pressure to crank them out was unrelenting. As for the participants they had too much to lose if they were ever to get religion, become remorseful and want to come clean.

No, they had been willing participants. Besides, a legal opinion by Ramsey, Ivy and Prince backed this up.

Sheila laughed to herself at the thought of remorse as she looked back over her own career path so far with Ramsey, Ivy and Prince. How had she ever gotten herself in such a fix?

For a while Sheila had tolerated Abigail as just being the price that a new associate had to pay when starting out at a big firm. She had been slow to realize that her treatment had not been typical. How stupid she had been; how blind.

She had arrived both thankful for her having been accepted as an associate for such a firm and committed to working all those billable hours. After a few years it would be paid back when she became partner. Daddy would be so proud.

At the beginning Abigail had actually been cordial, almost sweet. That phase had lasted a matter of weeks. The work had been pretty much what she had expected, involving legal research in various areas of tax laws. Abigail would often give her a memo of what this or that client proposed to do and have her outline the tax consequences. Her only surprise had been that there had been little feedback. It seemed to matter little whether her findings were favorable or unfavorable, legal, illegal, or in the grey zone. That had been disappointing as she had felt unappreciated. The little feedback she had received was when she had pointed out that a proposal was clearly illegal only to be told that surely she could do better than that and be creative.

One weekend she decided to come in and do her own follow-up on a few of the projects she had worked on. She was impressed with the professionalism of the letters that had been sent out to the clients under Abigail's signature. It was also rewarding to see how her inputs had made their way into these opinions.

The aggressive creativeness that was the hallmark of Abigail's work however often went overboard, she thought. Several opinions went right up to the limit as to what was even arguably legal. One thing she didn't understand was the frequent appearance in the margins of these client letters of faintly scrawled handwritten symbols. Had they only appeared in one or two instances that would have been one thing, but she had noted over a dozen. Had she not reviewed all these unrelated files sequentially, they would have gone unnoticed.

That little mystery was cleared up at a Friday's after-hours bash. Sheila had turned down several invites by the staff and secretaries to attend these weekly short parties, but this Friday Sara, Abigail's legal assistant, a title that had long ago replaced "secretary" in law firms, insisted that Sheila come along with her. Sensing that Sara was upset over something, she had accepted.

While Sara was into her second Amstel, Sheila broached the subject. Sara laughed, took a look over her shoulder and then confided.

"So you noticed?"

"Yep."

"You're the first."

"So they have meaning."

"Of course they have meaning; you think I'd have smudgy files?"

"And?"

Sara's happy, smiley-smirk slowly shrank. She looked seriously into Sheila's eyes for a moment. Then her smile returned.

"Promise not to tell?"

"Of course."

"Sure. Promises are like babies: Easy to make but hard to deliver."

"Sara, I not only delivered, I double delivered!"

With that Sheila took a prolonged, unladylike swallow on her brew. Sara watched and then followed suit.

"Touche'; Touche'-okay? Okay?"

"Okay."

"Those are places where the client was provided a little insert, if you will."

"Insert?"

"Yeah, a loose slip that tells the client how to get around the very thing that the lawyer has advised in writing. The symbol tells me which of the slips, which have now become forms, to insert."

"I'll be damned," said Sheila in surprise. "And where do you keep these slips?"

Sara took the last swig left in her bottle.

"I think I've said enough; more than enough. You know what they use to say: Loose slips sink ships."

"You are showing your age girl, but I think that was lips," said Sheila with a chuckle. "Those loose slips are for your boyfriends."

"Sheila, if you want to read some of those slips all you need to do is read some of your own legal memos."

Sheila looked away. Well that, she thought, explains the lack of feedback. I guess my work has been good and useful after all. I'll be damned.

"But what about my own memos? They are in the files, right?"

"Oh yes. Not only in the clients' files, but they have merited a file of their own."

"For my performance reviews?"

"I'd call it more like for your performance insurance."

"Performance insurance?" Sheila's mouth dropped open as her mind realized the implication of what it had just heard and as her body felt a chill running up her spine.

"Have a good weekend, Sheila."

Chapter 23

Nick Spenser waited for the light of the breaking dawn to become bright enough for details of his surroundings to become clear and distinct. Finally satisfied with that, he got out of the van. As he closed the door he now saw that he had forgotten to remove the sign that was held to it, magnetically.

His "Mallory Pests Control" sign came off easily which he placed back inside the van. It was a carryover from his prior afternoon work when he had "inspected" the rear entrails of Excelsoir's production plant. No pests had been found. More to the point however was the fact that no remains of the J and M slot had been found either. It was when he had made his inconspicuous exit out of the rear of the plant that he had noticed the dumpster which was now illuminated before him in the dawn's early light.

With the aid of a small Jacob's ladder Nick climbed into the dumpster - at least he tried to. The dumpster was almost full; full of debris. So once in he found himself to be exposed to anyone that might walk or drive pass. Hunched over he went through the upper level of industrial waste to find lots of empty cartons, wiring, metallic and plastic scrap of all shapes and sizes, a small engine, some tires apparently off of a front-end loader and some broken glass. Finding no discarded slot machine of any model or make he climbed back out.

A few minutes after eight o'clock he called the dumpster company and asked for a pick-up only to be told that that was already scheduled for that afternoon.

It is almost four o'clock before the truck arrives. Bam, bam, slam, bang, and the exchange for an empty dumpster is made.

Nick took up a tail as the truck drove off. It was some 15 miles out of the city before it turned off the highway and onto a dusty road. The truck kicked up so much dust that he felt that he was not likely to be seen as he followed along in a dust cloud.

A couple of miles down the dirt road and a series of mounds appeared off to one side of the drifting dust. Then he saw that a chain-link fence encircled the mounds. The truck ahead drove through an open gate without hesitation and on towards the smallest of the mounds which was to the far left. Only an old, battered sign aside the gate stood century against unauthorized entry. The only sign of the presence of other life was a filthy jeep parked outside of a hut that was just inside the fence near the gate. Spotting a shunt in the road to allow on-coming traffic to pass, Nick pulled off, stopped and broke out his binoculars.

There was not much to see. From the trail of dust he saw that the truck went around to the far side of the baby mound. Unlike an Egyptian baby pyramid aside that of its father pharaoh, this pyramid was in a state of daily growth.

Nick turned off the engine. Lord it was quiet, save for the rustle made by the faint breeze. Then movement caught his eye. The door to the hut had opened and a man was there looking his way. Nick started his engine and made his retreat as the man reentered the hut while shaking his head.

It was six o'clock before Nick saw the jeep enter the highway. That done, he made his way on foot back to the landfill. In no time he was at the exact site where the dump had been made. The fresh tire marks in the desert sand had left a clear trail.

The pile of freshly deposited debris was easy to discern from its lack of a covering layer of sand and dust. He climbed the pile armed with a crowbar, flashlight and pocket camera, cringing with each sound that he made. There just was no way to do this quietly.

After stumbling about for a couple of minutes he spotted a corner of a shiny machine jutting out. He climbed over to it and pulled off surrounding debris with his gloved hands. A screen appeared from out of the rubble. A slot machine! Eagerly he made a perimeter trench-like a moat about it. The letters "PON" suddenly appeared aside a folded dent. Prying the dent forward into alignment adds a "G," thus completing the word PONG.

Nick glanced about to find that no one was in sight. He snapped three pictures before continuing his excavation. In the fading daylight the flash had come on automatically. Then the J and M logo emerged and he snapped three pictures of it too. Then he moved back for a few panoramic photos. His jubilation was only mitigated by the worrisome flashes and all that noise that he had made.

His search for the guts of the machine proves to be to no avail; its innards were not there. Then he put the camera away and refilled the moat using the crowbar to inter the machine. When his feet were finally planted back onto the quiet, soft and comforting desert floor he took a deep breath which he had been holding without realizing it as he made his noisy retreat out from what seemed to have become the percussion section of a symphonic orchestra.

Later that day Dan Halsey's phone rang at Ramsey, Ivy and Prince. It was J and M with Mitt Johnson and Joe Turner on the line.

"Remember how we had asked you for a private eye?"

"Sure."

"Well he has come through, in spades."

"Good. Tell me about it."

"Actually it's pretty simple. He followed a trash pickup from Excelsior out to a dump. Guess what he found in the load that was dumped? No, I'll tell you. Our Pong slot, or what was left of it; the one that killed our rep."

"And you say that he followed the truck from Excelsior?"

"You got it."

"Where is it?"

"The slot?"

"Right where he found it; you see it was just the casing. The electrical components were gone. So there wasn't anything to examine to see what happened. But we have a good set of photos of it there in the dump."

"What's that man's name again? We need his affidavit right away."

"I'll email it over to you along with the pictures. But what do we do now, I mean once you have his affidavit?"

"Probably take it to the police. The insurance company would want that done."

"The Las Vegas police or the FBI; remember there was a kidnapping."

"An unreported kidnapping; don't think that would go unnoticed, Mitt."

"Hi, Sheila; how are you doing?"

"Hello Jimmy. It's been awhile."

"Sheila, I've just gotten off the phone with Mitt Johnson at J and M. Seems that they now have proof that Excelsoir was involved in that drama at Caesars Palace; you know, where their slot machine killed J and M's own sales rep."

"So? How does that involve you?"

"They are going to the police with it."

"Don't think there is anything we can do about that."

"There's more. They want to add the kidnapping."

"But there's no proof that Excelsior had any part in that."

"Come on now; how about the demands to drop the patent, the very patent that J and M has now sued them on?"

"But the 'accident' was on the Pong machine while the patent was on the smart card."

"You've kept up with this, I see."

"Jimmy, this would be trouble for us, for both of us. You just might recall that we didn't go to the police."

"I know, and we should have."

"Look, ask them to hold off on the kidnapping until they know that it is really needed. What they already have may be enough for the police to bring down Excelsior."

"Okay, I'll run that by Mitt, but I can't promise you that they will go along."

Sheila hung up the phone and headed for Abigail's office. No Abigail. She was out until tomorrow. From there she went down the hall to see Craig Chesterfield, another tax lawyer and an occasional date of late. Craig's face always lit up when he saw Sheila, and that was nice. He had been one that she could confide in.

Only average in looks, that was made up with his warm personality and support and as far as she knew he was not privy to the underhanded and illegal activities of the tax department.

"Something has come up Craig. Do you know where Abigail is?"

"Haven't the faintest, but come on in."

Sheila plopped herself down on a sofa and exhaled.

"What's up? Is your job becoming, well, becoming taxing?"

Sheila returned his smile.

"Craig, it's about J and M. Remember them?"

"Sure; they are the slot machine people; a real thorn in Excelsoir's side, as I recall."

"Right; well they have learned that Excelsoir, their competitor, was behind their slot machine disaster at Caesars Palace. They are planning to go to the police."

"Don't think that will please Excelsoir; not at all," he said as he pushed back in his chair and put his hands together behind his head.

"There's more."

There followed a break in the conversation as Sheila looked away to one side. Craig brought his chair back upright, put his hands together on his desk and rested his chin on them.

"I'm all ears; go ahead and try me."

"Well, I'm not supposed to say this but then you *are* on our team."

Sheila filled him in on the fake kidnappings that had been done in order to coerce Jimmy into failing to secure a patent on the smart card invention, and how they had not gone to the authorities, and how now J and M, who had known about the kidnappings, now wanted to include that in their report to the police to solidify their case.

"Craig, I probably shouldn't have told you this, it's just that I know that Abigail will fly off the handle when she hears."

"Sheila, I think you are overreacting and overworrying."

"It's just that I feel trapped. It's not only that; I've come across some other underhanded things that have been going on in this department. In fact an IRS special agent has been nosing about. I may be in deep shit over the twins."

"Oh come on now; so a mother sends her boys to visit the family farm . . . "

Sheila, who had been looking down somewhat sheepishly jerked her head up.

"Farm? Family farm; I didn't say anything about any farm!"

Sheila felt her blood start to boil as she stared at Craig. He had screwed up; screwed up royally.

"I'll be goddamned," she said in realization. "God damn all of you. You're *all* in this fucking thing together. I've been had."

Craig's face slowly makes a transformation sort of like the portrait of Dorian Grey. But in this case it contorts into a smug sneer. "In more ways than one, my dear; in more ways than one," he muttered, softly.

Chapter 24

"Ladies and Gentlemen. On each side of the cabin you can see the great Mississippi River as it meanders its way down to the Louisiana Delta and the Gulf of Mexico," says the co-pilot.

Jimmy looks down. Sure enough there it is all lit up on his side by reflecting sun rays. He takes out his cell phone.

"Juliana? Jimmy."

"Hi; where are you now?"

"On the Mississippi River."

"The Mississippi River?"

"Well not exactly on it. We are over it at about 35,000 feet."

"Good; then I'll be meeting you at Baggage Claim."

"I don't want to put you out like that. The hotel is far out of your way. I can catch a cab."

"You aren't staying at the hotel. You are staying with me. I have plenty of room."

"Juliana, there is no need for that. I can stay at the hotel. No problem, really."

"No you can't. I've already cancelled you out and I've got Angus ready for you to grill out back. Besides, remember the last time you stayed at a Las Vegas hotel?"

"Beautiful."

"Tell me what you're up to out here."

"I just told you: up to 35,000 feet."

"Funny. What was it; a deposition like you had said?"

"Yes, and more; I'll fill you in when I get there."

"I can't wait."

No sooner had he taken his seat in the Honda than the wonderful aroma of Juliana's perfume again filled Jimmy with reassuring pleasure. He took a deep breath and smiled in contentment which did not escape Juliana's notice. In instant recall his mind shot back to her welcoming hug at Baggage Claim that had earlier reintroduced him to that lovely fragrance.

"So fill me in. Que pasa, Jimmy?"

"What pasas? I tell you, plenty is a pasa-ing."

Jimmy looked over at Juliana. What a beautiful woman. She returned his look.

"You want it now or when we settle at your place for some casa-ing."

"Your Spanish is coming along quite nicely. Si, Senor, I want to hear it now. Damelo, por favor!"

"Well I am here to take the deposition of Excelsoir."

"Alone? I thought you were new to litigation."

"That's right, I am, and I didn't ask to go it alone but Charles Macguire thought I was up to it. Actually he is overloaded right now in litigation; said that he didn't have the time now to take off for Nevada. He said our local counsel could hold my hand if they starting making waves, but don't worry, we have thoroughly gone over what needs to be asked."

"Who will be interrogating Excelsior?"

"It's 'deposing'."

"That's too polite; it should be interrogation."

"It's what's called a 30(b)(6) deposi- - - , interrogation."

"Wonderful, that's just what I would have wanted, too. Yea,

nothing better than a good old 30(b)(6)-er to get things a-rolling."

Jimmy snickered. "We didn't name an individual; we named Excelsoir. They provide the person or persons that can best answer questions in the areas of interest that we have already specified. Our guess is that they will produce Mr. Bobby Bianco, the President."

"Good. But Jimmy you know he's going to really be tough to handle. It's going to be a challenge to bring him down."

"Juliana, I'm not here to 'bring him down.' I'm here for sworn testimony as to the facts of this case. You know, things like how and when and who designed their smart card feature. When did they learn about J and M's design? How many have they produced. How many have they sold? How much have they cost? What basis do they have in claiming that our patent is invalid?"

"Lot's of luck."

"Juliana, we already have a lot of this through their answers to our interrogatives and requests for the production of documents."

"What if he claims that he doesn't know the answers?"

"Then we'll ask him who does and depose him or her. But he probably already knows that and probably isn't very eager for us to depose his employees."

"Well I guess you are right. Anyway, it seems that you are on top of this. It's just that Mr. Bobby Bianco is a hoodlum. I just can't picture him sitting there quietly answering your questions. Do you really think he'll admit killing my Mario?"

"Juliana, this isn't about Mario or his demise. That had nothing to do with the smart card infringement case. As we say, that's irrelevant."

"Irrelevant? Irrelevant, you say?"

"Oh Juliana, you know what I mean. It's just not relevant to this law suit."

They drove on in silence.

"I'm sorry, Jimmy. I didn't mean to come on like that. It's hard to control this Latin blood of mine. It doesn't mix too well with staid Anglo-Saxon law suits. But on the plane you said that there was more. That you were coming out here for more."

"That's right; in fact you have already hit on it in bringing up Mario."

"Well? Don't keep me in suspense."

"I'm also going to the police."

"The police; hey, that's great. There's one right there ahead of us. Want me to honk?"

"Funny."

"No, that's really great. Excelsior, right? Not Caesars?"

"Right; Excelsior."

"What's happened? Why the change in heart? You all must have learned something."

"We have. J and M hired a private eye. He found their missing Pong machine in Excelsior's dumpster. Well not exactly in it but at a dump where a pick-up had taken it from Excelsior's plant. He actually followed the truck out there."

"Yes, I suppose that this is good and important news. By the way those lawyers who've called me - what did you call them?"

"Land sharks?"

"Ah yes, land sharks; well they are still swimming around. One in particular is really persistent, but not in a bad way. He's polite. I wouldn't feed Caesars, nor J and M for that matter, to him. But to Excelsior? Now that would be another matter. Excelsior as shark bait? Yes, I do think that might work."

Juliana pulled into her driveway and then gave Jimmy a house tour. It didn't take long as it was just one more modest ranch in a modern Vegas development where all of the houses had the same desert sand colored stucco walls and the same tile roofs of the same color of rust. It was the color of the doors and window shutters that distinguished one from the next, but even this pattern was repeated block after block. So the key was to keep sober enough to find your way home to the right block. All of that was how it had initially been planned but now it was the condition of the small lawns, or lack thereof, and the cactus beds that were more often the defining feature. Juliana's little yard was neat and well irrigated.

The house tour ended with the guest room. Jimmy was relieved when Juliana told him that that was his since this social experience was all new to him and he didn't know how to handle it.

After freshening up from his trip he found her on the back patio, which was shaded by a large awning. A wooden fence enclosed the back yard. A bag of charcoal lay unopened next to a grill.

"Here's to the chef," she said as she handed him a chilled bottle of Corona. "I'll take mine medium well, por favor."

"Si, senorita."

Juliana smiled. "Think I'm a bit on the mature side for senorita. But thanks."

"Si, sen- - senora."

"So tell me. What else do you have for the police?"

Jimmy took a swig of his beer before answering. Then he filled her in on the threats that had been made on him regarding his pursuing the smart card patent.

"But you have no proof that Excelsior was behind that."

"True, but who else? They were the ones with the most to lose."

Juliana turned that over in her mind. "I don't know. That's not much to go on."

"What about that little visit to me at the hotel?"

"Well, sure, that goes along with the threat notes. But was it Excelsior? How do you prove that?"

Jimmy finished his Corona before answering.

"I'll tell you how. Juliana, they also kidnapped my two boys; first one, then the other."

"What? They have your children?"

"Had; they had them. But they've been returned, one at a time."

"That's awful; God what you have been going through."

"Yes."

Juliana put down her beer and looked up to the sky.

"They weren't hurt?"

"No. They weren't harmed."

"But again, what proof do you have that it was Excelsior?"

"Damn it, Juliana, who else would it be for, for God's sake?"

"You're right; of course you're right. Now let's change the subject. I'm getting hungry, chef."

Jimmy ripped open the bag of charcoal and set about lighting some up on the grill. When he asked for another beer Juliana said that they were switching to wine. Angus was too good to waste on beer, even on good Mexican beer. As he put the steaks on she lit two heat lamps which straddled an outdoor table located beneath the awning.

They ate hardily as the wine and lamps warmed them and the sun proceeded to set. Once finished eating Jimmy poured what remained of the wine and they adjourned together to an outdoor sofa where an Indian blanket lay neatly folded. Juliana pulled him down beside her and spread the blanket over them. They sat together in silence enjoying the warmth of the meal, the wine, the heat lamps, the blanket, and their mutual body heat in full contentment. Eventually he spoke.

"This is nice; it's been so long since I've felt this good."

"Yes, it's like a fairy tale. I know that fairy tales can come true, they can happen to you if you're .."

"Yes, I know the song, but this fairy tale was pre-scripted, I do believe, and your song is a siren's song, I also do believe."

"This has been my fairy tale come true for you. Now you tell me one."

Jimmy thought. Then a smile of connivance came over his face.

"Tell you what. Since it's getting late for me I'll tell you the world's shortest fairy tale."

"Well I guess that would be better than nothing."

"Once upon a time there was a young man who met this beautiful woman. He asked her to marry him. She said no. And he lived happily ever after golfing and fishing, playing cards, drinking good whiskey and beer with plenty of money in the bank, and never having to justify leaving the toilet seat up. Thus endiths the world's shortest fairy tale."

Juliana set up and looked at him. "Endith? endith? I'll endith you. There's no such word as endiths, you chauvinistic pig!"

"And just how would a wetback piglet like you know?"

"I'll wet-back you," she said as she poured her last few drops of wine down his back and threw the blanket off laughing.

It was not until minutes before ten PM that Juliana heard his soft knock on her bedroom door.

Chapter 25

A young scout named Rafael Rivera was the first person of European descent to have found the valley back in 1829. It was filled with wild grasses and plentiful water. In 1855 the Mormon Church built a fort there being that it was located halfway between Salt Lake City and Los Angeles. With the discovery of minerals the area grew and in 1905 the City of Las Vegas was founded. In 1931 gambling was legalized in Nevada and has since become the backbone of the state's economy. There was no need for a state income tax here.

The streets of Las Vegas were developed in a simple north-south; east-west grid that only later became traversed by three interstate highways. Thus Jimmy should have had little difficulty in navigating them as he drove to the law office of his local counsel. His navigational difficulties were simply due to his mind still being back at the police station where things had not gone well.

Fortunately the detective who had been assigned to the Mario Moreno case was available and had heard him out. Yes, a file had been opened but with the Coroner's finding of accidental death the file had since been closed. And yes, as with any case it could be reopened and an inquest held in light of new evidence.

"But I've just provided you with new evidence."

"Mr. Davis, I hardly think the Coroner will find the shell of that slot machine in the city dump to impact his finding of accidental death, much less change it to homicide at inquest. Now if you had found the electric circuit, and it was an electrocution circuit, that would have impressed the Coroner, I'm sure."

"But what about you; can't you take action?"

"I know my Chief and I know he won't go to the District Attorney with just this. It's far too circumstantial. Excelsior and J and M are competitors. It's quite common for competitors to get their hands on their competitors' products."

Juliana had been right, Jimmy had thought at the time. The two men had looked at each with the pause in conversation after which Jimmy had decided to proceed. He filled Detective Harvey in on the kidnappings, the threatening notes and the assault in his hotel room.

"You should have reported the hotel room break-in and battery to us."

"I've already explained that."

"Why didn't you report the kidnappings, at least after your boys were safely back home?"

"I've already explained that, too."

With that the detective had excused himself. Inside of ten minutes he was back.

"Mr. Davis, I have spoken with my superior. I want you to know that Excelsior has been and still remains on our radar screen. We would like nothing better than to nail them. They have a history of malfeasance but we have to have a rock solid case. They are well represented by legal counsel, which we learned the hard way a couple of years ago. You must understand that Vegas is a rough town which continuously strains our resources.

"Mr. Davis I will add what you have told me to the extensive file we already have on Excelsior. What you have told me does show motive and for the Moreno death to have been a homicide, but at this time it remains just your word with no corroborating evidence when it comes to implementing Excelsior as the perpetrator. Your long silence doesn't help either. With regard to the kidnappings I am sure that the press would love to hear that story - sequential abductions and returns of twins would really sell. The tabloids would have a field day. But none of that was done in our jurisdiction. That's a matter for the Georgia authorities and, of course, for the FBI. I suggest that you go to them."

Suddenly seeing the street number at hand which had been lodged in his short-term memory, Jimmy's mind changed gear from recall contemplation to current events perception, much as seeing a traffic situation suddenly develop. He pulled in.

Hap Holiday, known to his friends as Happy Holiday, the lawyer, appeared to Jimmy to have been aptly named. His parents had to have had a crystal ball. A rotund, white man, who had since seen sixty, used suspenders to keep his trousers waist-high, suspenders of a color that matched his necktie whenever he sported one and when he didn't, which was more often the norm, which matched the color of his shirt. In greeting Jimmy he didn't bother to remove his stogie from his mouth, which was also the norm.

"Happy to meet you, my boy; please call me Happy."

"Happy to meet you too sir, I mean Mr. Happy, eh Happy."

"I'd offer you a good cigar but my guess is that you don't partake."

"No sir, I mean Happy; I'm not a smoker." Lord, thought Jimmy. Are all the big guys out here cigar smokers?

"The times they are a changing; they are a changing. Can't say they are for the better though."

"I wouldn't know if I hadn't been there, would I?" replied Jimmy now getting into Happy's jovial rhythm.

"Touche. Now logically that would mean that these will become the good old days for you. And since they are what they are, I guess that means that for you they will someday have been the bad old days. So then what will the expression be? Nothing like the bad old days?"

Jimmy tried to think that through but then lazily decided it was easier simply to laugh.

"Old man Macguire tells me that this will be your first deposition."

"That's right, Happy."

"Well you don't worry about a thing. Your sidekick here will be right there, right there at your, eh."

"Side?"

"I like you already, Jimmy boy."

"Well anybody out here in Nevada needs a sidekick. That's the way of the West. I guess I should bring you up to speed on the case."

"Up to speed, you say?" No, don't think so."

"You don't want to be briefed?"

"Hell no; I can learn all about that at the deposition."

"But shouldn't you be prepared?"

"Already am. The past thirty-odd years has seen to that."

"But . . "

"Getting 'prepared' sounds too close to working for me, son. I'm just along for the ride. But since that ride is at $250 an hour I don't think we want to wear out their old mare. I'd like to keep the carousel a turning."

"But . . "

"Jimmy boy, I'll hear about your case at the depo – from you. You know what needs asking, right?"

"Right, but.. "

"No but about it; you just keep asking away 'til you get all your answers. I'll be there if their horse starts in a bucking. The rules are pretty simple at depositions – not like at trial. Unless they get into privileged stuff you can pretty much just ask away. Let 'um object. The reporter can take note. And if they really clam up we can always give the judge a call. You got his number, don't you?"

Having used but one quarter hour of the two to three hours Jimmy had allotted for prepping with the happy Mr. Holiday, he found himself suddenly free for the rest of the afternoon. So he gave Juliana a call. She was thrilled with the unexpected chance to spend more time together. She told him to meet her at the Chapel of Holy Purification on Carson Street. It would be an easy walk from the parking deck adjacent the Neonopolis on Fremont.

Paradoxically there was a heavy concentration of chapels in Sin City which overwhelmingly catered to the wedding industry. They came in all kinds of package deals ranging from the sort in which an Elvis could marry you off, all the way to the truly opulent. This chapel however was atypical. It was like a miniature old Spanish mission which was accessed from the street by a meandering stone path.

He found Juliana in prayer in a back pew. The only others inside were an elderly couple in the front pew. The squeaking of the heavy wooden door caught Juliana's attention. She rose and joined him at the threshold.

"Lovely, isn't it?" she whispered.

"Surprisingly quaint and authentic to be so close to the bustle of Fremont," replied Jimmy.

"Yes, it's my secret place. When I'm downtown rep-ing I always try to come by. It's open from sunrise until sunset so I don't have to watch the time like when I go to Mass."

"I love the smell and the quiet. It's a real oasis."

"Come along; let me show you the town. I'll be your tour guide."

Together they ambled hand-in-hand back down Carson and onto Fourth Avenue with all its shops and fast food. During the remainder of the afternoon Juliana showed Jimmy several of the sights of downtown Vegas. These included the Blackhawk antique rail car which was built in 1903 and had served as the personal car for Buffalo Bill Cody and Annie Oakley. At the California Hotel Jimmy marveled at the rotund Buddha with its well worn belly which often was believed to have become that way by gamblers rubbing it for good luck. Then they gave the Neon Museum a good walk-through before ducking into Binion's Horseshoe with its old time gambling ambiance.

Inside Binion's Juliana excused herself and headed for the ladies room. Jimmy wondered through the sea of screaming slot machines until he thought he recognized a familiar sound. Ping – Pong – Ping – Pong. Sure enough there were two young men battling it out on a pair of J and M machines located at the end of a bank of slots. They were halfway yelling to each over the casino noise as buddies would during a match. Jimmy watched with some trepidation, the memory of Mario's last game having sprung immediately to mind. Then he realized that these two players must not have been on-line in a network but isolated as a stand-alone pair. Binion's had apparently set aside this first pair for friends to play together who didn't mind a short wait while one quickly caught up with the other who had already reached the bonus round.

"Come on man; how much more are you going to feed that mother. I'm a waiting for you," teased one.

Lord, Jimmy realized, he was actually getting a kick out of the wait while he taunted his buddy! He would have to tell Joe Turner.

Beyond them stood a few more Pong machines that Jimmy saw were most likely on-line due to the diverse appearance and behavior of the players that stood side-by-side. Two machines were in play and two were not. Just beyond them he saw Juliana waving him over to her. She was standing behind the player at the first slot in the next bank of slots.

"Look," she whispered.

This next bank of slots began as did the bank of Pongs with a pair of dedicated machines. These were called "Madison Square Garden" and bore the colored graphics of that famous boxing ring. At this pair of slots stood two middle-aged men watching simulated reels spin as they played away. Immediately Jimmy noted that each machine had a pair of joysticks instead of just one as Pong had. Just then the player got a winning line-up of symbols. The screen changed from spinning wheels to the boxing ring as a ringside bell dinged.

"Ladies and gentlemen; In this corner I present the Dynamo Dastard from Denver." A cheer goes up from the crowd. "And in this corner - - and in this corner; well where the hell is our other contender? Somewhere throwing his money away, I'm sure," he taunts.

On and on this goes, to the delight of the waiting player and to the frustration of his tardy opponent. But then a trumpet fanfare is heard as the other player enters the ring after having achieved a winning line-up of symbols on his machine. "Let's give a hardy if belated welcome ladies and gentlemen to The Tardy Truant from Tampa." And the crowd goes wild again.

A bell announces that the match is on. Jimmy watches as the player next to him uses one of his joysticks to move Dynamo Dastard about the ring. The other is used to swing his two arms and gloved fists but not for long, for in less than a minute the Tardy Truant had landed a right cross squarely on Dastard's chin. Down he goes. Further movement of Dastard's joysticks merely serves to raise him slightly only then to fall back down in futility until the count reaches ten. As the ref raises Tardy's arm in victory "Ching ching ching ching" rings on Tardy's slot as he collects the prize money.

As the losing contestant turns to rant at his opponent Jimmy seizes the moment to lean down to read some small script on his machine. "Madison Square Garden" is the registered trademark of the Excelsior corporation for electronic gaming devices.

Chapter 26

Juliana selected Hugo's Cellar at the Four Queens Hotel and Casino for an early dinner. The Four Queens was located in the very heart of Fremont next to the Golden Nugget. It was definitely up-scale dining for downtown but they were already dressed for the occasion as Jimmy was still wearing his lawyering attire, albeit minus the necktie. As for the cost, forget that; they both were on J and M's expense account. Besides, Juliana's gracious hospitality had saved the company the cost of a hotel room. Jimmy would just put in a per diem charge to avoid any rising of eyebrows.

They started off by ordering a bottle of French Chablis and the Hot Rock Specialty for two. Mini medallions of marinated swordfish, chicken breast and shrimp were to be served on a sizzling slab of granite. They settled in for a scrumptious meal to be savored with gusto with the appetites they had worked up with their walking tour.

"What do you make of that Madison Square Garden machine?" asked Juliana.

"I think that will be my return trip ticket to spend more time with you; that's what I think."

"What a smoothie my lover here is. You must be a lady's man."

"Hardly, I'm just a patent scribe who is showing promise."

"And he's a Mister Modest, too."

"Actually I've been trying to recall the claims I put in the Pong slot patent application to see if they covered that boxing game. I may be okay but I can hardly wait to be sure."

"You could call your office."

"Back there they will have already gone home some time ago. Anyway, I can always add some more claims."

"That doesn't seem fair after you've seen theirs."

"Let me explain later. This Hot Rock is just too good for me to be putting my patent-nerd hat on now."

Just then the waiter returned to see if they were ready to order their entrée.

"Got room for an entrée Jimmy, or would you like just to order another appetizer." I think that's what I'll do. Yes, I'll have the crab and portabella."

"An excellent choice, madam; that's one of my favorites."

Jimmy gave the waiter a look and then a look at Juliana who twinkled a smile in return.

"You want to break off from the plates for two, huh? They do have a Cellars Champion: chateaubriand and lobster for two for a snappy $135."

"I'll pass."

"Then I'll go with the Tournedos – Hugo."

"Very good sir," replied the waiter as he collected the menus, refreshed their wine glasses and withdrew.

"One of my favorites, indeed; must they all say that? I mean like that must be on the waiters' bar exam."

"Only the bartenders have a bar exam."

Jimmy smiled.

"How are the twins doing?"

"I wish I knew; I see so little of them but I am taking them to the Atlanta Aquarium on Sunday."

"They should love it. That will be a treat."

"I don't know if they are old enough yet to really appreciate it, but so what? The funny thing is that Sheila asked if she could come along."

"What did you say?"

"I was disappointed and thought of it as an intrusion on my personal quality time with them."

"I don't blame you; it would be."

"But I said yes. I just didn't see how I could say 'no' what with me having no adult friend going with me."

"I would have said 'no'."

"Actually she may be changing somehow; perhaps mellowing; go figure. Then again maybe 'confused' is the word."

"How is your house selling? Had any luck?"

"There's been a little traffic, but the market stinks."

"Maybe you should try selling The Saint Joseph Way."

"The Saint Joseph Way?"

"Yes, the Saint Joseph Way."

"And just what might that be, pray tell."

"You're on the right tract with the praying part since praying is the last step in the ritual."

"Are you serious? What are you talking about?"

"You've seen people with a Saint Christopher statue in their car, haven't you?"

"Why sure."

"Saint Christopher is the patron saint of the traveler. Well Saint Joseph, the carpenter, is the protector of the family. What you do is bury a statue of him in your backyard, head down with his back to the house, and say a prayer after refilling the grave. That will surely bring you a speedy house sale."

"Good Lord."

"Why yes, of course," Juliana replied with a broad smile.

"And just where do I go to purchase this Saint Joseph statue only then to bury it?"

"At any Catholic store, of course."

"Catholic store? Is that where they sell the Catholics, sell 'um like they do Cadillacs?" The wine was making him talk silly.

"Jimmy, just go on-line; that way you won't have to darken a Catholic den of religious icons. No, tell you what; I'll get one for you. In fact I'll get a Saint Christopher also to protect you in your travels between here and Atlanta; that is if you promise to carry it along with you."

The entrees arrived and the waiter reluctantly departed with the crab and portabella, it still being "his favorite." Serving of the tournedos followed.

Jimmy and Juliana both found their meal to be excellent. They ate quietly for a short while before Juliana spoke.

"Are you protestant, Jimmy?"

"I'm not much into religion."

Juliana looked up at him. He sensed that she was waiting for him to elaborate.

"I mean it's good to have faith. Religion can instill good moral values in children and it can provide comfort for adults and the elderly. But I think that over the eons it has done as much harm as it has done good. Way too much evil had been practiced in the name of God."

"Do you believe in God?" she asked.

"Believe in God? After all is said and done "God" now is

just a word, isn't it? Sure I believe in Gods, in the Sun God, the Moon God, and the Rain God; they are all part of nature which I do indeed believe in. It's the supernatural, you know the super – natural, that I have trouble with. Now many of those ancient stories in the bible are good and full of wisdom. And Jesus Christ? To me his story remains today the greatest one ever told and he the greatest religious figure of all time. Yet it is puzzling why nothing like Him has come along since."

"Then so much then for your protestant's Apostles Creed; you do remember it?"

"Of course, and I can still recite it."

"Then you must recall that it recites belief in the holy Catholic Church."

"Hey, hold now. I think they took that part out. Yes, they took that out and replaced it with 'Under God.'"

"That's the Pledge of Allegiance, you nit. But then maybe now you've broken that pledge too. You know that during the cold war the communists substituted the word Nature for God."

Jimmy laughed.

"No, I haven't broken that pledge, but tell me about your own religion. I really was touched seeing you there in prayer in the chapel. You looked so beautiful and serene. I can't believe myself, but I actually envied how you must have felt. I hope you never lose your faith."

"Being a good Catholic can place you close to a state of grace. On a daily basis you can consciously appreciate the mercy and love of God."

Jimmy listened intently as she expounded briefly. Then he realized that they needed to lighten up.

"Amen to that. I know this may surprise you but actually I've been thinking about establishing a new church of my own."

"Really? What will be its name?"

"The United Church of America."

"The United Church of America?"

"Yes, the United Church of America. That's UCA for short."

"Not to be confused with UCLA, I presume," she replied as she now lightened up and joined in the banter.

"Of course not; I know L.A. is the City of Angels, but I would never locate it there."

"And just where would you locate it? Where would be its birthplace - its genesis?"

"In Kansas, of course; that's the geographic center of America."

"Of the lower forty-eight, you mean."

"Well yes, I guess so. I don't know where the geographical center is for all fifty. Further west, I'm sure. Maybe it's in the Dakotas but if it's in the Pacific, that now might present a problem."

"The geographical center for the continental USA is located near Lebanon, Kansas," continued Juliana. "And guess where?"

"Okay, where?" said Jimmy. "Enlighten me."

"In a hog farm."

"In a hog farm? I thought it was in some kind of park, a park with a statue."

"True, but that park is on the hog farm."

"Well that won't do; no, that won't do at all. I can't have all my followers kneeling in prayer facing a hog farm. But say, why is it that you know such trivia about America?"

"It's just different for us immigrants. At least it was different for this immigrant. Some of us are more motivated to learn."

"So you studied up on America?"

"You and your 'America'; you know there is more to America than just these states here. There's a North America, a Central America, and a South America. Will you unite them all in your United Church of America?"

"That would solve the hog farm problem."

"Europe has tried to go secular, you know, and it hasn't worked."

"What?"

"No, it has not worked. As you technical types well know, nature hates a vacuum. A society without religion has never worked for long."

"The expression is 'nature abhors a vacuum.' "

"Yes, as I said, and that void in European religion is being filled as we speak."

"How is that?"

"Islam is replacing Christianity and Judaism there. Mosques are being built all over Europe."

"But that doesn't count; those are for the immigrants and you know how those immigrants are."

They laughed in unison.

"Well if I'm to bring in all of the Western Hemisphere I guess I would have to call it the 'United Church of the Americas.' "

"Then you could have your first church in Manhattan – at number 666, Avenue of the Americas."

Jimmy nodded an appreciation of her banter. It seemed that he had met his equal at that.

"I don't consider Manhattan as really part of America. It's not mainstream; it's not even mainland but a frigging offshore island. No, my new church isn't going to sell out the good old USA like that. But wait; hold on now. That statue out there in Kansas; it isn't by any chance a Saint Joseph, is it?"

"Jimmy, some day you'll learn that the old saying is true: There is no prophet in being an atheist."

From the restaurant the new lovers had a waiting period of just minutes before the on-the-hour Fremont Street Experience show started. Juliana agreed with the hype that "glitter gulch" was indeed a Las Vegas experience that was not to be missed. The ninety-foot high canopy extended for five blocks above Fremont Street. Over twelve million LED modules were synchronized to produce spectacular animations that were accompanied by equally spectacular music. Aside from card decks snapping, that music was mainly country western to which cowboys danced and buffalo stampeded to the play of honky-tonk fiddles. When the show commenced they simply stood still and simply marveled for a couple of minutes along with several hundred other spectators. Then they ambled hand-in-hand down the pedestrian mall. How could any day have gone better and then be capped off like this, thought Jimmy. He was in heaven and in seeing that so was she.

When the ten minute spectacle ended Juliana asked Jimmy to walk her back to her car. She had found a parking space on a street a few blocks away from the hustle and tussle of Fremont and it was now dark.

They made their way down a side street lined with some

quirky shops, some of which were in the process of now closing. A tattoo shop remained open while a barber shop right next to it, complete with illuminated rotating red and white striped barber's pole, was closing. They came to a fortune teller's establishment in front of which a dimly lit sign swung gently from a hangman's post. It was swinging slowly in a small front yard enclosed by a small, dilapidated picket fence. "Madam Magda - palmist," it proclaimed below a weathered rendition of two spread-open, yellowed hands.

"What do you think?" asked Jimmy with a promiscuous smile.

"Why not?" answered Juliana.

Jimmy swung open the gate in the fence and led her down a dirt path to a ramble shack of a house and up onto its front stoop. A small bell was mounted next to the front door with a suspended clapper. To one side of them light briefly came through a window of a room that had probably been converted from a garage at one time, as a drape was briefly pulled back. As they stood there they heard soft voices speak in a foreign tongue. Jimmy looked at Juliana who just shrugged her shoulders. Apparently it wasn't Spanish. Then an old and diminutive woman opened the door. Stooped over as she was she could have stood no more than four feet high.

"Come in; come in, my children," she said with a smile that revealed a set of yellowed teeth smack out of the pilgrim era.

The old woman wore a black robe gathered at the neck much like a Roman toga which bellowed out behind her slightly as she led them over to a table. Upon the table set a small lamp with a green shade. The color of the shade almost matched the emerald color of the old gypsy's bandana and front-laced vest. Other than the dim lighting provided by two wall sconces, the room was only lit by this solitary lamp.

"Please," she said with a hand gesture pointing to a chair in front of the table.

Jimmy and Juliana exchanged glances and Juliana took the chair in response to Jimmy's nod. He took a stand behind her with his hands laid gently on her shoulders as the gypsy took her seat.

"How much is it for a reading?" Jimmy asked.

In response Madam Magda simply took hold of Juliana's hands and turned them face up upon the table.

"How much, please?" he repeated.

"Please take a seat good sir as I cannot concentrate with you standing there."

Jimmy looked about and found another chair against a wall of the small room. He pulled it over beside Juliana and sat down backwards on it facing her. The gypsy took brief note and returned to gaze and feel Juliana's palms.

"Have you ever had a reading, Miss?" she said with a look of some concern.

"Why no; this is my first."

"Are you widowed?"

"Why yes, I am."

"Recently?"

"Yes," She replied as she looked at Jimmy, questionably.

"Why, what do you see?"

Madam Magda folded Juliana's palms together and cupped them within hers. Juliana felt their comforting warmth. The woman gazed into her eyes with a sad expression and then slowly shook her head.

"Perhaps we use the cards," she said as she released Juliana's hands and pulled open a small drawer beneath the table top.

Hollywood couldn't match this, thought Jimmy. He was just about to ask the price yet again when the gypsy spread out two decks of cards. One deck looked the size of ordinary playing cards and bore an ordinary checkered design. The other deck was made of cards of a larger size which bore an artful design in a mixture of shades of blues.

The old gypsy began to shuffle the smaller deck. This was done with professional dexterity that was mesmerizing in this setting. The smooth action of her long and boney fingers was so captivating to watch that Jimmy abandoned the question of price. At this point that would be inappropriate or even rude.

On and on the old woman cut and shuffled, cut and shuffled, methodically as with the finesse of a concert pianist plying her trade. On and on she cut and shuffled, cut and shuffled. There seemed to be no end of it. To Jimmy it appeared that she herself had become mesmerized as into some kind of a trance; into a sad trance. It even looked like she may have teared up.

Suddenly she stopped and reached for the larger deck. She made three shuffles and then handed them to Juliana who received them solemnly with trepidation.

"Please make the cut, my child."

Juliana cut the deck in half but before she could put the upper half under the bottom half the old woman grabbed her wrist that was holding the upper half. Juliana looked down at the surprisingly strong hand of the old woman holding her hand still and then up into her face and eyes. Slowly the old gypsy rotated Juliana's hand that was holding the upper half between her thumb and her third and fourth fingers. She looked at the card that had been buried in the deck but was now exposed to her. Then her eyes shifted slightly and she proceeded to study Juliana's palm. Suddenly in a fit of sad frustration she slapped the cards from Juliana's hand which went scattering in disarray.

The fortune teller's face did not look at the disarray. Instead her head turned slowly to one side and she looked at a side door which was slightly ajar and backlit. Then her head turned back and she looked at Juliana.

"I am sorry. I am so sorry, Miss. I apologize. Please forgive."

"But I don't understand. What happened? What did you see? What does all of this mean?"

The old woman took hold of both of Juliana's hands and held them softly in hers.

"You are not from here, I can tell, but from another land. Return; return to your home. You must go quickly; hurry home before it is too late. Hurry home, my child."

Chapter 27

Sheila tossed and turned as she tried to sleep without success. Her mind and state of consciousness would not shut down. The night demons were out in full force tonight.

The demons had devilishly created a dilemma. When she was asleep they would orchestrate a nightmare. The nightmare would tediously reach a crescendo that would rudely awaken her. Briefly she would find relief in realizing that it had only been a nightmare, but then the while-awake demons would take over, for it would now be their shift.

The little while-awake devils would present her with a field day, or make that a field night, of real life problems and worries. Often she was as scared of not being able to get to sleep as she was of getting to sleep. Relief seemed to be found in turning on the light, getting up out of bed and turning on the TV. Instead of TV sometimes just making a list of things to do the next day in addressing her problems seemed to work in bringing about drowsiness. With that done she need not worry about forgetting that which she had thought through during the fitful night. Total relief would only come when the normal time arrived for her to get up. She had then made through yet another night.

This night found her sitting at her small, yet stylish, bedroom desk at two o'clock in the morning ready to make a list of things to do during the day. Then she thought of going instead to the root of her problem instead of merely treating its symptoms.

She turned on her laptop and Googled "insomnia," its definition, causes and cures. Did she awake un-refreshed in the mornings? Did she have difficulty concentrating during the day? Was she irritable during the day? Bingo, bingo, bingo; triple bingo. As to its causes she could rule out menopause but she clearly tested positive for stress and anxiety. For its cure she found an enumeration of prescriptive drugs. She had only heard of one. Drugs though were not answer, at least not tonight. But she found solace with this Google-confirmed diagnosis. She was not alone in this either. Misery loves company and it appeared that millions of others suffered from insomnia. She turned off her computer, returned to bed and drew the comforter up to her chin. Ah; contentment at last.

Later in the morning she quietly heard out one of the regular complaints of her father. These complaints would be about Andy's latest disruption to the household quiet, or her failure to move on with her life by selling the house or finalizing the divorce or making partner. The daily special on today's menu was career advancement and the fact that she still was just an associate at the firm. This status quo in her life was giving him nothing to brag about at the club.

Once at the office she took out her frustration on her legal assistant, only immediately to realize what she had done and apologized. This insomnia was really making her irritable. She tried to break that spell by thinking about something pleasant. Ah, Sunday, she thought; going to the aquarium with the boys and with Jimmy would be a refreshing change of pace. Actually it should even be fun. Just how long had it been since she had had any fun?

Now out of their terrible twos the twins had become a pleasure to parent when she had the time. As for Jimmy, she now saw him with somewhat different eyes.

Before Sheila had seen Jimmy as being timid and unambitious to a point that boarded on nerd-dum. When they had first met there had been that physical attraction to the tall and lanky, sandy-haired young man so full of life and wit, plus the fact that he was entering the legal profession right alongside her. Not only that but he had that specialty with his computer science degree and actual work experience. But when it turned out that he brought nothing to the table at night with his boring patent drafting practice, documents drafted in a language that was foreign and unintelligible to her, her shining knight lost his luster. Crap, he never once brought to the table any juicy office gossip. But now she realized that Jimmy had simply been being Jimmy. He had not misled her one iota. Quite the opposite, it had been her who had misled him with that deceitful kidnapping. That scheme had also hurt him as it would have anyone else. How could she have expected him to act any differently than he had? Yes, she had been entirely too hard on him. She would try to take a fresh look at him on Sunday and make an attempt at making amends. She now could use a friend and companion away from Ramsey, Ivy and Prince, and from her parents even if he couldn't be a confidant.

Her phone rang clearing her mind. Abigail wanted her now, right now. Fuck it, she thought, I'm not in the mood to take any shit from her.

Unbeknownst to her, neither was Abigail. The two ships were approaching each other on an unchanging bearing that inevitably could only lead to a collision. The first warning of imminent collision was Abigail's closing of the door after Sheila, which left the two women alone.

Abigail wasted no time in reaming her out. Sheila could only see her as some female drill sergeant at Parris Island. She responded as any stone-faced marine recruit would have. Seeing no fight in Sheila Abigail eventually tired of her tirade. "Sorry, I may have gotten a little carried away there, but you know . . ."

"Abigail, this is what I know. The time has come for me to make partner; this is what I know."

Abigail appeared to go into shock.

"What did you say? What did you just say?"

"You heard me; I want a partnership and I want it now."

"A partnership is it? You want a partnership."

"That's the size of it."

"You want a partnership; just like that you want a partnership. You think you can just waltz into my office and demand a partnership. You make it sound like an ultimatum."

"Yes you probably should take it like that – like an ultimatum. I'm sick and tired of all of this."

"Or you'll leave with all your clients and go elsewhere. Is that it? You know partners do have clients. It's the partners who are able to hand out work to associates, to associates like you, because they have clients; they have the business. Indeed, they *are* the business."

"I realize that I don't yet have a client following and because of that I am only looking to be made a junior partner. But a partnership I want now."

"You're quite the brazen little bitch, aren't you," said Abigail in a whisper to herself as she studied Sheila's face. "You haven't put in the time yet for partnership and you know it," she said as she tried to figure out just where Sheila was coming from.

"I've put in plenty of time here. I've worked my ass off for you. It may not be the time that Ramsey, Ivy and Prince normally requires of an associate to make partner, but then my time here hasn't been normal in any sense of the word, either, has it? I think you know what I mean."

"If you are thinking about that harmless little kidnapping scheme you can forget it. You were as much a partner-in-crime to that as anyone. I don't think the authorities would think much of a mother having kidnapped her own children without their father's knowledge. You do that and you'll watch your boys grow up at a rate of about one hour per month. At least I think that's what the federal pens allow for inmate visits. And once released you can forget going back into law for you'll have long since been disbarred."

"Abigail, a mother can't kidnap her own children as you well know. But regardless, I don't have to go to the authorities; I don't even have to go outside of Ramsey Ivy now do I, really?"

"What are you saying?" asked Abigail softly, now realizing that this was going well beyond just the tirade of a fed up and stressed out associate.

"I can go to the managing partner. You see I know all about the little problem the firm has long had with their tax department; all about how its percentage of overall firm revenue that far outstrips the norm for large firms. And I know all about how it has put all the tax partners on easy street in a quite illegal and criminal manner.

"I'm all ears."

"It wasn't the kidnapping that increased the billing hours for the tax partners. That had nothing to do with it. No, it was all the many other schemes, all quite illegal and sufficient to tarnish and besmirch the name of Ramsey, Ivy and Prince, forever. Would you like me to name one?"

"Pray tell, do."

"Okay, I'll name one, one that involved not just one client but a whole host of clients. It has to do with a matter of little inserts having been placed in tax opinion letters, inserts that were to be discarded once read by the clients."

Abigail sat there quietly. Slowly she started to nod her head. Then a broad smile spread over her face."

"Congratulations, Sheila. You have just passed our little test. You have graduated!"

"What? I have graduated?"

"Yes, you have graduated. You are now a part of the select inner sanctum of the tax department of Ramsey, Ivy and Prince. You have proven to possess the intelligence, fortitude, determination, cunning, deviousness and selective lapse in moral turpitude that we require for membership. Welcome to our little secret club. You've earned it."

Sheila sat there stunned.

"Sheila, there is a partners meeting next Friday. Your name will be presented for internal promotion to Junior Partner. The following Monday I will formally induct you by introducing you to all our other members. In the meantime not a word; not a peep; understand?"

"Of course."

"Oh Sheila, I am so happy; so thrilled for you. Congratulations, again," said the human chameleon.

Chapter 28

Sheila awoke the next morning feeling fully refreshed. She had slept like a baby.

After the confrontation the day before with Abigail she had sat alone in her office dumfounded. What route to take had been determined for her by overtaking events. She was in! No longer would she have to face that dreaded decision on whether to leave the firm or to stick it out; whether to be a good little girl or bad. That decision had been made for her. The devil now owned her professional soul.

The work at the office that morning was a joyous labor of love. Her feelings were an odd blend of excitement and self-satisfaction. Her legal assistant even commented that she looked like a woman in love. At coffee break time she walked the halls of the tax department looking at the attorneys working away in their offices for any sign that they had been informed yet. Those who saw her simply smiled back. Were they all-knowing smiles? She couldn't be sure for she didn't yet know just who was and who was not a member of the club, a member of the inner-tax-sanctum. Abigail walked past her once and gave her a knowing wink. Sheila snickered. After she had just passed her Abigail turned around and faced her.

"Oh Sheila, my car is getting a new set of tires put on down at the Chevron station today. Could you give me a lift back there when you leave this evening?"

"Sure, I'd be happy to. What time would you like?"

"I'm afraid it will have to be a little late. Let's say 6:30. But I must run an errand before that. Can I use it now, too?"

"Sure."

That evening Abigail appeared at the open door to Sheila's office just before 6:30. As she was sporting a shoulder bag Sheila knew that she was ready to go. They made their way to the elevator through a now virtually empty office.

"What level?"

"All the way down. I had to park on the A level."

The elevator opened for them on the subbasement A level and Abigail led the way.

The car was parked at a remote, far corner of this lowest level, a corner which was poorly lit. Upon arriving at the rear of the car with its identifying plate Abigail reached into her bag to retrieve the car keys for Sheila. She fumbled about rummaging for them. "It's so dark," she said as she looked up at the ceiling lighting and then panoramically about them. Sheila then saw that she must have finally found the keys by feel as her head came to a halt in her panoramic scanning.

"Voila," she said having finally located them at the bottom of the bag. Then she slowly removed and inserted the key into the trunk lock and finagled with it but the trunk remained closed. She wasn't used to these keys.

"Here, let me get it," said Sheila.

Sheila took the keys and worked the lock with ease. Just as the trunk sprang open two burly hands grabbed her head from behind in a strong, vice-like grip with their fingers overlapping her mouth. Her head was immediately swung violently to the left over and past her left shoulder. After a momentary pause, and before she could get off even a muffled scream, her head was violently yanked back all the way over and well behind her right shoulder. This produced a sharp cracking noise that was immediately followed by her body going limp. The attacker then grabbed her hair with one hand to steady her now limp and disjointed head. With the palm of his other hand he rammed her nose bone deeply up into her skull and then flung her body into the open trunk. With military precision the assault and body disposal had taken but seconds.

Abigail looked at the huge man, nodded her approval as she handed him an envelope, and walked off back towards the elevator.

It was pushing midnight before Jimmy got back home from his trip to Las Vegas. He pulled into the drive, parked, grabbed his bag and went inside through the front door. He flung his bag and himself on the sofa and reached for the remote. Then he laid it aside. He didn't need to sit and watch television. He had already sat for hours on the plane. No, what he needed was a walk. He left the house without bothering to turn off the lights.

As he walked his mind was occupied by memories of the trip and what a trip it had been. Las Vegas was a great place to enjoy, particularly with a new love. And did he ever have a new love. Yes, he realized that he was in love with Juliana and believed that she was in love with him. And the sex they had shared. Fantastic! She certainly lived up to the reputation of hot-blooded, Latin lovers. It had never been like that with Sheila.

Jimmy turned the corner and continued his walk still immersed in thought.

Then there had been that strange reading by the fortune teller. Apparently the blood of gypsies was just as hot as that of the Latinas, what with that tantrum that Madam Magda had so strangely thrown. Go back home; go back home, indeed. Don't you dare, my sweet Juliana. It was a shame that that had tried to spoil the perfect night out. The evening could not have gone any better, at least up until that little tantrum that had come out of nowhere.

Later when they had discussed it, Jimmy had said that he had found the gypsy's den to have outdone any that Hollywood could stage on its back lot. Even the romantic room odor given off by the incense had been quite the touch. To this Juliana had replied that it had smelled more like cigar smoke to her. So much for the scented room ambiance; apparently even the little old ladies of Las Vegas smoked cigars.

Jimmy continued his walk.

Then there had been the deposition of Excelsior. Their counsel had offered to make its offices available for it, which Hap Holiday had readily accepted on behalf of J and M. Let them be host. What the hell, let them provide the coffee and doughnuts.

Jimmy had been pleased with himself for having been well prepared. He had had all of his documents indexed and in good order and Happy had provided a good supply of exhibit stickers on them. His list of questions was clearly written out on his legal pad in logical order. Where they related to a document, or to an interrogatory answer, he had so indicated with a red pencil so that he could quickly and smoothly pull it out to have Bianco amplify once he had identified it. Happy had arranged for the court reporter who had showed up timely and had made her setup at the conference room table while Jimmy was arranging his seat at command central.

As expected, Excelsior had provided Mr. Robert Bianco to answer Jimmy's questions. They had not attempted to produce low level employees who would often have answered that they didn't know the answers to Jimmy's questions. Earlier Happy had headed them off at the pass, spoiling that possible gambit. Jimmy had only just started his engines however with a couple of background questions when Hap had interrupted and stopped the proceedings. Jimmy had neglected to have the witness sworn in by the court reporter. How embarrassing! Next time he would be sure to put that first on his list.

From there on however the deposition had gone as well as could have been expected, except for the cursing. "How the fuck would I know?" Then came a "screw that, and screw you." He hadn't known how to handle that sort of thing since he had at first thought that it might be a plus. But then Bianco's own counsel had put his hand on Bianco's arm and whispered something in his ear. After that there had only been a couple of "shits." Later Hap had explained that Bianco had been headed for contempt of court and his counsel had no doubt told him so.

Jimmy had pushed Bianco to admit having known about J and M's patent application. As foreseen Excelsior's counsel had instructed Bianco not to answer whenever that line of question edged close to communications between Bianco and his own counsel or patent counsel. That was privileged attorney – client information. He also had run into that same problem when he had asked questions that could have led to information to prove that the infringement had been willful and deliberate – which would have led to enhanced damages.

If there had been one theme to Bianco's responses it was that the smart card patent thing was clearly invalid and everyone knew it. J and M had not invented the smart card and its application to the slots had been obvious to everyone. It had only been J and M that had been so presumptuous as even to try to get a patent on that idea. Thus it was J and M that was being the industry jerk here. It was J and M that was trying to run up all of their legal bills and our little fraternity of slot makers don't appreciate. For shame, Mr. Davis.

Jimmy turned around and started walking back. Now he was getting really tired and that was good.

Finally there had been his discovery of that brand new Madison Square Garden slot which might well be covered by the pending application on Pong. He couldn't wait to review the Pong claims and to tell Joe and Mitt about that. What if it covered the boxing game? Wow!

Yes, it had been one hell of a trip.

As he neared the house a car slowly drove pass him. Lord, he thought, that looked like Sheila's car! Then he saw its brake lights come on just as it approached the house. It stopped. Yes, it must be her, but at this hour? Something serious must have come up. He quickened his stride but just as he approached it the car drove on. He must have been wrong.

He went inside, locked up, doused all of the house lights and went to bed. He had been asleep less than a half hour when the car had returned.

Chapter 29

The next morning at the office Jimmy eagerly, yet anxiously, pulled out the Pong patent application and turned to its claims.

Claim 1. A slot machine with added game of skill feature which comprises, in combination:

a plurality of symbol bearing rotatable reels or video display thereof;

a controller with a random access number generator for determining the relative arrangement of said reels when all are brought to a halt after a spinning or simulated spinning thereof to indicate a winning or losing combination;

a video game of skill having a joystick;

and wherein said controller is programmed to enable said video game upon a specified symbol or combination being displayed following a spinning or simulated spinning thereof;

and means for discharging coins from a bank of coins or a credit slip in response to a player winning the game of skill.

Yes, yes, said Jimmy to himself. Claim 1 was but one of many claims in the Pong application but this one would cover the

Excelsior Madison Square Garden slot machine. It embodied the same concept. No doubt that many others would too. It didn't matter whether simulated paddles or fists where used in the interactive game portion of play.

He picked up the phone and called Joe Turner and asked him if he could come over the next morning. They had a lot to talk over. He had no more than put back the phone when it rang. It was Sheila's father asking if he might know where she was. She had not come home last night. He said "no" but that they would be going to the aquarium together on Sunday.

Jimmy spent the rest of the day playing catch-up with some other clients and their cases. Charles Macguire invited him to lunch. The lunch turned out to be a business one. Charles again apologized for having thrown Jimmy to the wolves in not having assisted him at his first deposition. Nonsense, Jimmy replied – Happy had worked out just right.

Jimmy then asked a number of questions regarding the taking of depositions which Macguire was glad to answer. They also discussed how best to go forward from this point on the case. The business lunch turned out to have been timely, what with his meeting with J and M being set for the next day. Back at the office both of them wrote up a time slip, thus putting J and M as the paying host, the consultation justifying that.

The next morning as he pulled into a visitor parking space at J and M Jimmy decided to leave a window cracked. The weather had turned quite warm; actually it was going to be a hot one and he would be inside the building for several hours.

Both Joe Turner and Mitt Johnson listened to Jimmy as he gave a recap of the deposition. They found the Excelsior's sales to have been higher than expected and were surprised that they had been turned over without a fight. Jimmy responded that they could have tried to get them treated as business confidential and for attorney eyes only, but Happy had said that Bianco had been only too happy to brag about them.

When asked what lay ahead Jimmy said that soon they would be making a motion for summary judgment since there were no facts in dispute that needed to be tried. Excelsior's defense was mainly patent invalidity which was a legal issue. Joe and Mitt were pleased that there was that chance to bring the case to a speedy conclusion. If that didn't work, cautioned Jimmy, they would have to go on to trial and the money spent on the summary judgment motion would have been for naught. Mitt thought it was worth the try anyway.

After that they turned to the Madison Square Garden machine. How could it be covered by their patent application, Joe asked? That game wasn't anything like Pong. Jimmy read aloud Claim 1. But their game has two joysticks? Is that covered by any of our claims? No, but it doesn't matter. Our claim doesn't say one joystick or only one joystick. No, it says "a" joystick and Madison Square Garden clearly has "a" joystick. As an analogy, don't corsages have a flower? Yes but a corsage is a bouquet which by definition has a bunch of flowers. Ah yes, but then we didn't claim a bunch; we claimed "a" joystick and Madison Square Garden does have a joystick. You can't just add more to escape infringement."

"Jimmy, I guess you are right. By definition any garden, including the Madison Square one, does have a flower. . . or two." That proved good for a laugh.

"Should you amend our application now to include boxing as one of the video games?" asked Mitt.

"No, I don't think that is necessary. It should already be covered, as I've explained. Besides, one could argue that we had derived that embodiment from Excelsior, were we to do that now."

"Whatever you say."

"Moving on," said Mitt, "I think Joe would agree that this Madison Square Garden slot shows that we should be moving faster on expansion of our Pong slot to other video games. The E3 is coming up real soon now and you know that the cursed Mr. Bianco will be there trying to get his hands on the most popular; on the tried and true. We need to nail down our niche quickly. Our backroom boys want us to be the first to get in the Battlestar Galactica franchise. In fact they have already jumped the gun and started work there. They also want us to try for Epic and Inferno and for Grand Theft Auto. For another multi-player version their first choice is Red Dead Redemption, you know, that Wild West ringer. As they explain it a lot of the software should overlap, which would save us time and money."

"I agree, Mitt," chimed in Joe. "We need to get Jimmy up to speed here as the licensing will probably get a little hairy."

Lord, though Jimmy. I've done next to nothing in the way of licensing. I'll need to get up to speed myself back at the office before Joe adds yet more speed.

"And who knows, we may run into Bianco there and be able to settle the law suit."

Lord, again, thought Jimmy; this entire thing could be over in a flash. Unreal!

"Good. Then Jimmy why don't you get with our Jack, our Jack-in-the-back, aka our Jack-in-the-box, who can fill you in on just what we are looking for as far as these other video games go.

And put the E3 Convention down on your calendar to be coming along with Joe and me."

It was after four o'clock before Jack walked Jimmy out to his car. Jimmy got right in and put his briefcase on the passenger seat.

"Take it easy," said Jack as he leaned over to the still cracked-open window.

"Thanks. You all really are keeping me busy and I love that."

"Say, what's that smell," asked Jack.

"Smell?" Jimmy sniffed. Yes there was an odor; an unfamiliar and quite nasty one.

"You think it's coming from my car?"

"Seems like it."

"I'll check it out when I get home. Bye now."

Rather than go directly home though, Jimmy drove back to the Concourse. This time of day in the late afternoon there were several vacant parking spots in Visitors Parking which was much closer to the front entrance of the high-rise office building than the parking deck. He grabbed one and quickly went inside and up to his office. He unloaded his briefcase and set up three new case files. He was just beginning to write up his time slips for the day when the phone rang. I hope it's Juliana, he thought.

"Mr. Davis?"

"Yes?"

"It's Ralph here from Security."

"Yes, Ralph."

"I believe that your car is parked in Visitors Parking; at least it's your decal."

"Yes, but see I just parked it there a few minutes ago and I'll be leaving in just a jiffy."

"There's another problem with it. Would you mind coming down?"

"A problem? Sure, just give me five minutes. As I said, I was just about to leave."

Jimmy finished up and left the office. I hope it's not a flat, he thought. As he exited the revolving front door of the building he saw a motorized building security scooter parked by his car with its yellow light flashing. The security man was standing there talking with a police officer.

Jimmy walked over wondering what this was all about.

"Is this your vehicle, sir," asked the officer.

Just as he was about to reply he smelled that foul odor again. Now it was more than foul; now it was a stench. It must be coming from the car after all since it had followed him all the way here.

"Wow, that's quite a smell. Yes, it's my car."

"Would you mind opening the trunk, please sir."

"Sure."

Jimmy pulled out his car key, inserted it into the trunk lock and turned it. The trunk popped fully open. All three men gasped at the grotesque sight before them as the rancid odor escaped into their faces. Sheila's face looked out at them from a head that was faced backward from her curled up body still attired in a business suit. Her eyes were wide open and milky as was her mouth. But it was her nose that was her most horrifying facial feature. Having been rammed up deep into her skull she looked like that of a pug-nosed dog.

Chapter 30

The six o'clock news on Atlanta television stations had scant coverage of the murder as it had just happened. The newscasters simply reported that a woman had been found dead in the truck of a car parked in front of the Concourse in Sandy Springs. "We will let you know as soon as further details are made available," was typical.

Within an hour more intriguing details had indeed become known. CNN had a news crew on the scene well before any other member of the new media. The Concourse was now abuzz with police cars, an emergency vehicle and a tow truck. A section of Visitors Parking had been cordoned off with yellow tape designating it as a crime scene. The CNN cameraman captured all of that in the background of the reporter Jessica Brown.

"Breaking News: CNN has just learned the identity of the woman found at the Concourse late this afternoon. Her name is Sheila Frazier who is, that is was, an attorney at Ramsey, Ivy and Prince. She was found in the truck of her estranged husband's car a little before six this evening.

"Mrs. Frazier's husband is a Mr. Jimmy Davis who also is an attorney. He is with the Atlanta firm of Knight and Macquire. Her body had apparently been in her husband's car for some time according to the building security officer who had smelled the stench of a decaying corpse and had summoned a nearby police officer. He had called Mr. Davis from his office to open the truck at the request of the officer who had explained that he had smelled decaying corpses before and that once you have smelled one you're not likely ever to forget it."

Release of the victim's name was made unusually quickly since the next of kin was her husband."

"Jessica, do you know if they have any suspects yet?"

"Not yet, Mike."

"Is the husband, this Mr. Davis, still there?"

"Yes he is. He's standing over there by an unmarked police car with its blue light still flashing. He is talking with what apparently are two plain clothes officers - detectives. There, over there: you can see that he is now getting into their car."

"Are they arresting him?"

"Mike, I can't tell, but it looks like they are just talking."

"What can you tell us about the condition of the victim?"

"Mike, I'm told that her neck had been broken and her face mutilated. The security man said that it was grotesque. Her head was turned around almost completely backwards and her face smashed in. Said her face reminded him of *The Exorcist*, the horror movie, you know.

"Did he say what she was wearing? Was she in fact dressed?"

"Yes, she was dressed; dressed in a woman's smart business suit."

"Then she was dressed as a lady lawyer would be dressed?"

"Yes, I guess you could say that."

"Fine, keep us in the loop."

It was nine o'clock when Jimmy arrived home by taxi. The police had impounded his car for testing. There were 13 calls on his answering machine. As to be expected most were from the media. One though was from Charles Macguire offering his condolences and help. Another was from Sheila's father with his hope that he roast in hell. Then there was one from Juliana who simply said that she was out the door and on her way to Atlanta. She would be there in the morning and not to worry. She would find him.

The next morning he went to the police station as he had promised the police detective back at the Concourse. They now had a time of death established. Where had he been between the hours of four and eight pm the day of her death? On a flight from Las Vegas to Atlanta, he answered. How was the house titled? Joint tenancy, he responded. Is that with right of survivorship? Of course; we were husband and wife. Was there a life insurance policy on her life? Yes, there was. Who was the beneficiary? Me, of course, but you see there was also one on me in favor of her. How much insurance did you carry on her life? Five hundred thousand. Who instituted the divorce proceeding? She did. Would you take a lie detector test? Sure.

Jimmy took the test and apparently passed. They thanked him for coming in and cooperating in their investigation. They would let him know when he could pick his car up.

The next morning Jimmy asked Patty, his legal assistant, for a lift to a car rental agency. From there he drove back to the Concourse. As he drove into the complex, which was comprised of several high-rise and low-rise office buildings with multiple parking decks, the scene seemed surreal to him in that it appeared as if nothing had happened. Well, for most folks nothing had, he realized. Visitors Parking was already full as usual and now free of yellow tape. He parked in his usual area and went up.

Everyone in the office was supportive. Condolences however

were given somewhat perfunctory since they already knew that they were divorcing. Nevertheless Jimmy's children had just lost their mother. Any thought that he had had some role in Sheila's demise was dismissed. He was not at all the type. The media coverage was insensitive to say the least, one assistant told him. And beware, it will only get worse.

He called Sheila's parents house. Fortunately it was her mother who answered for a change. The body would be released this afternoon. The children had been told but they had thought it best to let them go back to preschool today. They were taking care of the funeral and burial arrangements and she would be letting him know the time and place. He had no sooner than hung up the phone when Juliana appeared at his office door. He stood and walked over to her prolonged embrace.

They talked behind Jimmy's closed door for over an hour before deciding on leaving the office. On his way out he stopped by Patty's desk.

"Patty, this is Juliana Moreno."

"Hi there, Juliana."

"Hi."

"Juliana is J and M's sales rep out in Las Vegas."

"I heard about your husband. I'm so sorry."

"Thank you."

"Patty, I'm going on home. I can't get any work done today. I'll give you a call in the morning."

"Do you know when the funeral is?"

"Not yet, but I'll let you know."

"Jimmy, I heard that Nancy Tate will be on CNN tonight talking about Sheila. Eight o'clock, I think. Thought I'd give you a heads-up."

JACKPOT!

"Great; that's just great."

———◦———

CNN NEWS: "And here is Nancy Tate with an exclusive."

"Thanks, Mike. The body of Sheila Frazier was found yesterday in the truck of a car that was parked in the Visitors' Parking lot of the Concourse, a large office building complex in Sandy Springs. CNN has learned that she was a rising star lawyer in the prestigious Atlanta law firm of Ramsey, Ivy and Prince. Indeed, she was a mere days away from officially becoming a partner in the firm. Instead of reaping her due, however, it was the grim reaper that she had met in the grimmest of manners.

"The stench of a decaying corpus drew the attention of a police officer who was on patrol at the Concourse. Upon opening the trunk a horrid scene lay before him and a Concourse security guard. There lay the body of Ms. Frazier still dressed in a fashionable black pants suit with black high heel shoes. She lay in the trunk in a curled-up, fetal-like position with her back facing outwardly. But not only was her back facing out of the open trunk, so was her face! You see her neck had been broken. But wait, just wait; there's more. You see someone had also rammed her nose up into her skull as if breaking her neck hadn't been enough. That someone was full of hate. This, ladies and gentlemen, is raw evil. This is the very face of evil, personified.

"And guess whose car it was in which the body of Sheila Frazier was found in this condition. Was it her own car? The answer is no. It was not her car. Then whose car was it? Why none other than that of her husband, her estranged husband, that is. For you see she and her husband were in the midst of getting divorced.

"As it turns out her husband is also an attorney in Atlanta. Her husband is one Jimmy Davis who works there at the Concourse. We have learned that the police have now named him a person of interest. Duh.

"Finally we have learned that Sheila Frazier's life was insured for $500,000. The beneficiary? One Jimmy Davis, double duh.

"This is Nancy Tate, reporting."

Chapter 31

The long line of cars in the funeral procession entered the cemetery and then crept along under the vast canopy of oak trees to the burial ground. As Jimmy drove with Juliana at his side he watched for camera crews along the way. He breathed a sigh of relief in finding none. Soon a white tent came into view off to one side of the cemetery lane. Three or four men in dark suits were milling about the tent.

The hearse came to a halt at the direction of one of these men while the police escort drove away. The black limousine in which the Fraziers rode behind the hearse came to a halt as did another limousine behind it that was in front of Jimmy and Juliana. The rest of the procession followed suit as each driver was reminded to turn off their headlights.

Jimmy and Juliana set quietly in the still of Jimmy's car and watched as pallbearers received the casket under the guidance of the funeral director and made their way to the tent. A few minutes later the director returned and escorted Mr. and Mrs. Frazier to it. Sheila's father Harold glanced at Jimmy and then scanned the line of parked funeral vehicles. His scan returned to Jimmy's car with its out-of-place color in this sea of black. For a moment he held back his wife Betty and glared intently at Jimmy in disgust. Jimmy felt like he was naked. Sheila's father had provided vehicles for all of the family members, except him.

From a distance the funeral director now beckoned all others to proceed to the tent. The first to do so was the young man who had gotten out of the limo ahead of Jimmy and then leaning back against it as he surveyed the scene. Jimmy recognized him as the reclusive younger brother of Sheila, who he had heard was an alcoholic. Then others from their rear began to make their way over. Juliana motioned for them to join but Jimmy held back. "Let's give it a minute."

After that minute had passed Jimmy got out and opened the door for Juliana. As they walked hand-in-hand towards the tent he found relief in the fact that many were walking ahead of them with their backs towards them. The less eye-contact, the better.

Under the tent the elevated bronze casket took center stage. It was impressive, and it was closed. Candles to each side gave off a reverent scent.

Jimmy and Juliana made their way down an aisle between several rows of folding chairs, many of which were already occupied. Soon they reached the front row and started down it. There were but two chairs still vacant but they were spaced apart. No one offered to slide down. Jimmy and Juliana stood before it for a moment feeling all eyes of the hushed assembly on them. Juliana whispered for him to take one.

Jimmy stood staring at the single empty seat before him. Then he looked at the several others now seated in the front row, some with their heads bowed. A couple more were looking solemnly at the casket while others were looking up at him. Included among those was Sheila's father whose face now bore a smirk seeing that no one on the front row was offering any help.

Jimmy turned towards Juliana and motioned for them to leave. As soon as she turned and began her retreat Jimmy fell in line behind her. Four rows back he found two adjacent seats still unoccupied and took them. The Frazier's social set and the curious were having a field day, thought Jimmy. This was an event not to have been missed.

By the time the service started there was a small overflow of standers. The Episcopalian priest delivered a liturgy from the Book of Common Prayer. It was an Easter liturgy which found its meaning in the resurrection. Since Episcopalian funerals were for worship, graves side services were not encouraged, but Harold Frazier had wanted one. He also wanted to deliver his own liturgy.

"Sheila was my . . . was our daughter . . . our only daughter." - pause - "Sheila was our little girl. -pause – tearing - "She grew up to become a fine young woman, a woman whose life was wrenched away in its . . . in its prime." - pause – tearing while staring at Jimmy - "Sheila was our daughter . . . our . . . our . . . our . . ."

Seeing him starting to break down the priest stepped forward, hugged him briefly and then escorted him back to his seat.

At the conclusion of the service Jimmy and Juliana waited for most of the assembly to make their departure. Then they walked out again hand-in-hand which Jimmy found to be comforting. Feeling the same, Juliana gave him a smile which he returned.

When they got back to the house Jimmy again found several messages on his answering machine. Media calls again. Two however were from the Fraziers.

"Don't waste your time trying to get custody of the boys.

They are my boys now. And don't think you can get your hands on Sheila's trust either. I'll see you roast in hell first. Oh yes, and the insurance, well you can forget that too, not that there would be much you could spend it on where you are going to be for the next 60 years." With that Harold hung up.

"Trust?" said Jimmy out loud. "Sheila never said anything about any trust."

"What about custody?" asked Juliana.

"Doubt he has much of a chance with that. Grandparent over parent? No way."

"What did he mean about insurance?"

"There's a rule that one cannot profit from one's own misdeeds. I don't think any insurance company is going to pay out a death benefit to the deceased murderer."

The phone rang again. What had the old fart forgot? He let the answering machine handle it. Much to his surprise it was the voice of Betty Frazier.

"Jimmy, this is Betty Frazier. I'm calling about the twins. We thought it best for them not to attend the funeral or the graveside service. They are just too young. I thought they might be disruptive and not really understand what was going on. I do so hope you approve.

"Andy and Alec had been so looking forward to going to the aquarium that I don't want to deny them that, too. If you could pick them up around eleven tomorrow, I'll take care of Harold. No need to call back, that is unless you cannot do this."

CNN NEWS:

"What is the latest on the Sheila Frazier case, Nancy?"

"Mike, I'm out here in L.A. but I can tell you that the case of Sheila Frazier right there under your nose in CNN's hometown just gets more bizarre. Haven't you got a window there in the Omni?"

"The nearest window to me is about a football field away, I'm afraid."

"Well this 'person of interest', as the police refers to the husband, Jimmy Davis, has become ever more interesting, at least to me. Take a look at this picture."

A picture of Jimmy and Juliana smiling at each other as they strolled from the burial tent came up on a million television screens around the country.

"Mike, that is our person-of-interest, Jimmy Davis. The attractive lady holding hands with him is one Juliana Moreno, another person-of-interest, you might say."

"Do you know where the picture was taken?"

"Oh, yes; this is the widower leaving the graveside service for his wife Sheila."

"How do you know that?"

"Mike, we, that is we CNN, took the picture; this is an exclusive."

"This Juliana Moreno, what do you know about her?"

"Remember that bizarre scene at Caesars Palace that CNN aired just recently?"

"Do you mean the one where a slot machine player died when his machine malfunctioned?"

"You got it. Well the name of the unfortunate player was Mario Moreno."

"Unfortunate indeed; but say, is this Moreno related to our Moreno, Juliana Moreno?"

"Bingo. Mike, you never fail to amaze me with your penetrating insight. Yes, as you have guessed, the late Mario Moreno was the husband of Juliana Moreno."

"Then this picture of Jimmy Davis and Juliana Moreno is a picture of a widower and widow."

"Yes, it is a picture of a widower leaving the graveside service for his deceased wife with the widow of the man who died while playing the slots at Caesars."

"Nancy, Sheila Frazier's death has or obviously will be ruled a homicide, but what about the death of Mario Moreno? Wasn't it under investigation?"

"Mike, we've spoken to the Las Vegas police about just that. You are right; it was carefully scrutinized by the Coroner's Office. It has been tentatively ruled as accidental."

"Tentatively ruled?"

"Yes, tentatively ruled upon. The case will not be closed until a year has passed. Even then it could be reopened if new evidence warranted."

"Nancy, do you know how this Jimmy Davis and Juliana Moreno happened to meet?"

"Glad you asked. Jimmy Davis is an attorney for a slot machine manufacturer in Atlanta by the name of J and M Gaming. Juliana Moreno works for a company in Vegas called Moreno Distributors. Her now deceased husband was the owner of Moreno Distributors. Mario Moreno's alleged accidental death at Caesars came about as he was demonstrating a new J and M slot machine. In attendance was none other than Mr. Jimmy Davis, the only person-of-interest named so far in the grisly murder of Sheila Frazier."

"Well Nancy, one would guess that her murder has not gone unnoticed by the authorities there in Vegas."

"The tentative ruling has, shall we say, become more tenuous. I'm sure the Coroner's Office will be taking a renewed interest in all this."

Chapter 32

Jimmy pulled into the driveway of the Frazier's house.

"What a lovely old house," remarked Juliana. "All these trees; they are magnificent. This is just beautiful."

Jimmy led her down the short, stone path and up the wooden stairs. There on the porch were the twins in a glider, rocking back and forth. Mrs. Frazier rose from a rocking chair and made her way over.

"Juliana, I'm Betty."

"Mrs. Frazier, I'm so glad to meet you. I didn't have a chance at the service to give you my condolences. Please let me extend them to you now."

"Thank you."

"These, of course, must be the twins."

"Say hello to Juliana, boys," said Jimmy.

The boys studied her in a silence that was only broken by the soft squeaking of the glider. Then one smiled at her.

Jimmy walked behind the glider and gave the smiling one a soft pat on the head. "This one is Andy," said Jimmy as he gave the glider a shove.

"Then this one must be Alec," said Juliana as she reached to shake his tiny hand.

The three year old Alec examined her outstretched hand and

then took it. Juliana shook it while swaying in tempo with the movement of the glider.

"Don't they look precious in their little sailor suits," declared Juliana.

The twins were dressed as twins with white shorts, white socks and shoes and blue sailor jumpers with their traditional collars with white stripes.

"They are precious and getting more so every day," said Mrs. Frazier.

"They are indeed," said Jimmy as he gave the glider another push.

"Can I get y'all something? Would you like some ice tea? I've sent Harold on some errands."

"No thanks, Mrs. Frazier," responded Juliana as she squatted down in front of the glider and brought it to a halt. She looked approvingly into the eyes of both boys. "Are you ready to go to the aquarium?"

"Yes, yes," they replied almost in unison. I want to see the whale sharks," said Andy.

"Me too; I want to see the whale sharks," chimed in Alec.

"Well then, let's do it!" said Juliana as she stood up.

"What time do you think you'll be back?" asked Mrs. Frazier.

"Is six alright?" responded Jimmy.

"Six is fine; I'll be on the porch watching out for you. You need'en get out of the car. And be sure not to honk. I'll come and fetch 'um. Now off you go. You'll have fun."

"Thank you, Mrs. Frazier," said Juliana as she took the hands of both boys. "Your home here under all of these huge trees is just beautiful. This would be an oasis in Nevada."

"It's Betty, Juliana," she responded with a sad smile.

After parking, the four of them marched off to Centennial Olympic Park which was on the west side of downtown Atlanta. The aquarium loomed ahead of them on the north side of the park. It was enormous. Jimmy stopped for a moment and turned around to face the opposite way.

"See that building?" he asked as he nodded to a large modern structure of concrete and glass that bordered the southwest side of the park. "That's the home of the devil."

"The devil?" responded Andy with his eyes wide open.

"I was talking to Juliana, Andy. Yes, the devil, for you see that is the devil's lair."

"What on earth do you mean?"

"That's the home of CNN. In fact that is the *world* headquarters of CNN. The building is called 'The Omni'."

"It's looks weird to me; I mean it was just minutes ago that we were in the shade of a deep forest at the Frazier's home and now look around here where we are now in a sea of concrete and glass. We might as well be back in Nevada."

"Make that a concrete jungle," laughed Jimmy. "Tell you what, boys. There aren't any amusement rides in the aquarium but there is one in The Omni. Want to ride it before we go in the aquarium?"

"What are you trying to do, Jimmy, tempt the devil. It's never smart to tempt the devil."

"Oh come on. It will only take a few minutes."

"What if *they* see us together?"

"I don't think the devil will be looking for us in his own lair."

They reversed their walk and made their way over to The Omni. Upon entering it they found themselves suddenly in a darkened and cool, immense atrium. For a moment they just stood there and looked agog.

"Well this is impressive, I must say," said Juliana. "But an amusement ride? I don't see any amusement rides."

"Over there in front of you, see it?" said Jimmy as he pointed to an escalator.

Juliana's eyes opened wide as she tried to take it in. She had never seen such an escalator. Upward and upward it extended to its end which was swallowed up by a giant globe of the planet Earth. There was a line of people already on it about fifty feet away. They looked like they formed the end of a line of a tour group. Indeed, there was a tour sign at the bottom of the escalator but at the moment it was unattended.

"It's the largest freestanding escalator in the world. It extends, that is ascends, eight stories high."

"First the world's largest aquarium and now the world's largest escalator. Is Georgia trying to out-Tex Texas?"

"What do you think, boys? Want to ride it up?"

The three year old twins looked it over, or rather up, but said nothing.

"Come on now, let's go."

The boys stood on the ramp before the escalator steps that were emerging from out of nowhere from beneath the ramp. Jimmy and Juliana stood side by side behind them but nobody moved. Jimmy and Juliana exchanged looks and then reached down and sat them side by side on the next step to emerge. Then they themselves boarded the next step side by side behind the boys. Off the foursome rose as Andy squealed with unbridled delight.

Up and up they ascended. The boys peered about over the moving handrail. When Andy would place his hand on the sidewall beneath the moving rail Jimmy would place it back atop the rail.

In the CNN security center two security officers sat in a darken space before an array of television monitors. "Hey Paula, take a gander at the escalator."

"Yeah; what'cha got?"

"Here; look at that couple with the small kids."

"Bring it up."

The officer manipulated a couple of controls on the panel before him. The camera came to be centered on their moving target with its image greatly enlarged.

"Those two look familiar. Yep, I know them from somewhere."

"Hey, they look like that couple – you know – what did they call them?"

"Widow and widower," he responded softly.

"By God you are right! Call the newsroom."

"The newsroom? Shouldn't we be calling the Captain?"

"No time. Call the hot tip line; NOW!"

Officer Charlie threw up a phone number index on another screen for the general public tip number and made the call.

"CNN tip line. May I first have your name please?"

"My name is Charlie. I'm a CNN security officer here in the building. This is urgent."

"What do you have, Charlie?"

"The widow and widower – you know – from last night's broadcast; they are here in the building."

"In the building? In this building? Are you sure? Where?"

"They are on the escalator – approaching level six now. We have them with two small children on a monitor."

"Quick; patch it in."

"Patch it in? I can't patch it in. This is building security. Our network is – well, it's secure. There's no patching in to broadcast, for God's sake."

"You are taping, right?"

"Yes, that's done automatically. Hey, they are about there, now – level eight. They are now going into the globe and off my screen."

"Get the tape over to us pronto and don't lose them. Switch over to extension 8010."

As alarms of the human variety were going off in the newsroom Jimmy and Juliana and the boys were readjusting to life inside the globe where inside it was dark with theatre-like settings where people sat watching CNN footage at interactive kiosks.

"Where are the fish?" asked Alec over the babble.

"What did you say, Andy?" asked Juliana as she bent over.

"I'm Alec. Where are the fish? I don't like this aquarium."

Juliana smiled. The child had seen the escalator enter the blue South Pacific on the globe and thought it was the aquarium.

"No fishes here, Alec, but soon. Jimmy, this isn't for them. Let's find an elevator."

Soon they emerged from the coolness and din of the CNN Center back into the sunshine and started across the park towards the aquarium. Their stroll was in stark contrast to the bustle going on in the CNN newsroom. Images of the couple from yesterday had been compared with those received from security of the couple on the escalator. There was a match in no uncertain terms. Security was alerted. Find them inside the globe. Delay 'um if seen at an exit. Hurry!

Jimmy led them over to the huge glass structure of the Georgia Aquarium. It was in the shape of the bow of a ship. The aquarium was the brainchild of philanthropic Bernie Marcus, a co-founder of Atlanta based Home Depot.

Once past Admissions they had to go through security. "Any chewing gum?" asked a guard.

"Chewing gum? no, no chewing gum."

"Even chewing gum," mumbled Jimmy to Juliana as they clearing Security. "What's next? No sucking your thumb?"

Then they heard a commotion and looked back. There stood a lady reporter all out of breath with a field cameraman in tow. CNN was blazed across his shoulder-mounted camera. The man was sweating and panting even more than the reporter. Apparently they had run across the park from the CNN Center in hot pursuit.

"All professional photography requires advanced approval in writing from the Aquarium," the guard was explaining out of earshot of Jimmy and Juliana.

"But this is an on-going news event as we speak. How could we have known and asked for permission in advance? Hey, be neighborly. We're CNN!"

"I know that you are CNN and I know that you need written permission."

Although Jimmy and Juliana could not hear the dispute, it was obvious that there was an impasse.

"We're alright. Come along; let's go."

"You said you had tickets for the Kids Corner show. When is it?" asked Juliana.

"Three-thirty; we have plenty of time."

"Do you know what it is?"

"It's for ages 2 to 5. They have music, crafts, puppets, and storytelling."

"Sounds perfect. Hey look there - African penguins!"

Time had passed before they knew it. They barely made it to the Kids Corner show in time. Jimmy had made a good choice. Andy and Alec were soon in seventh heaven. Jimmy was torn between wanting to explore the aquarium and staying with the boys. He elected to stay.

When the show ended they were just leaving when none other than Harold Frazier suddenly appeared.

"There you are. I thought so!"

Jimmy and Juliana stopped with the boys in hand and stood gaping at the man. He was obviously in distress.

"Thought you could go through the backdoor, huh? Thought you could go behind my back. Come boys; come with me. Right now!"

The old man reached for Andy who shrank back away.

"Mr. Frazier, please," said Juliana as she put both of her hands around the boys and nestled them close to her body.

Frazier paused and then started to reach for the boys again.

"Mr. Frazier," said Jimmy as he put one hand on his shoulder only to have the man grab it. Frazier turned to face Jimmy up close still holding his wrist.

"I can explain . . . "

Harold Frazier was in no mood to hear an explanation.

"You, you .. you won't have these children, ever. Understand? Understand me?"

Frazier's face and mouth started to contort.

"You won't have her trust. No trust; no children. You, you, you . . ."

Harold Frazier's face continued to contort as his eyes widened.

"Her will – you can't . . ."

"Her will? What will?"

"I will . . . Sheila's will . . . I will . . . I . . . "

Just then he started gasping and grew weak-kneed and tipsy.

Seeing a bench out of a corner of his eyes Jimmy guided him over to it as Juliana continued to nestle the children. Harold set down but continued to gasp. His eyes looked around for help.

"Juliana, get someone."

Minutes later a man in a light blue jacket with a caduceus insignia on it came rushing up and immediately took charge. His name plate read Jim Owens LPN.

"Sir, can you hear me?"

Harold nodded while still breathing heavily.

"Sir, tell me you name."

"Frazier," came out weakly.

"Tell me your full name in a complete sentence."

"Frazier . . . Frazier . . ."

"Mr. Frazier, please raise both of your arms over your head."

Harold slowly raised one arm bent at the elbow. The other remained on his lap.

"Can you raise your other arm, sir?"

Harold nodded. The other arm remained on his lap.

"Sir, please stick out your tongue."

Harold's lips slowly parted.

"Please stick out your tongue, sir."

Ever so slowly the tongue emerged but it was all twisted to one side.

The medical attendant stood up, turned his back and pulled a phone from his jumper pocket. A minute later he turned back around.

"I believe he has suffered a stroke. I've summoned help." He then reached in the other pocket of his jacket and pulled out a stethoscope.

Chapter 33

"Jal, get your big ass in here; there's something I want you to see," summoned Bianco.

"Be right there, boss." Minutes later Jal walked into Robert Bianco's office.

"Hi there, big man. Here, take a seat. I want you to watch som'um. I taped this last night."

Bianco turned on a computer monitor that was on his desk and turned it sideways so that both he and Jal, who was sitting in a chair in front of Bianco's desk, could watch together. Bianco hit a button on his computer keyboard and an ad came on telling TV viewers what a great investment gold was in these uncertain times. Bianco hit fast forward. Moments later the interminable gold ad was over and the CNN Evening News with Mike Taylor came on.

"Good evening, ladies and gentlemen. I'm Mike Taylor. And I'm Ann Cochran. And welcome to the CNN Evening News.

"There is a lot of news to report this evening. But first I want to start off with something that happened today right under our very own noses here at CNN in Atlanta," said Mike. "Take a look at this picture."

A still shot of Jimmy and Juliana and the twins appeared fuzzily in black and white with the time shown digitally at the bottom. It was a security shot of them while they were on the escalator. "Maybe you can't quite make out their faces. So let's bring it up."

The image suddenly enlarged with greatly enhanced clarity. Now there was no mistaking just who these people were.

"Yes, we have Jimmy Davis and his lady friend Juliana Moreno riding the giant escalator right here in the world headquarters of CNN. Rather brazen, wouldn't you say, Ann?"

"Brazen and gutsy, I would say, Mike."

"Ann, what do you think? Are they actually looking for publicity?"

"Mike, it's too early to tell. We don't yet know that much about these two; however I doubt it."

"What makes you say that?"

"The twin boys are with them. Those are Mr. Davis's children."

"They sure are cute in their little sailor suits."

"That they are, Mike. They are dressed for the occasion."

"Dressed for the occasion?"

"Yes, you see they weren't really here for one of the CNN tours which start every ten minutes. They were in and out in less time than that. I think they just gave the boys a ride, for just minutes later they were seen walking across Olympic Park. They were on their way to the Georgia Aquarium which is on the opposite side of the park from us."

"Therein the sailor suits."

"That's right, Mike."

"Did they do the aquarium?"

"Yes they did, but the strange thing is that they rendezvoused at the Aquarium with Mr. Harold Frazier."

"Frazier? The name sounds familiar."

"Well it should, Mike. He is the father of the just murdered Sheila Frazier."

"You mean to say that they all went touring together, this Jimmy Davis, her widower, his girlfriend, the twin boys and the father of the deceased? I thought this Davis guy has been named a person-of-interest by the police in her case. This makes no sense."

"Yes, the widow and the widower were on the move again here. And there's more, Mike. Just our reporter and cameraman were at the entrance of the Georgia Aquarium an emergency vehicle arrived at a service entrance in the rear. And who did they drive off with minutes later? None other than Mr. Harold Frazier who had suffered a severe stroke right there inside of the aquarium with this Davis and his twin boys and his girlfriend."

"With the widow, and the widower."

"Precisely."

"Well that's enough to give anyone a stroke. How is his condition, Ann?

"He is now listed as being in serious condition. And Mike I doubt he would have made it at all if he had seen his daughter's face after her attack. We can't air it but I can tell you that it was absolutely hideous. Her head had been wrenched completely backwards when her neck was broken and her face smashed in. There wasn't even an attempt to repair it, postmortem. All they could do was rotate the head back around."

Bianco turned off the monitor and turned his attention to Jal.

"What'cha think, Jal?"

Jal raised his eyebrows and shrugged his shoulders.

"What'cha think, Jal? Looks kinda familiar-like, don't it?"

Jal looked at Bobby but remained noncommittal.

"Fess up, Jal; out with it."

"Out with what, boss?"

"Jal, this Davis guy is the fucking lawyer who interrogated me. That was his wife that went down."

"Then it ain't such a bad thing."

"She was taken down with a nose jab. Sound familiar?"

Again Jal shrugged.

"Isn't that the trademark of someone I know?"

"Well then, how about this? Does it look familiar?" With that he flung a pair of airline ticket stubs at Jal.

"Bobby I went to Atlanta on my own time. I was going to pay for the fucking tickets, I swears."

"Jal, this Davis guy is the attorney for J and M, in case you didn't know it. J and M is our fucking competitor – my competitor."

"Sorry, boss. I didn't think. I, I . . . "

"You didn't think is right. These little side job you get from time to time don't interest me. But when they get connected to Excelsior they damn well do."

Jal sat there with his head down like a scolded child. "Sorry, boss."

Bobby Bianco sat there staring at the gypsy, at the 230 pounds of meek gypsy. Then he swung his chair to the side and changed his stare to the space outside the window. Finally Jal spoke.

"Bobby, it was you who had me rough up that lawyer. I didn't think you would mind if I took that job."

"Really now; and who the fuck was it that gave you that job?"

"Oh come on boss; don't ask me that. You don't wants to know that."

Bianco turned that over in his mind. Well maybe he really

didn't after all. That dead woman meant nothing to him. And yet he always wanted to know everything that went on in his own little world.

"Boss, it didn't come from Vegas; I swears."

"Atlanta, huh?"

Jal kept quiet as he studied the floor.

"Jal, I'm tempted to fire your ass. I should fire your ass. I've warned you about killings. I don't need people killed. I can get jobs done without that. You know that. I've told you that. I've warned you."

"Don't fire me, Bobby; I'll make it up to you. You'll see."

"Well I guess it was me that started giving you those little outside jobs from time to time. Now I realize that I shouldn't have. You do what you do damn well enough back there in the shop. You know the slots insides and out. I do need you."

"Boss, let me give you a new slot. Okay? I'll come up with one of them new ones – you know, the ones with the bonus playing."

"A new slot, huh?" Bianco set back and looked back out the window again.

"A new slot; hummmm. But you aren't really a fucking designer now are you?"

"Boss, the box will be about the same; same old; same old. What's new will just be the flashy artwork. You know I can handle that.

"I can do it boss. Just give me one more chance."

"And no more outside jobs?"

"No more outside jobs, boss; you got my full attention. You'se gots me exclusive-like.

"Okay then, it's a deal. But listen, these proactive slots

aren't going to kill off the old slots. No, I don't think so. I've been watching. I sure as hell have been watching. The young studs are playing them; that's for sure. But I sure see plenty sitting there with empty stools. It's the women who aren't playing them. The little old ladies aren't playing and what the little old ladies don't play don't gets played enough. Can't be long before the casinos pick up on this. No, they ain't going to be the end to end all.

"Tell you what, Jal, give me an new old-fashion slot. Give me a new one of the old ones that's fresh — one that will bring back our little old ladies. I miss our LOLs. Yes, a slot that I won't have to bid for at the upcoming show for video game rights. Yes, yes, that's it! I'ves God damn gots it. I'll just up the bidding for our competition; make J and M bid through their fucking nose and what will they end up with? A nose bleed. They'll bid through the nose and then bleed through the nose. They don't know it but they are about to become blooded licensees, I guarantees it."

Madam Magda looked at the half finished dessert before Jal.

"What is it Jal? You haven't said two words during dinner. What's wrong, child?"

"Ma, I thinks I may have bitten off more than I can chew."

"Well, tell me about it. From the looks of your plate I can't see that you've chewed much of anything."

"I've gone and promised Bobby that I would design a new slot for him. Now I don't know."

"Design; did you say design?"

"Yea; design."

"You mean like a brand new one?"

"Yeah."

"Now what came over you? You've never designed one before, have you?"

"Not really, but you see, he wants me to design one of the old ones – you know, ones with just the spinning reels. All's I got to do is to come up with a new, a new – you know – theme."

"Well now there, that shouldn't be so hard now, should it? You just need an inspiration. Tell you what; let's do a reading. Maybe it will come to you."

With that they stood up from the kitchen table, put the dishes in the sink, and walked out of the neon kitchen lighting and into the front room. Jal took the same seat that Jimmy had taken when he and Juliana had had their reading but he sat properly on the chair. His ma lit two candles.

"Jal, since this is a freebie I think I skip the Celtic cross and the Star Spread. Simple is, simple gets."

After resting quietly for a minute Jal's Madam Magda shuffled a deck of Tarot cards and then laid out three, side-by-side. Jal knew that the left one represented the past, the middle one the present, and the third one the future. Madam Magda turned over the one that represented the past. It was The High Priestess, inverted. Magda nodded.

"Emotional instability; clouded thinking; and recklessness. Overly emotional attitude and impulsive actions have produced negative consequences." She looked up into Jal's face. "Sound familiar?" Jal nodded solemnly.

"That's not fair, Ma; You already knows me."

"You think I planted that particular card there?"

"No, I saw you shuffle. It's just that . . . "

"Jal, there are 72 cards in this deck. That's roughly one chance in seventy-two I would guess. Now let's move on."

Slowly she turned over the middle card. It was Temperance; it too was inverted.

"Very unsettling and volatile period. You have an inability to juggle multiple responsibilities. You are overcommitted. Your situations are out of your control. Are you in an unsettling and volatile period, Jal? Are you overcommitted? Now isn't that why we are sitting here?"

To this Jal simply nodded in agreement. The Queen of Tarot then reached and turned over the card on the right which represented Jal's future. It was The Chariot which also was inverted. Since all three were inverted, all of their images were upright facing Jal.

"Ah, The Chariot! *Quel surprise*! You will achieve success through underhanded means. You will be ruthless in dealing with others. You will exploit others for your own advancement and will win by intimidation. I guess we have the wrong Questioner here after all," said Magda, the Diviner as her voice rose. Isn't that right, son?"

"No, you know that's not right; it's Jal sitting here alright."

Jal sat there solemnly absorbed in the dim light and the smell of residual incense and the candles. He looked at the colorful images facing him. There sat the high priestess with her blue gown and cross. Next to her stood Temperance in his white robe and bearing red wings. And finally there was the Charioteer.

Back and forth Jal scanned the images silently as Madam Magda followed his eye movement intently. Slowly he touched them and began to manipulate them. One by one he slowly slid them up and down upon the table like passing elevators. Suddenly he stopped. His eyes opened wide with a revelation. He looked up at his adopted gypsy mother.

"That's it; that's it ma. I has it!"

As if this had been expected, Madam Magda softly asked.

"And what do you have, my child?"

"Why this; why this here, right here."

"The cards?"

"Yes, the Tarot cards. A Tarot slot machine!"

Madam Magda looked at him in amazement as Jal leaned over and kissed her. She leaned back away.

"Jal; no."

"No? What do you mean, no?"

"That would be blasphemous."

"Blasphemous?"

"Can you see our divine Tarot cards spinning away in some raunchy casino; spinning away in the clamor of a gambling casino. That would be a wrath unleashed to end all wraths."

"Ma, please; we are gypsies. Ma, please!"

Madam Magda looked at the rare eagerness and happiness of her son. Further resistance would be wrong.

"Voila, the cards have spoken and in their own mysterious way revealed the answer. But The Chariot; *this* Chariot gives me worry."

Chapter 34

The funeral for Harold Duckworth Frazier took place at the Cathedral of Saint Phillip in Buckhead. The Episcopalian cathedral was prominently situated at the crest of a hill that was approached by a lengthy stretch of Peachtree Street. Though it was most impressive at night when it was beautifully illuminated, it remained impressive at eleven in the morning for those in the procession of limos and automobiles that had followed the hearse from the Patterson Funeral Home on Spring Street that morning up Peachtree to it. This is what Harold had wanted and this is what his widow Betty had arranged.

Harold had mercifully succumbed some twenty-two hours after having been admitted to the hospital. His stroke had been so severe that he would have been paralyzed had he survived. His last words were those he had spoken in the aquarium. His only response to words and gestures and touches made by Betty at his bedside had been his squeezing of her arm and hand.

Jimmy and Juliana paid their last respects at the funeral home. While there Betty had pulled them aside. She seemed to be quite calm and collected amongst the bereaving. It was she who suggested that they, and she did use the word "they," take Andy and Alec with them. That would be the right thing to do, she explained. Jimmy readily agreed.

The day of the funeral it was they who met the boys at the end of their day at Buckhead daycare. They drove directly to Jimmy's house. Miss Clara was there to welcome them back home. Now it almost seemed as if nothing had happened. Sheila had simply been replaced by Juliana who had immediately started to assume the role of mother as though without realizing it. It was all so impossibly natural, it seemed to Jimmy; it was so harmonious.

"I like you, Miss Julia," said Miss Clara.

"And I like you too, Miss Clara."

The boys beamed.

"Are you staying on here with Mr. Jimmy?"

"I'll be here for are a few days. I've made arrangements with my business people back in Las Vegas. They can handle things for a bit."

Jimmy spent the next day rounding up the vestiges of all things Sheila. Except for a photo album and some loose photos that he wanted to keep for the boys to have sometime some day, vestiges of her image had been swept away. At least they had been swept into the back of Jimmy's car for delivery to her childhood home and her mother Betty.

Later he rounded up Juliana, the twins and Miss Clara out in the yard where he had set up a game of croquet with a layout of spaced hoops and poles. He took pictures galore of the boys, pictures of them with Juliana, and pictures of them with Miss Clara and with Juliana. He finished up the photo feast by having Miss Clara take pictures of him and Juliana and with him and Juliana and the boys. Some were mixed in with crazy antics with the croquet mallets and ball. The next day they would go to a frame shop and do this up right. Before that however he would deliver Sheila's things.

For continuity Jimmy brought Juliana and the twins along

with him when he went to Virginia Highlands. He wanted everything to appear natural to them. It would be enough for them to handle not having their mother Sheila. The Frazier's black, live-in cook and housekeeper, Stella, met the call at the door and showed them in to see Betty.

"Where do you want her things to go, Mrs. Frazier?"

"Put them in her old room if you would, Jimmy."

While he did that the boys extracted some toys from an old wooden toy box, which was like a chest, and went out with them to play on the front porch. In the meantime Betty led Juliana to the sun parlor at one side of the house.

"This is beautiful, just beautiful Betty," Juliana said as she looked out through the spacious glass windows onto the back lawn which was shaded by several one hundred-fifty feet high oak trees.

"Thank you; this is where I find refuge, although I do host our ladies bridge games regularly in here."

Just then two squirrels came into view scampering about beneath the oaks. One apparently had stolen a nut from the other. Then again, perhaps it was mating season.

"It must be so very, very hard on your losing both your husband and your daughter in such a short time span. Life can just be so unfair."

"Yes, you could say that."

"If there is anything I can do, just ask. Please, just ask."

"Juliana, you may not know it but you already have. The twins have snuggled up to you like a bug in a rug. I think providence had a hand in your appearing on the scene just when you did."

"That is so kind of you to say, Mrs. Frazier."

"It's Betty, please."

"Betty."

Just then Juliana saw two more squirrels scampering about in the mixed outdoor lighting of shade and sunshine. Then two more caught her eye. These cute little varmints seemed to be all over the place. Then, as if on cue, two small dogs came bounding into the parlor.

"Well, who do we have here?"

"This is Gizmo and this is Gigot."

"Lhasa Apso?"

"No, they are Shih Tzu."

"They are gorgeous; just gorgeous!"

"They make great pets; they really do."

"Hello?" came a voice from the front door.

"I'm in here girls," Betty answered, loudly.

Two ladies of Betty's own generation came bounded in. One was wearing a bright red hat while the other one was sporting a bright pink one. Both of their dresses bore some purple. One was carrying a plate of brownies and the other a bowl of fruit salad.

"Just in time; I think I too was on the edge of expiring. Juliana I want you to meet my two sisters. This one here, sport'en the fake Louis Vuitton handbag, is Gracie."

Juliana absorbed the tall Gracie, who was rendered taller by her red hat with red feather. Her shinny red handbag was no fake.

"I don't think so," replied Juliana with a smile.

"What's that, honey."

"I don't think it's fake. You see, I'm from Las Vegas and I've never seen a real Louis Vuitton one before now."

All the ladies got a laugh out of that.

"I'm Juliana."

"Honey, I know who you are," replied Gracie.

"Everyone knows who you are these days," chimed in the other sister.

"Unfortunately, yes."

"I'm Cynthia – Cynthia from Tulsa," said the other sister who was holding the bowl of fruit salad with both hands.

"Here, girls; just put them on the table. But you really shouldn't have."

"Now don't go think'n too highly of yourself darling. We shouldn't have and we didn't have. These were smuggled out from the luncheon."

"Juliana, these ladies are members of the Red Hat Society."

"I think I've heard of them. But Cynthia, your hat is pink."

"It's pink until you turn fifty."

"Then aren't you a tad bit out of uniform?" asked Betty.

"Well I just haven't had the time to get around to that. I hate waste, you see, and I just can't come to see it go on sale at the Goodwill – for all of three dollars."

"Well let's catch up with them, Juliana. Would you like some tea?"

After the visit Jimmy came inside to find Juliana and Betty taking a breather after the onslaught of the lively sisters. He pulled up a chair.

"Mrs. Frazier, just before his stroke down at the aquarium Mr. Frazier mentioned something about a will."

"I wouldn't exactly call it 'mentioned,'" said Juliana.

"It's Betty, Jimmy."

"Betty, Sheila never mentioned anything to me about a will."

"Do you mean her will, or yours?"

"To be honest, neither."

"Do you have a will?"

"Well no, Betty, I don't. I know I should, but I haven't made one."

"At your age I'm not surprised. People your age are too alive to be thinking death. They think they'll live forever, but they rarely do."

Jimmy nodded. "Yes, I guess so."

"What about when the children came. Testimonial wills must have come to mind then."

"It did, and that's why we took out our life insurance policies."

"Well Jimmy Sheila never mentioned any will to me either. She was always so much on the go, you know."

"Mr. Frazier also; at the aquarium; Mr. Frazier said something about a trust."

"A trust; yes there was - - that is there *is* a trust, you see."

"I wonder if I might – not now, of course - - but later see it."

"I don't have it. I suppose it might be in the safe deposit box down at the bank. But I don't know much about these things. Maybe you should speak with the trustee first."

"The trustee, yes; may I ask just who is the trustee?"

"I can't recall her name just now. But you know she's with the firm."

"The firm? She's not at the bank?"

"No, the firm; the law firm, of course."

"And that is?"

"Why her firm - Sheila's firm; the one Harold got her all set up with: Ramsey, Ivy and Prince."

Back in the kitchen Stella sat on a stool working over some string beans before a small TV on the kitchen counter. The ad was coming to its usual conclusion. Yes, I'd love some gold, she thought, but they'll probably wants money for it. The ad for gold ended as it was now the bottom of the hour and time for the latest news.

"What do you have for us, Nancy?"

"Mike, the Sheila Frazier case just gets weirder and weirder."

"What have you got now?"

"Mike, what this CNN reporter has not been able to do up until now has been done by another. Mike it appears that insurance investigators carry more weight with the police that us lowly news reporters."

"You simply haven't looked in a mirror recently, Nancy."

"Thanks fellow," said Nancy as she glanced down at her figure.

"In all seriousness, we have just learned that Mr. Jimmy Davis, the suspect, I mean the person-of-interest in the death of his wife Sheila, himself went to the Las Vegas police about the time of her murder."

"Do you know why, Nancy?"

"You want believe this but he went to them to report a kidnapping."

"A kidnapping, did you say? A kidnapping, of whom?"

"Mike, he went to the Las Vegas police to report a kidnapping of his own two sons, the twins."

"Do you mean the twin boys that we saw riding the escalator here in the CNN world headquarters?"

"Yes indeed I do; the very same; the very one in the same, or perhaps I should say the very two in the same."

"Was that before or after the ransom was paid?"

"That's a good question, but I don't know. You see the insurance investigator wasn't investigating that."

"Do they know if Mr. Davis's lady friend with the twins on the escalator may tie into this – this kidnapping?"

"You mean Juliana Moreno. Not that I know of, although she is from Las Vegas. But I do know this; the police out here are now treating the death of Mario Moreno as a homicide."

Chapter 35

Mitt Johnson passed the serving plate around. Tuna, pimento cheese or Peanut butter and jelly sandwiches, together with an ample supply of potato chips, pickles and Cokes. Mitt sat at the head of the table there in his own office. The others sitting around the table were Joe Turner, Jack Partus, Juliana and Jimmy.

"I guess it's no secret that Juliana and Jimmy have teamed up in more ways than one. Is that CNN supposition right, Juliana?"

"I can't deny it, Mitt; that's about the only thing that CNN has gotten right."

"Jimmy, why don't you sue the bastards for slander?" asked Joe.

"If I lose my best client that I'm sitting with here now, I just might do that."

"Yes, you could say that Jimmy and I are rather fond of either."

Jimmy laughed. "Yes, I guess you might say that we are both *fond* of each other."

"I never saw J and M's line expanding into the cupid business," said Mitt. "Think that might work for a new slot, Jack?"

"Why not? I imagine the copyright on Cupid has expired by now. There would be no license needed."

"Caesars might go for it. Wasn't Cupid a Roman God?" asked Joe as he reached for another pickle.

"The ancient God of love," answered Juliana as she batted her eyelids with a look of feigned innocence.

"Speaking of copyrights and licenses," said Mitt, "the G3 Show is coming up real soon now. Joe, why don't you give these folks a recap of where we stand?"

"Except for our bank balance, we are in great shape. We've got an exclusive license on Death March game play modes. Had to pay through the nose for the exclusive but it should pay off. You know it's integrated into many RTS computer games but our license is just for commercial slots. Jack says we'll have three in time for the trade show."

"That's right; they'll be a lot of fragging available for the military and ex-military guys."

"They all will be on the Smart Card, right?" asked Mitt.

"That's all we are using on the new slots."

"How do we stand on the Excelsior suit, Jimmy?"

"We are waiting for the judge to rule on our summary judgment motion. They've asked for an oral hearing and the judge hasn't ruled yet on that either. Anytime now we should be hearing."

"How do we stand with our booth at the Convention Center, Juliana?"

"Last thing I heard we were in good shape. The pens and banners and floor decals are all in. We've also got a good location on the floor, I think."

"I'm telling you Mitt, with that exclusive license we are going to double our money."

"Some seer once said that the quickest way to double your

money was simply to fold it and put it back in your pocket. But really, I think this show could be a defining moment for J and M. I think we just might make a break-out there and find ourselves heading for the big leagues. I want all of you to be there, and that includes you, Jimmy."

Jal looked up from his workbench to see Bianco heading his way.

"Good morning, Jal. You're looking good."

"Thanks, boss; I am doing pretty good."

"Are these the new ones for the show?"

"Yep; here's Capture the Flag and here's Rise of the Triad."

"Nice artwork; did you run them by the lawyer?"

"Yeah; said it shouldn't be a problem."

"Did he now? Well I haven't heard from him. Guess I'd better give him a call.

"Now these are the multi-player slots. What about our new one for the little old ladies? How're you coming with it? I'd like it ready for the big show."

"Boss, you're going to love it. And Boss, you ain't going to have to run it by no lawyer; at least I don't think so."

"Do say now. Well we'll have to see about that, but where is it? Let me take a peek."

"It ain't ready for you to see just yet."

"Oh come on now; it's just our standard slot with a new theme, right?"

"Yeah, that's right."

"Well then?"

Jal looked at him and then put down the tool he had been holding.

"It's over here."

Jal led Bobby over to another workbench where a slot machine sat under a hood. For a moment they stood looking at the hood in silence. Then Bobby made a hand gesture for Jal to lift the hood.

Jal put his hand under the hood and hit a switch which turned the machine on and lit it up. Using both hands he lifted the hood off. There stood Tarot – The Game of the Gypsies!

Bobby's eyes opened wide in amazement. Then he started to smile from ear to ear."

"Goddamn it Jal if you haven't gone and done it. It's beautiful, just beautiful!"

Bobby slid his hand gently over the glass face of his new slot and studied the symbols on the three reels. Of course they weren't actual reels but electronic generated images of reels.

There were nine images in total with a row of three above and a row of three below the center, winning row of three. The winning, center row had three beautifully colored renditions of The High Priestess. In the row above there was The Hermit, The Devil and The Fool. In the bottom row was another one of The Fool and one of the Lovers and one of Death.

"Jal, you have fucking outdone yourself. This is great. Mind?" he asked as he put his hand on the spin button.

"Sure, give it a try."

Images of the three wheels started their spin. One by one they came to a halt.

"There's no sound. Where's the frigging sound?"

"It's been recorded. All I have to do is to load it."

"What did you record?"

"Gypsy music overlaid with an old woman's eerie voice."

"An old woman's voice, you say?"

"Yea, an old gypsy fortune teller woman - my mom."

"Your mom, by God. Then you're right; no fucking license fee, but I'll make it worth her while. You tell her that."

"What's the jackpot?"

"You wanted the little ladies so I made the jackpot three of The High Priestess. See, it's there on the payout table."

"Oh, yeah; I remember."

Bobby looked over the payout table. "I see you've thrown in a little twist here."

Jal smiled. "Yea, that Death is a real downer, isn't he? Catch him and you lose and you lose all if you've been sequencing."

"But why did you say this wasn't ready? Was that just because of the soundtrack?"

"No boss, you see I've been worked at home with a big demo – for promotion at the show, you know. You could also use it in a casino, if they'd let you. I just wanted to show you both at the same time."

"A big one, you say."

"Yea, it's a big one; like life-size, you know."

Chapter 36

"Mr. Parsons, it's George Prince on line one for you."

Phillip Parsons was the Managing Partner of the Atlanta office of Ramsey, Ivy and Prince but George Prince was one of the esteemed founders of the firm, a named partner, and a former Managing Partner. Though largely retired now, he still remained entitled to the use of his old office at the firm's headquarters in Los Angeles, even though on most days it would be vacant and dark. People there knew however when he would be coming in as Minnie, who now was in her late sixties, would arrive early that morning and lay out his mail, messages and the latest monthly financial report of the firm. The word would get around quickly on the twentieth floor whenever Minnie arrived. Desks would get straightened up in minutes and the water cooler oasis would become devoid of its usual gatherings. In any event, no matter who you were in the firm, you answered a call from George Prince.

"Good morning George. It's good to hear your voice."

"And a good morning – no I guess it's afternoon back there now – to you Phil. Roger is here too, so I'll put you on the speaker." Roger was Roger Allgood, the current Managing Partner of the nation-wide firm.

"Morning, Phil," said Roger.

"Is this line secure?" asked Mr. Prince.

"All of our attorney lines are secure, George," explained Allgood. "You have to render unsecure any call coming in or going out of any attorney's office in the firm in order to patch in a third party."

"Oh, I didn't know that."

"What, may I ask, can I do for you folks this fine day?" asked Parsons.

"Such a shame about the demise of the young lady lawyer there in your office," said Prince.

"Yes it was. That was a horrible murder; just horrible."

"What department was she in?"

"She – Sheila Frazier – was in our tax group. According to Abigail Carmichael, who heads that group, she was a rising star."

"Tax group, huh; I see."

"I can't imagine who would have done such a thing or why. A crime of opportunity, I guess. Maybe someone just had to have his fix."

"Phil, her body was found in her husband's car for God's sake," said Roger. "No, I can't see this as any crime of opportunity," said Roger. "It's quite the contrary."

"I heard that our name came out on TV during the news reporting of her murder. That's not the kind of publicity we need," said Prince. "Never in my life have I seen my own name on the same page as a murder, or any other crime."

Only faint static could be heard on the phone line for a few moments.

"Yes sir; I would imagine," said Phillip.

"Phil," said Roger, " the firm has just been served with a summons."

"On the Frazier murder?"

"Perhaps that's behind it, but I rather doubt it. Then I guess you can never be sure. No, it's been served by CI, you know, the Criminal Investigation arm of the IRS."

"Mrs. Frazier was in our tax group but she never worked in Los Angeles."

"It's not about the Los Angeles operation; it's about your shop, Phil. Why they served it to us out here I don't know. I guess it's just because I am named in Martindale as the Managing Partner."

"Well I don't think they will get very far with that. We aren't bloody accountants. We're lawyers warmly clothed by our attorney-client privilege blanket."

"Phil, I think we have to assume that this isn't the first time they have investigated a law firm. I'm sure they are well acquainted with privilege. Besides, it's the client's privilege, not that of the attorneys."

"Phillip," said Prince, "needless to say but I don't like this. First here is this murder of one of our attorneys and now an IRS investigation. I can just see the media tying the two together. That's all I need in my retiring years after a life-long career that was free of scandal."

"I don't know what to say, George."

"How about telling me that you will keep this from the press?"

"Well I sure will do my best, you know that. What do they want? Who do they want?"

"Witness interviews are to be conducted in the IRS offices there in Atlanta," said Roger.

"Witnesses; do you mean us – us attorneys?"

"Phil, I'll send it to you. Yes, it names three tax attorneys of yours. But this may just be the beginning – the first round."

"Well damn it; we can't be letting the cats out of our clients' bags."

"Phillip," said Prince, "Mark Twain once said "letting the cat out'a the bag was a whole lot easier than puttin' it back in."

"Rather than cats," added Allgood, "maybe you should be thinking ostrich."

Phillip Parsons swiveled his chair, leaned back and looked out the window in contemplation. This had to come sooner or later. Perhaps Roger had been guessing, but "ostrich" was indeed the operative word. He had been playing ostrich for too long now.

Money had been the root of it, as usual. What else was new in the world of American large law firms. Yes, once again money had been the root of evil.

A chill came over him. Evil, he thought; evil, evil, evil. Sheila Frazier's death had been the vilest display of evil. Could someone in the firm have been behind it? God don't go there, he thought. Well the person of interest in her case was a lawyer, but a lawyer at another firm. Of course the spouse *is* always the first suspect to come to mind, and usually for good reason.

Yes, money had been behind the ostrich behavior of Phillip, he thought to himself, but not murder. That was just too far out. Phillip's mind turned back to the deep recesses of his brain where his long-term memory resided.

Several years ago the Atlanta real estate market had gone bust. Commercial transactions had come to a halt. Closings dried up, both commercial and residential. The real estate group's workload dropped precariously.

After a few months, cuts or transfers in personnel would have to be made. The bottom line of the Atlanta office was suffering. That had not reflected well on Phillip who had only recently been named its Managing Partner. But cutting back was also painful. Having himself just left the ranks of partner he was loath to send any partner in the real estate group packing. There would be no work for them at any other Atlanta firm. They would have to start over in some other field of the law. So his cuts had been rather cosmetic, limited to a few new associates and staff. The real estate partners did have to go back to doing some of the grunt work themselves, of which there was plenty in the practice of real estate law. One even took up title searching at the courthouse for a while.

The cutback quickly proved to be inadequate. Bonuses were cut across the board. The litigation partners were up in arms. Litigation was doing well. Bankruptcy was also thriving. How long are we in litigation and bankruptcy going to have to subsidize the real estate group, they asked. Other groups joined in the protest. One of the most vocal to protest was the tax group. Look at our numbers for God's sake, Phil. We deserve good bonuses.

Phillip finally acted. The real estate partners not only lost all bonuses but lost shares in the firm as well. It was rare to make such a cut in shares prior to the end of the fiscal year, but he did so anyway. The bleeding had to be stopped. By now he had learned and matured on the job with some tutoring by a managing partner at another firm. Being a good managing partner entailed having a working atmosphere in which the support staff was happy and productive. His tutor pointed him to some books on firm leadership, ethics, modern office technology and finance. The latter included overhead control and the division of firm profits.

For some reason there was an imbalance at Ramsey, Ivy and Prince in the financial area. The tax group was doing well above the norm. That factor was not just recognized by him. All partners regularly received financial reports, which included the number of shares held by each partner for the current year, and thus their income, resentment grew. I can't win, Phillip thought. There is resentment if one group can't pull its weight; there is resentment if another is taking home more bread. Typical was the comment "I'm a lead trial counsel. I put in eighty God damn hours a week. And here is a tax guy with bankers' hours taking home more than me! Something has got to be going on down there. Something is just not right."

So after downsizing the real estate group Phillip started to pay more interest to the tax group.

"Wow you all are doing well here," he would say to a taxation law partner.

"Yes, isn't that great!"

"You sure brought the bacon home here."

"Yes we did. How about that!"

"I don't quite understand this program you have."

"It' just a rather clever integration of TD 8875 – you know, with Reg. 122379. Imaginative, don't you think?"

Well no, not really, for he had no idea what the guy was talking about.

Next he turned his attention to the tax associates and staff. He vaguely remembered having spoken with Sheila. All that he could recall however was her fresh, young eagerness and smooth handling of him. He had gotten nothing of substance from her.

He did now recall a rather strange and awkward incident when he had pulled up a chair to chat with Abigail's secretary, Sara. During the course of some small talk he noticed how she was holding and shifting some legal papers on her desk in a clearly defensive manner. He took one of the papers in hand but just as he started to scan it Abigail had walked up.

"Spying on us, Phil?"

"I wish I were that smart, Abigail. I'm afraid that all this tax stuff is far over my head." With that he had put the paper back down.

"I hear that you've been nosing around our little tax department."

"It's my job to keep up with what's going on, and that includes your group."

He finally came to the conclusion that the abnormality in the success of the tax group didn't merit further concern. At least he didn't see anything to be gained by further investigation other than further upsetting the apple cart. The litigation and bankruptcy lawyers might remain jealous with their success, but there was no reason for resentment. They were getting their fair share and even if they didn't understand it, they still knew it. Besides, the tax people's contribution to the Atlanta's office's bottom line made him look good to Los Angeles.

Just then he sensed that someone had entered his office. He swiveled his chair around to see that it was Jeffrey Davidson, one of the tax attorneys.

"Got a minute Phil?"

"Sure. Have a seat. What can I do for you?"

"Phil, I'm not sure if you know this but I have been acting as trustee for a trust set up by Harold Frazier."

"No, I didn't know that."

"As you may know though, Mr. Frazier has just died – died from a stroke."

"Yes, I caught that on television."

"I feel certain that you know that he was Sheila's father."

"Unfortunately, I know that all too well."

"Well the trust was set up with the assumption that he, the father, would not survive his daughter. That was a pretty reasonable assumption, of course."

Phillip nodded in agreement.

"Unfortunately, it didn't work out that way."

"What are you getting at?"

"Phil, it was a revocable trust."

"A revocable trust? Who the hell would set up a revocable trust?"

"Harold Frazier."

"Why on earth would he do that?"

"Harold was a control freak. He couldn't come to giving up control by setting up an irrevocable one. With an irrevocable trust he would no longer be owner of its assets."

"What benefit would he have by setting up a revocable trust?"

"To eliminate probate. The trustee in a revocable trust is usually the Grantor himself as well as the beneficiary. When he dies the successor trustee becomes trustee thereby avoiding probate. Mr. Frazier assumed that his daughter Sheila would survive him and become successor beneficiary. When she didn't Sheila's heirs, her children, did because the successor trustee the way this trust was structured. But as her children are minors their guardian stands in for them until they reached their majority. Their guardian is their father, the surviving parent, Jimmy Davis."

"You mean to say that this Davis guy has taken over the trust?"

"That's right. I feel sure that Frazier was going to change it. It's just that he didn't have the time. His stroke came virtually right on the heels of his daughter's death."

"How is it that you know all of this, Jeffrey?"

"Because he was having us manage the assets of the trust. I kept on him to name me as alternate trustee in case of his death or disability but he kept deferring. As I said, he really was a control freak."

"Have you informed Mr. Davis about this yet?"

"Not yet. Abigail said to hold off. She wants to go over the trust agreement herself. I'm sure she is concerned about losing our management fee. Look Phillip, I only came to you because of all this publicity that has been going on with these folks. If the media gets a hold of this, well . . ."

"You say that Abigail is looking it over now. Do you have a copy?"

"No, I don't have a hard copy, but since I drafted it, it should still be on disc."

"Tell you what we do here, Jeff, for a little damage control..."

Chapter 37

Jimmy couldn't believe his good fortune. The Federal District Court had granted his Motion for Summary Judgment in the patent infringement suit against Excelsior. Not only that, but the Court had also issued a Preliminary Injunction pending appeal. The injunction however was limited. Excelsior was enjoined from making, using or selling any slot machines with the Smart Card feature. However the preliminary injunction did not apply to slot machines with that payment feature that were already in commercial use. No, the Court would await the outcome of the inevitable appeal before going that far. By doing this the Court was in essence trying to maintain the status quo until the appeal had run its course.

But Jimmy's good fortune was not to be limited to this great news on the litigation. No, also laid out on his desk that morning was a Notice of Allowance from the Patent Office on the Interactive Slot Machine and Video Game patent application. All that remained to be done was to pay the patent issue and the patent would be granted, albeit that would take some time. He put in a call to Joe Turner and gave him the great news. A half hour later Joe called Jimmy back with Mitt Johnson on the line.

"Jimmy, this is great news. Congratulations are in order."

"Thank you, sir! I still can't quite believe it."

"I'll tell you what I can't believe and that is the timing here.

The timing could not be better with the G2 coming up in just days. Tell me, Jimmy, how can we use this at the show? Now don't tell me that we can't."

"Well the approval of the patent application we can certainly announce."

"Who, besides us, knows about that?"

"No one yet should know about it outside of the Patent Office, my office and your office."

"So what can we say?"

"You can say that a patent with broad coverage has been approved on the Pong slot machine. The patent is expected to cover a wide range of usages of interactive play bonus rounds on slot machines."

"And you think that it will cover Excelsior's Madison Square Gardens' slot."

"Absolutely; I've checked that out already."

"What if people at the show ask us that directly?" asked Joe.

"You can say yes; that we believe it will."

"I think that will come up what with us just having won the law suit against them," said Mitt. What can we say about that, Jimmy?"

"Before you quote me on that let me run it by Charles Macquire here."

"Good idea; we'll hang on."

"Hang on?"

"Jimmy, it's in three days. The G2 is in just three days."

"Okay, hold on. I'll see if he's in."

Several minutes later Charles Macquire came on the line.

"Hi there, Mitt; it's Charles. Jimmy is here too so I'll put you on the speaker.

"Good morning, Charles. Joe Turner is here with me so I'll do the same. There we go."

"Good morning, Charles," said Joe.

"That's fantastic news that Jimmy has just given to us. Good work, you two."

"Thanks, guys. Yes, it is indeed a good morning."

"Now what can we announce, Charles? Our big annual convention is just days away."

"Yes, Jimmy told me. I understand he also will be out there with you."

"That's right."

"I think that you can announce that your patent application on Pong has been allowed. In fact I think you can add that broad claims covering interactive play bonus rounds on slot machines have been approved. Hopefully that will slow down your competitors, especially those that have not yet gone to the expense of designing some."

"Good; that's real good, Charles," said Mitt.

"Now with regard to the Summary Judgment and Preliminary Injunction against Excelsior, I think you should be cautious."

"Why do you say that?"

"I say that because of the reaction of your customers – the casinos."

"By that you mean what?"

"You don't want to tee off your customers."

"Of course we don't."

"To put yourself in their shoes, I'll give you an analogy. When you buy prescription drugs would you rather have the brand name or the generic?"

"If I could trust the generic, then I'd go for the generic. It would be cheaper."

"Exactly, and for the same reason casinos would also like to run with generic slot machines. Leave it up to them and they would like to see no patents on slot machines."

"Go on, Charles."

"The last thing they would want to see is to have all of their slot machines with the Smart Card recalled or retrofitted back to old fashion technology – at least it's becoming old fashioned now.

"True, but what's the point of getting a patent if you aren't going to use it?"

"You are going to use it, but you want that message to get across to your competitors without getting the customers all riled up."

"So what do you suggest?"

"You could say that the court has upheld your patent on the Smart Card but that you expect Excelsior to appeal and that that will take quite some time. That should both notify and mollify them without getting them too exercised. The future is always full of uncertainties. Don't you agree?"

Charles and Jimmy could hear the J and M men discussing this quietly for a few moments.

"Charles, we think you are right. We'll get the message out but soft pedal it to the casinos."

"You might think about setting up a licensing program. You could even announce that licenses will be made available to all on quite reasonable terms. That might even give you a better bottom line in the end, what with the Smart Card now being so widely used."

"We'll crank the numbers."

"And Mitt, you know the reputation that Excelsior has for,

shall we say, hitting below the belt. I wouldn't get them too pissed off."

"Listening to CNN you would think they would be scared of Jimmy here, Charles, not vice versa."

"Listen, all of you; I've been hit by Excelsior literally below the belt," came in Jimmy.

"You would have us keep all of this private, Jimmy?" asked Mitt.

"Well I do want Excelsior to keep off of my privates." That brought a chuckle from Joe.

"Better run your plans by your general counsel," said Charles.

"With regard to what?" asked Mitt.

"You want to keep him in the loop. There can be more involved here than just patents. You know, stuff like antitrust, commercial contracts, and the ever present issue of taxes. Your counsel, he's with, with, with . . . "

"Ramsey, Ivy and Prince."

"Mr. Bianco; it's Abigail Carmichael here."

"Yes, Abigail. What can I do for you?"

"Have you heard the news from your patent lawyer yet?"

"News? No news. Gotta be bad news that he dreads telling me."

"It could hardly be worse. The Court has granted Summary Judgment against Excelsior on the Smart Card case."

"Shit."

"It's also issued an injunction prohibiting Excelsior from making, using or selling any more slot machines that have the Smart Card feature."

"What the fuck?"

"There's even more, I'm afraid. I've learned that J and M's patent application on the interplay bonus round on slot machines has also been granted. Would that cover your new Madison Square Garden machine?"

"Good God woman; you got to be fucking kidding me. Hell, I don't know."

"You'd better find out."

"But the G2 is about to open."

"So I have heard."

"That God damn patent guy of theirs; that idiot just don't pay no attention. Think he's got to go. That way the others will get the fucking message."

"I think I may have a better idea."

"Yeah?"

"Moreno's death is now being treated as a homicide. He – Jimmy Davis – was at his side when he died violently there in Caesars palace. After that his wife was murdered and found in his own car truck."

"I know that."

"Three strikes and he will be out, trust me."

"Hum . . . "

"Get him indicted and all his work against you will be so tainted and damned that J and M wouldn't touch it. In fact they might get accused of being involved right from the start with him, their attorney."

"I get the picture. You're saying to finish the job."

"Make CNN's Nancy Tate's day. Make this Davis guy the villain – not the victim. That would clear up a lot of things."

After that conversation Bianco sat at his desk, thinking. Then he slowly made his decision to change *his* way of thinking. He picked up his phone again.

"Jal; we needs to do some talking. I've changed my mind about som'um."

Chapter 38

Jimmy and Juliana lay there in Juliana's bed in serene contentment. They had just finished making love for the second time inside of the hour.

"That was wonderful, Jimmy."

"I can't believe how natural it is with you, Juliana. With Sheila it never was completely natural. It was never so comforting – so comfortable. Sure there was wild excitement at first but it was never like this. There was always tension in the air; edgy; you know, rough around the edges."

"Well you are home now my Jimmy man but don't go thinking I am always a warm blanket – comfortable like an old shoe. I still have my Latin blood."

"I can't wait to be unleashed. Can I have a preview now?"

"That will be a future attraction."

"You mean here in Vegas?"

"You know what I mean."

"Well I won't argue with you. Mark Twain said that there are two theories to arguing with a woman: Neither works."

"You and your Mark Twain."

"I guess he is a little out of place here in Las Vegas. Okay, then; do you want to hear the world's shortest fairy tale?"

"No."

"And he lived happily . . ."

"I mean no – I don't want to hear it again. Once was once too often, I thank you. Looking forward to the G2 tomorrow?"

"Now that's a change of pace. Sure I am. I've never been to any trade show before."

"It's a real doozy, as they say."

"You are beginning to talk like me."

They went together to the Convention Center after eating a leisure breakfast on Juliana's back patio. Juliana already had their badges. Jimmy had expected it to be big, but good Lord it was humongous. Not only the sheer size but the lighting and sound was like – well like a light and sound show.

"Are most trade shows like this?" he asked.

"Not at all; there's a lot of noise and goings-on at others, but nothing like this. The products make the difference. You can't compare gambling machines with, say machine tools, cosmetics or shoes."

"Or tractor pulls?"

"Or tractor pulls."

"What about trade shows for the cruise ship industry? There ought to be some romance in that, no?"

"I wouldn't know. I think they are usually held in Miami. Their casinos are too small for us to get involved with."

"I bet a lot of things must go on sort of under the table here, huh?"

"You do have to watch yourself. For one thing there are a lot of scams."

"Like?"

"You can be scammed even before you get here. You have a confirmed room at the Bellagio, only once you arrive the Bellagio has never heard of you. You've paid for an ad in a promotional journal for the show, only there is no such journal. Then there are prepaid billboard ads but no billboard. The list goes on. Many of the scams are operated out of Mexico."

"Speaking of scams, look over there."

"That's the Security and Surveillance Institute. People sign up for a whole day's training on the latest in casino security and surveillance."

"And what's that there?"

"Those are tours – off-site tours. You can sign up there for some behind-the-scene insider tours at several casinos.

"And here I only expected to see the latest in gaming products. Speaking of that, where is J and M's booth?"

"Follow me."

As Juliana led the way they happened to come across the Excelsior exhibit. The exhibit was featuring two new slots. One was called The Gypsy. An old lady's crackling voice was alternately enticing "Come, let me read your fortune," and, "I see good fortune in your future." Jimmy stopped, pushed the play button and images of reels spinning sprang to life. He hit two of the Tarot cards, The Lovers which depicted a naked man and woman, a la Adam and Eve in the garden, and one of The Fool.

"Appropriate, wouldn't you say?" said Jimmy.

Juliana gave him an elbow in the side as an eerie voice of an old fortune teller announced "You've been foiled by the fool. Better luck next time."

"Wow!" exclaimed Juliana, "the audio follows the spin. I've never seen, uh heard, of that before. Excelsior must have an imaginative designer." Then she hit the play button.

Three reels came up: The star, The Sun and The Moon, a winning, celestial combination. The audio sound of ten coins clanging into a metallic collection tray was heard as well as the old fortune teller declaring: "Just as I predicted." Being a demonstration model, no pay out was actually forthcoming.

The other featured slot machine was Madison Square Garden with which they were already familiar, including its sound of the bell and roar of the crowd. Both machines accepted the Smart Card. Just then a comely young lady approached them wearing a blue blazer embossed with the Excelsior logo, and an enticing smile. Jimmy and Juliana turned and moved on.

They arrived at the J and M exhibition booth to find two Pongs in play, on automatic play with phantom players. Joe Turner and Jack Partus were sitting at a table and gave them a wave. Jimmy went to one of the Pong machines and took over control. Moments later his paddle missed the bouncing ball. Juliana laughed.

"Want to take me on?" he asked Juliana as he nodded to the other machine which was still vacant.

"No thanks."

They walked over to the table.

"Guess who was here a while ago?" asked Joe.

"I can't imagine," replied Jimmy.

"Your nemesis, Nancy Tate, no less."

"Oh God, is she in town?"

"Said she wouldn't miss it."

"Well she missed me," said Jimmy.

"So far," responded Juliana.

"How are things going so far?" asked Juliana. "Did the guys from The Sands and Excalibur show yet?"

"They did; good work. But Juliana, do keep Jimmy away from Nancy Tate," replied Joe.

"We'll be on the lookout."

"Have you seen the Excelsior booth?" asked Joe.

"Yes, we were just there."

"Notice anything surprising?"

"No; not really; we saw their Madison Square Garden slot and their new one – The Gypsy."

"Did you notice that The Gypsy had no bonus round with interactive play?"

"That's right, it didn't. Think we've scared them off from that?" asked Jimmy.

"I have no idea, but I did find that interesting," replied Joe.

"Joe, I'm going to mingle and see if I can't round up a couple more buyers to send over."

"Go to it. And Jimmy, why don't you hang close in case anyone asks about licensing. Here, pull up a chair and watch our little world go by."

As soon as Juliana had left, who was to appear at the J and M booth but none other than Bobby Bianco with Jal at his side. As Joe was rubbing his eyes in disbelief, Bianco casually began to examine one of the Pong machines.

"Mr. Bianco," said Joe as he stood. "I'm Joe Turner."

"A pleasure," replied Bianco without turning to face him while continuing to examine the Pong machine. "Jal, give me a game."

Joe just stood there in disbelief as Jal took his place at the competitor's slot machine. Jal hit the play button and the reels on his machine sprung into action.

"No need for that," said Joe as he hit a switch on the back of each machine. With that the Pong screen came up on each machine along with the audio.

Bobby and Jal began to battle it out. It wasn't any time however before Jal got a ball past his boss for a winning point.

"Shit," said Bobby under his breath. Then he turned to face Joe and extended his hand.

"Nice machine; it's making quite a splash."

"Thank you, Mr. Bianco. Here, meet its designer."

Jack stood up and extended his hand. "Jack Partus."

Bianco took his hand, limply.

"Yeah; nice machine you got here."

"Thank you," responded Jack as Jal and Jack sized up each other. Then Jal's gaze shifted to Jimmy who had remained seated. Jimmy instinctively sniffed the air. When Jal saw that Jal's own nose twitched, along with a knowing wink.

"Where's the boss?" asked Bianco.

"Oh he's around – making the rounds, you could say."

"Aren't we all? Can you get him? We needs to talk."

"Sure; I'll call him on his cell."

"Tell him to meet me in conference room 144. I gots it booked all morning. Second floor; thirty minutes."

With that he turned to leave. "Oh, and no lawyers," he hissed as he looked at Jimmy.

Mitt Johnson with Joe Turner at his side and Jack Partus just behind, walked down the row of meeting rooms towards room 144. These meeting rooms at the Convention Center had a room capacity which ranged from 20 to 2,500. Jal was standing outside the door to one. He raised one hand in recognition as they approached and then opened the door for them.

"Good morning," said Mitt.

" Morning."

There was a coffee tray and some yellow roses in a vase on the conference room table. At the head of the table sat Bobby Bianco.

"Welcome, gentlemen," said Bianco as he gestured them towards a seat without rising. Mitt walked to the other end of the table but as he was about to pull out the chair Bianco stopped him.

"Come on down here, Mr. Johnson. What the hell, there's only us five."

They did so but neither Mitt, Joe nor Jack took a seat next to Bianco. Finally Jal took one of the still empty seats next to his boss. Bianco sat there absorbing the seating arrangement and then opened his gaudy sport coat and smelled under one of his arms.

"Smell anything Jal?"

"No, boss."

"Then serve them some coffee there."

No one was about to decline.

"Now gents I've called you here perfectly legit-like, so if you are wired, forget it. I ain't going to propose any price fixing, territorial allotment; nothing like that. This here is a perfectly legit meeting. Got it?"

"Good," replied Mitt.

"Look, you people at J and M have done good, real good. You can be proud of what'cha done."

"Thank you," replied Mitt.

"And you are gutsy – real gutsy, man; I like that, being newcomers and all. I mean who would take on the whole fucking industry with that Smart Card thing? You ain't going to see anyone out here do that. And maybe, just maybe, that's just why. You all ain't from out here. You are way back East but not even *The* East. God you're in a fucking state that don't even allow gambling. If you'se were here you probably wouldn't have even done it – I mean this patent thing."

"Thank you again," said Mitt. "We are just trying to protect our investment – you know, our research and development investment."

"And now I hears that you'se gone and gotten yourselves a patent on the action play slot too. I tells you, that Davis lawyer you'se got must be some good. Hell, people in Vegas wouldn't even have thought to try. But then he's something else. I means like according to TV he *really* is something else, if you get whats I mean. I don't think I'd be crossing him. No sir."

"Mr. Bianco, where is all of this headed?"

Bianco looked at Mitt for a moment before he spoke.

"It's heading for a merger; a fucking merger, I'm thinking."

"A merger? You mean a merger of Excelsior and J and M?"

"You'se got it. How'sa 'bout that!"

"You are kidding, I hope. I mean our two company cultures are so far apart that that would never work."

Joe Turner and Jack Partus exchanged glances as if to say "thank god" for Mitt's response.

"Hey, don't just jump to conclusions so fast."

"Okay," said Mitt. "What would be the name of this new company?"

"Name? Why Excelsior, of course."

"And where would be its headquarters?"

"Vegas; where else? Don't go telling me 'lanta, Georgia."

"Any idea who would be its President?"

Bianco stared at Mitt while Jal lit up a cigar.

"Mr. Johnson, Excelsior has been 'round lot longer than you guys. It's bigger than you'se guys. You merge with me and together we make music. Hell, we'll make a fucking symphony. We'll be in the big league. You see, I've been looking at the numbers."

Mitt looked to Joe who was looking down at the table top in disbelief while he shook his head with a faint smile.

"Mr. Bianco, with all due respect, the answer is no; it simply would not work."

"Thought you might have a problem with that. Okay then, no merger; we'll buy you out — you know — acquisition-like. Want to hear the number? The whole deal?"

"Mr. Bianco, before we go any further I think we need to have our lawyers present."

"You mean that Davis guy?"

"No, he's just our patent lawyer. We would need our General Counsel."

"Is he here in Vegas?"

"No, he's back in Atlanta."

"Then get him out here. We could meet again tomorrow."

"He's a very busy man. Look, I seriously doubt that anything will come of this. It's just that I don't want even to hear your offer without legal representation present."

"Well just get that Davis guy if you just want a fucking legal witness. I think he could make a witness without rubbing us all out." Bianco snickered as Jal blew cigar smoke almost straight up over his head and joined in with his own snicker.

"Tell you what. We gots a big demo on for tonight over at Caesars. We're introducing our new Gypsy slot. I think you'll find it very impressive. Nine o'clock is show time. Have Mr. Davis there. Oh yeah, and have your rep there too, Ms. - - "

"Moreno," provided Mitt.

"Oh yea, Ms. Moreno. Sorry I goofed up about wanting no lawyer at this here meeting, but I know you and your patent guy are going to be impressed. Maybe you'll want to telephone conference in your counsel tomorrow. You know, your patent man on the scene and your counsel behind the scene-like."

Mitt turned and looked at Joe and Jack. Jack was curious from a design viewpoint and Joe was curious as to why they had not gone with the interaction feature. They both nodded a yes to Mitt.

"After you see The Gypsy demo I think it will be you who throws a number out. It's dynamite."

Bianco neglected to add that Nancy Tate had also been invited.

Chapter 39

By eight-thirty all members of the J and M entourage to Las Vegas had finished their dinners and had entered the casino at Caesars Palace. In what other industry could competitors see the best of their competition's wares at a trade show and then see them in use on the same day? What was hot and what was not was right there in front of their eyes as well as the demographics of the users. Sure you could read up in the trade journals on all of this but any printed information was always in the past compared with information gathered in real-time. Of course Caesar's was hardly the only game in town but it was as good a representation of the upscale end of the market as any other.

Jimmy was playing a video poker game while Juliana messaged his shoulders when the fanfare was heard throughout the casino. The flourish of trumpets was followed by the now familiar voice of Sid Riley.

"Ladies and gentlemen, may I have your attention, please! This evening Caesars Palace is honored to have been chosen as the venue for the introduction of the latest slot machine from the Excelsior Corporation. For all of who are interested in knowing your future you will absolutely love The Gypsy. Yes, The Gypsy will tell your fortune with her deck of Tarot cards. If you've never had your fortune told, you are in for a rare treat. Who knows but your new found fortune may be just one spin away. So please make your way now over to the casino entrance by following any one of the roving centurions. The Gypsy awaits you."

Jimmy and Juliana were among the first to arrive at the exhibit. From his earlier experience he knew where it would likely be set up. The demonstration consisted of two rows of The Gypsy slot machines arranged in the shape of the letter V with its bottom cut away. In the cut-out area of the V was an enclosed booth with a glass front window and a small side door. The booth was bathed in an eerie, green light. On the outside of the booth appeared "The Gypsy" logo below the window. Inside the booth a holographic image of a gypsy woman could be seen through the window. She was seated, holding an illuminated crystal ball. Her head moved ever so slowly between a position gazing at the ball and gazing out of the booth window. The color of the ball would slowly change at the end of her gaze at the ball, only to fade back to white as her head turned back to the ball.

Above the booth was a large, vertically oriented, roulette wheel. Rather than having alternating red and black numbers however it bore almost life-size dolls that represented the twenty-two major cards of a tarot deck. The dolls were molded in a thick, plastic-like material much like that of a child's doll from the eighteenth century. Only the eyes moved under the force of gravity as the wheel slowly revolved about its horizontal axis. It was spun from time to time by a short woman in gypsy attire who had her back to Juliana and Jimmy.

The demonstration area had its own localized sound system. It was playing a rendition of the 1945 song *The Gypsy* as sung by Dinah Shore:

"In a quaint caravan
There's a lady they call The Gypsy
She can look in the future
And drive away all of your fears . . ."

This was overlaid by the voice of the gypsy inside the booth as she beckoned the curious to come forth.

"Impressive," said Juliana.

"Very much so," said Jimmy in agreement as he studied the image of the gypsy woman inside the booth. He walked over to the booth and peered in. Since the image was three dimensional he concluded that it was a hologram straight out of a Disney World ride. He walked back to Juliana who was studying the rotating wheel.

With a gentle wave of her hand the costumed gypsy spun the wheel. Being so large however it would only spin about a couple of revolutions before coming to a stop with a Tarot card character located beneath an arrow above the apex of the wheel. Jimmy pointed out to Juliana that the gypsy hand wave was over an electric eye which actually triggered the spin. As he was pointing that out he felt a hand touch his back. He turned to see Bobby Bianco with a broad smile.

"Mr. Davis, I must apologize for dis-inviting you to our little meeting today. It was a mistake. You should have been there."

Jimmy looked down on the man-of-the-hour who still was wearing his gaudy sport coat. "No problem, Mr. Bianco. As much as we lawyers would like to attend all of our clients' meetings, sometimes it's better to leave them out."

"The show is about to start and I wants to ask you a favor."

"Sure."

"They are going to ask for some couples to participate in our little show and I sure would appreciate if you and your pretty lady here would volunteer. You know, to give me a boost for the merger."

Jimmy looked at Juliana who was enjoying the excitement and the after mat of the good meal and wine.

"Oh, I don't know, Jimmy," replied Juliana.

Bianco shook his head while smiling. "Mr. Davis, give the booth a checkout."

Jimmy hesitated.

"Oh go on."

Jimmy walked over to the booth and peered in the window again. Then he went around the side and opened the small side door. Bending over he entered. Since the booth was too small for him to stand erectly he sat down on the bench. The spring-hinged door shut beside him. Dinah Shore's lilting voice continued to sing.

> "But I'll go there again
> 'Cause I got to believe
> The Gypsy
> That my lover is true . ."

By now a sizeable number of people had gathered in the demonstration area. Just outside of the V-shaped space stood several centurions in full dress regalia, they having now completed their shepherding duties.

Jimmy remained inside the booth alternately looking out its window and looking at the holographic projectors. It was quite a setup. Although no live gypsy was present, her crystal ball was.

He saw that its light was powered by an electric cord that extended out of its bottom. He was just looking under the ball when he heard a rap on the door.

"Mr. Davis; are you alright?" asked Bianco. "Are you still with us or have you turned into a zombie?"

Jimmy took the door handle but it wouldn't turn.

"Mr. Davis?"

Jimmy tried the handle again. It was locked.

"It seems that I am locked in," he muttered but the music drowned him out.

Then with an over dramatic flourish Bianco opened the small door. Spectators behind him glimpsed Jimmy still bent over. Then he slowly extracted himself from the confined space.

Bianco stuck his head inside the booth and looked around for a moment before he stepped back and closed the door. Then he gave Jimmy a stare that was interrupted by Sid Riley giving another short announcement over the casino's sound system.

Moments later two of the centurions made a clearing in the gathering for the arrival of Sid. In he walked with a portable mike in hand to join Bianco. By a visual signal he had the centurions clear the area inside the V space with a gentle nudging of their staffs. Then he took up a position in front of the booth.

"Ladies and gentlemen I am Sid Riley, the casino floor manager tonight. On behalf of Caesars Palace I want to welcome you to witness and hopefully participate this evening in the official introduction of a fantastic new slot machine from the Excelsior Corporation. With me here is the President of Excelsior, Mr. Bobby Bianco. Mr. Bianco, please gave us a little introduction, if you would." With that he handed the mike over to Bianco as the people about stared at the man in his gaudy sport coat.

"Good people, as you can hear I'm no public speaker. But what we gots here is our newest slot. It's called 'The Gypsy.' It was designed by a real life gypsy who has worked for Excelsior for a long, long time. He's a real wizard at slot designing. So Jal, take a bow."

Jal raised his hand and nodded to the gathering with a slight smile. The striking difference between Bianco and his line-backer built sidekick fascinated the audience.

"And Sid, if you don't mind, I'd like to get in a plug for Jal's mom who also is a real life gypsy and fortune teller. She is the one giving us a hand tonight – the one that is operating the wheel there."

Jimmy and Juliana looked. The costumed gypsy was now facing the audience. She wasn't hired help in costume. She was the real life gypsy that had warned Juliana that night at her reading!

"Madam Magda is her name and she is always available to give readings right there in her own home just off Fremont, downtown. Her business cards are in that tray there for the taking.

"Now The Gypsy slot machine here is nut'in fancy. It's an old fashion slot . . simple-like, you know. Just three reels of spinning Tarot cards. Simple as them old cherries, grapes and bells, you know. There's a couple of new twists but they are just side shows. When you have a big winner your fortune gets told. The Jackpot is three of them High Priestesses. Another good winner is a line-up of three of The Emperors. Oh yea, and the full sky one -The Sun, The Moon and The Star - is another good'un that gets your fortune told with the payout. But just watch out for Death; man, he's a real bummer. He will wipe you'se out every time. . . even if you've bet cumulative – you know – let it ride. He'll crash that ride. Anyhows, the pay off schedule is on each 'chine. So enjoy it, folks."

"Thank you, Mr. Bobby Bianco," said Sid as he took the mike back to a sparse smattering of applause. The whole scene was too bizarre for much applause. "And thank you Excelsior.

"Now folks, as Mr. Bianco said he's not much of a public speaker, so he has asked me to emcee this little show tonight.

"Now we are going to have a little fun. Here's the deal. If you have a friend, a lover or what-have-you with, you then one of you will enter the booth and the other will spin the big wheel when you signal that you are ready. Now you give that signal by gripping the crystal ball with both hands and hold it tight. As you do that you give us your best, intensive even reverent stare into the ball. The ball will know when you have reached a state of karma and begin to pulsate. That will be the signal for your partner to spin. Our old hag here, oops, I mean gypsy, will show you how."

To that the audience gave an authentic chuckle. By this time the audience included not only Jimmy and Juliana and the two from Excelsior, but also Mitt Johnson and his wife, Joe Turner and Jack Partus. Nancy Tate was also there but in hiding behind her cameraman. She wasn't the only one hidden from view.

"Now folks if you would please line up in pairs over to the side here. Excelsior and I thank you for your attention and participation."

To that there was a smattering of light applause as some in the audience spoke to each other about giving it a try. Within a couple of minutes a line of some eight or ten pairs had been formed into a line. As a result of Bianco's coaxing Jimmy and Juliana found themselves to be fourth in line as observed by Nancy Tate and her cameraman.

Chapter 40

The "Spy in the Sky," sometimes called the "Eye in the Sky," is ever vigilant above casino floors. It is a network of cameras that are housed in glass bubbles mounted on the casino ceilings. They constantly feed images to security rooms where shrewd observers conduct surveillance around the clock. Of course there are other hidden cameras as well. Indeed, a large casino can have several hundred.

This evening there were two visitors in the security center at Caesars Palace. They were the detective that Jimmy had spoken with at the Las Vegas Police Department, Detective Price, and Nick Spenser, the private eye that had been hired by J and M. They were seated together before two monitors that were trained on The Gypsy demonstration. The images displayed were also being recorded. Two casino security guards were standing behind them.

"Quite a show," muttered one guard.

"And you're positive no one from Excelsior has opened the power box in the booth since Nick made the switch?"

"Absolutely; the ape checked the leads but didn't unscrew the lid."

"And security has their power supply guts, right?"

"That's right. Just as you said to do, we filmed Nick as he removed it and tagged it. It's all locked away."

"And you filmed Nick as he made the switch."

"That's right too. Out with that bad old ramped-up A.C. and in with the good old D.C.," added the guard.

"The demo may be electrifying, but there'll be no electrocution tonight," said Nick. "She'll just get a little shock to show that they did indeed try to execute their little plan and the little lady. Whereas their stepped-up A.C. would grab her hands and not let go, the battery will just shove her hand away, maybe with a little spark and sting. I tell you they had that A.C. stepped up to a lethal level, believe me."

"I guess a sting operation does have to have a little sting in it, huh?" said the detective with a smile. "I'd rather have an attempted murder charge on my watch than a murder one."

"And you said the feds also have a hold on these too?" asked Nick.

"Yeah, the tax guys have done that. They need 'um for some take down of a bunch of lawyers in a big Atlanta firm. That's a shame because it went way beyond tax finagling. A lady lawyer was murdered back there."

"Why, a shame?"

"Cause they'll plea bargain away the death penalty. Just watch; they'll snitch to save their asses."

The first couple in line was a middle aged woman and a young man in his early twenties.

"And who are you, may I ask?" asked Madam Magda.

"I'm Loraine Davenport and this is my son, Dan. We're from Wichita, Kansas."

"Very good; please follow me, Mrs. Davenport."

With that Madam Magda led her over to the booth and opened its door. The lady entered and sat down on the stool.

"Please lift the ball and hold it in front of you. It's light. Good, a little lower now so that we see your face through the window. Very good; now after I have returned to your son's side, and you are ready to learn your fortune, just look at your son through the window, nod your head twice and then look intently into the ball. Understand?"

"Yes."

With that Madam Magda gave her a reassuring pat, closed the door, walked over to the wheel beside the son, Dan, said a few words quietly to him and then turned away from the wheel to face the audience. She then lowered her head as if in prayer. A moment later the wheel began to spin when Dan, having seen his mother's nod and look into the crystal ball, passed his hand over the electric eye. After two full revolutions the wheel slowly came to a halt on the Tarot card, Temperance. With that the image of Temperance appeared in the crystal ball that his mother was holding in the booth and its color changed from white to green.

"Temperance. Madam Davenport you are one who works well with others and have a gift for good management. You may now exit the booth as I give your son Dan here a one hundred dollar casino token as a token of Excelsior's appreciation." To that there was a light applause.

The next couple was two young ladies in their twenties which were holding hands. They obviously were an item. The routine was repeated. Not surprisingly they drew The Lovers whose image appeared in the crystal ball as its color changed from white to pink. There was a chuckle from the audience as Madam Magda informed them that the card meant physical beauty, a beautiful soul and the beginning of a romance – to their delight. But Jimmy did not join in the chuckle as his mind was focused on the wheel rather than on the make-up of the all-female couple. He and Juliana stepped into the second position.

The third couple was a married couple, one Mary Joe and Ted Hasbro from Los Angeles. The routine was repeated and they drew The Empress. "Mrs. Hasbro, The Empress shows that your success will bring you freedom, material comfort, security and protection."

Jimmy hardly heard the words as his analytical mind was totally concentrated on the winning Tarot symbols on the wheel. There was a pattern here. Yes, there definitely was a pattern. but what was it?

"Jimmy, Jimmy, we're being called," said Juliana as she nudged him forward to center stage.

Madam Magda looked at the two of them as they stepped forward. Then her mouth opened slightly as she recognized them. Instantly she recalled the warning she had given Juliana earlier.

"May I have your names please?"

"I am Jimmy Davis from Atlanta and this is Juliana Moreno from Las Vegas."

"Do you wish to proceed, Juliana?"

"Yes."

"Are you sure?"

"Why yes, of course," she answered, questionably.

Madam Magda looked deeply into Juliana's eyes as Jimmy's eyes returned to the sequence of the Tarot cards on the wheel. Damn it; I've almost got it, he thought as Madam Magda began to escort Juliana to the booth. She opened the small door and Juliana stepped in and sat down on the stool. Then she turned back to the gypsy who nodded to the crystal ball. Juliana lifted the ball off its pedestal and held it out in front of her near the booth window. It was surprisingly light. Madam Magda, seemingly with reluctance, closed the door and returned to the wheel and to Jimmy who was still staring at the symbols.

By now Nancy Tate had emerged into the open beside her cameraman who was recording it all.

"Are you ready?" Madam Magda asked Jimmy softly.

Jimmy really wasn't ready but feeling that the spotlight was solidly on him he softly muttered "I guess so."

"Are you ready, son?"

Jimmy felt the presence and pressure of the audience on him. "I guess so."

Jimmy looked over at the booth to see Juliana holding the crystal ball that glowed white and looking expectantly into it. Then she looked up and nodded her head. Jimmy looked at Madam Magda who was now facing the audience as if in prayer. Ever so hesitantly he passed his hand over the electric eye thereby momentarily blocking its beam to generate a signal. The wheel began its spin of pre- orchestrated doom.

The sound of the spinning wheel energized Jimmy's mind. Suddenly he realized what the outcome was destined to be. The wheel had been programmed to stop on the next fourth card succeeding the last one after too revolutions. It was as simple as that. In line for that was the Death card. He turned to see Juliana still peering intensely into the crystal ball, her face illuminated by the ball's white light. He broke into a run towards her.

"No Juliana; no. Drop the ball!" he screamed as the wheel slowed. But Juliana continued her intense study of the ball as if mesmerized by it.

As Jimmy ran he had to decide whether to split for the side door to the booth or run straight towards her there behind the booth's window. As the wheel's spin was now slowing to a crawl he opted for the window.

As soon as he reached the window he began to pound on it with both hands. Juliana ever so slowly raised her head to face him as the wheel stopped: Death.

The crystal ball instantly turned bright red as did Juliana's face from its glow. Simultaneously the two sides of the crystal ball sparked brightly throwing Juliana to her side against the door of the booth. The door sprung open as Juliana fell out of the booth and onto the floor. Only her feet remained within the booth.

"No!" screamed Jimmy as he ran to her motionless side.

Madam Magda's solemn pronouncement of death was heard by the hushed and stunned audience.

"Juliana!" cried Jimmy. There was no response. He started mouth-to-mouth resuscitation.

"What the hell?" cried Detective Price in the security center. "What kind of battery did you use, Nick?"

"Just a car battery; you know, twelve volts."

"Twelve volts! That's too much. You see what twelve volts can do." With that the detective spoke into his mike. "Move in; move in; MOVE IT!"

Juliana's eyes opened wide. Feeling smothered by Jimmy's efforts at resuscitation she shook her head from side to side. Jimmy backed off.

"Oh God, he tried to kill you too!" It was the voice of Nancy

Tate who had moved in as the audience had moved back with her cameraman who was continually shooting away.

Juliana looked at Nancy and then the cameraman and then back at Jimmy. Then she gave Jimmy a big smile that grew and grew.

Jimmy leaned back down and kissed Juliana. Juliana responded by wrapping her arms around his neck and returning his kiss.

Nancy Tate's eyes open wide in amazement. Then hearing a commotion behind her she turned to see two uniformed policemen enter the area. Quickly she had her cameraman swing his aim around to the couple.

"Let's give them room," she instructed the cameraman, assuming that they were headed for Jimmy. But to the surprise of her life they instead walked over to Jal and Bobby and cuffed *them*.

"Gentlemen, you both are under arrest. Now about Mr. Moreno, and your Miranda rights . . . "

CNN NEWS: "Breaking news," began Nancy Tate. "We have shocking, truly shocking new developments in the Jimmy Davis case tonight."